T0195856

A KNIGHT'S TIME SERIES

BOOK ONE: BY FAITH WE LIVE

D. S. DEMAREE AND S. E. WILLBANKS

BALBOA.PRESS

A DIVISION OF HAY HOUSE

Balboa Press books may be ordered through booksellers or by contacting:

Balboa Press
A Division of Hay House
1663 Liberty Drive
Bloomington, IN 47403
www.balboapress.com
844-682-1282

Because of the dynamic nature of the Internet, any web addresses or links contained in this book may have changed since publication and may no longer be valid. The views expressed in this work are solely those of the author and do not necessarily reflect the views of the publisher, and the publisher hereby disclaims any responsibility for them.

The author of this book does not dispense medical advice or prescribe the use of any technique as a form of treatment for physical, emotional, or medical problems without the advice of a physician, either directly or indirectly. The intent of the author is only to offer information of a general nature to help you in your quest for emotional and spiritual well-being. In the event you use any of the information in this book for yourself, which is your constitutional right, the author and the publisher assume no responsibility for your actions.

Any people depicted in stock imagery provided by Getty Images are models, and such images are being used for illustrative purposes only. Certain stock imagery © Getty Images.

Print information available on the last page.

ISBN: 979-8-7652-3078-7 (sc)
ISBN: 979-8-7652-3080-0 (hc)
ISBN: 979-8-7652-3079-4 (e)

Library of Congress Control Number: 2022912050

Balboa Press rev. date: 09/15/2022

CONTENTS

PROLOGUE

The demon stared at the three boys sleeping in the moonlit room. Well-built, strong and handsome boys, he thought. The youngest interested him the most, so sensitive, honest, trusting and innocent, devoted, of course, to Jesus, the Virgin and the disciple Mary Magdalene. Unfortunately, that protective tutor from India had told the young one about Buddha and Krishna. Soon the boy would travel to the land of wars and also learn about Mohammad. All enemies of the demon. But the creature chuckled. Already he'd slipped into the boy's dreams and encouraged thoughts of doubt and darkness. It was easy. The malignant spirit had long ago inserted himself in the mind of the boy's father. The father had unknowingly transferred his memories of horror and sacrifice from the crusade into his sons. The youngest would suffer, the demon thought, from my mind games. He would take me from his thoughts into his reality. Then, he would martyr himself and sacrifice his soul.

As the young boy turned in his bed he saw something dark flit across the wall. He sucked in his breath and lay still. If he didn't breathe, the thing wouldn't notice him. He squeezed his eyes shut then peeped through the narrow slits. The blackness was there, in the upper corner just above his sleeping brother's bed. Red flaming eyes stared at the boy. Watching.

The wall dissolved into a deep, dark pit behind the colorless creature. The boy could hear screams, pleas and threats inside his head. He knew they were coming from the blackness. A dark world was there. He knew it. He could smell something foul coming from it. The horror beckoned with one long, bony finger. His brother turned over catching the shadow's attention. His other brother coughed and the demon flew toward him. He was going to devour him! The boy shouted "No!" waking his two older brothers.

In the bright sunlight of the morning they made fun of his dream. But he knew it was real and when he grew up he would find the demon.

And kill it.

CHAPTER ONE

THE FATHER

1119 A.D.
Marets, France

The tall, well-built man, looking every inch the noble that he was, watched from a distance, as his gamekeeper patiently answered the three boys' questions. He nodded in silent agreement, as the keeper carefully showed them how to set the new, improved trap. Impulsively, the youngest boy grabbed a stick and snapped the trap, making the keeper frown and the father smile. It was typical of Baldwin, the youngest and most softhearted of the trio.

Armand DesMarets scratched his graying beard as he contemplated his intelligent and inquisitive offspring. His more serious and studious first son, Reginald, would never think of interrupting a lesson. He would try to figure out how much profit he could get for the trapped creature. His second son, Goswin, might try to take the trap apart after the lesson or see if any of the parts would float.

All three boys–men now, their father realized–were more educated than he'd been at their age. They were also more curious and well trained in weaponry. Each was creative in his own way. Reginald spent hours designing buildings and weapons and then figuring the cost of each. Goswin loved floating the green glass bottles, used for bottling their vineyard's bounty, to see how far

1

they'd go. And Baldwin was excellent at sketching, painting, and etching out designs in metal. He could create very lifelike portraits. All three asked many questions, which Armand knew was a sign of intelligence. At the moment, the three were excitedly discussing a "better way" to catch an animal.

"A deep hole is what we need," Reginald advised. "One deep enough where a deer, for instance, could fall in but not get out."

"But deer can jump high and almost straight up," Goswin countered.

"Plus, we just can't have a hole along a path that a man might accidently fall into, or a woman or child," Baldwin said thoughtfully.

"That's why," Goswin cut in, "we need it near the lake. Then I can make a channel into the hole and run water into it, drowning the thing."

Baldwin made a face as Reginald said, "Cruel but effective. How would you do it?"

As the father listened to the boys' ideas, a woman with long, brown braids walked up beside Armand and put her arm inside his. She was wearing a modest but finely woven linen dress, with detailed colorful embroidery, a matching beige cloak, hemmed in a design to match the dress and a kerchief as a headdress.

"Why must they always learn such things Armand when the gamekeeper can do it for them?"

Armand smiled down at his lovely wife, Angelica. Although they were just a few years apart in age, his world-weary, lined face, perpetually tanned skin, and graying hair made him look, at least, twenty years older. "Knowing how to catch game fed my hungry belly more times than I care to remember on the march to Jerusalem. The more they know how to survive on their own, the better. Plus, they like to design traps. It amuses them, even when Baldwin sometimes lets the poor, entangled creatures go."

"But Armand," she countered, "you had your servants with you. Surely they did those things."

He patted her hand and looked into the distance. He frowned

2

and a shadow of sadness crossed his face. "Where are they now, my dear? Not with us, where they should be."

"No Armand, but in a greater place. They died serving our Lord. And you. What greater service is there?"

"If I'd died in the service of our Lord, or to be exact, Pope Urban the Second, we would not be the proud parents of three boys, who are about to be men." He kicked at a stone, sending it flying.

"Shame Armand! The Pope does God's work."

"The Pope does ..." but he stopped. His wife was too devout a Catholic to understand his exact opinion of Pope Urban II or of the religious men who took his place. In 1095, the pontiff influenced thousands of men, women, and children to leave their homes, travel to the Holy City and take it back from Muslim rule.

For that, they were *guaranteed* a place in heaven. If they didn't sacrifice themselves and regain Jerusalem from the infidels, they would go to hell. Armand had been in Clermont, France and heard Urban's rousing speech and the crowd's reaction. There'd been a collective gasp when the Pope had promised absolution and remission of sins for all who died in the service of Lord Jesus.

When he left for the crusade with his fellow noblemen, Armand thought there was only one true religion and way to worship and live. Everything in the Bible was true, and the Pope was God's authority on earth. He was proud to do God's will, kill the Saracens, and take Jerusalem from the infidels. At the age of twenty, Armand left his parent's estate, enthusiastically joined the other nobility and took part in the battles along the way, to free the Holy City.

It was a three-year campaign, where peasants and nobles alike killed non-believers in the name of God. Muslims, Jews, and even Christians who looked foreign to the rampaging mob of peasants were slaughtered on sight. Only the nobility, who'd organized and left weeks after the peasants, showed order among the troops. They killed and confiscated lands for themselves, eventually making them all the richer.

Upon arrival in the blessed city itself after a seven-week, bloody siege, he'd followed his commander, Godfrey of Bouillion, through the gates and cut down every one he saw. A powerful kick, just above his left knee, from a falling horse was the only wound he received, but it was a harsh one. He'd fallen into a pool of blood and carnage, which soaked him. He stood and someone's severed hand stuck to him.

"Damn it to hell!" he cursed, threw the hand over the nearest roof, and went on slashing. The stench was horrendous—one he'd never forget. Bloody-faced and angry, he strode through the masses, maiming and killing. He then limped through the flowing blood of the "others" to serve his religion. His blood was on fire!

He felt righteous, proud and truly noble. He'd done his duty. He didn't look beyond his sacrifice, to the dictates of Pope Urban, into the sadness that wrapped around his heart.

It took him three days to wash all the blood and gore off. The stench remained. A shadow took up residence in his soul. He spent several weeks slowly healing his wounds and painfully treading the path where Jesus had walked. He looked at sacred relics and prayed at holy sites. He kissed the wall of Temple Mount and thanked God for giving him strength in battle and righteousness in his weary heart.

Almost twenty years later he had a broader view of other people's thoughts and lifestyles. It was still the mood of the time, to be fanatically religious, but he was no longer convinced of the all-knowing, infallible opinion of the church. Over the years, he'd gotten to know the peasants he owned, as part of his estate, and showed them respect.

Angelica also treated them as people rather than chattel and let them use the estate chapel for worship, an unheard of practice in other parts of France. In return, these moral, hardworking, and humble people were devoted to the DesMarets family.

After the crusaders made Godfrey of Bouillon the ruler of Jerusalem, Armand left. He'd commandeered a shaggy, desert-colored camel. It was not his ride of choice but almost all of the horses had either starved or been killed. He traded his saddle for the camel but kept his chainmail, helmet and sword.

He would not take the long overland journey back and decided to travel by sea. It was a shorter trip but equally as perilous. When he got to the coast, he sold the stinking camel, boarded a ship at Acre, and sailed to Italy, on a sailing vessel the Vikings would have admired.

The trip was long, dreary, and not without danger. He signed on to row, an unusual step for a man of his background. The salt water, sun, and monotonous pace of rowing helped numb his memories, harden his muscles, and strengthen his resolve to create a better life.

Once back on land, he bought a sturdy-looking, black stallion and made his way home. He found his father was dead, and his mother was doing her best to save their home. He arrived in time to thwart several brigands, who thought they could take the estate away from her. They, obviously, didn't know her strength.

Armand had served the Pope well in the great three-year crusade. He'd defeated the infidels, returned to France, and married the beautiful Angelica. She'd given him three strapping and rambunctious boys. Except for the constant nightmares, the physical scars, and his slight limp, he thought himself a lucky, God-fearing man.

After he'd left the Holy City, the invasions and battles didn't stop. Now he'd heard the rumors of other problems. Pilgrims, on the way to visit the Holy Land, were being robbed and slaughtered because there weren't enough knights to protect them. There might be another crusade, he didn't know.

He shuttered at the thought. He'd seen too many atrocities to ever have a charmed and carefree life, as he had been when he was young. He'd been twenty when he left on the great campaign, to rid the Holy Land of all non-believers. His boys were now twenty, nineteen, and eighteen. He was making sure that, if the passion to defend the Holy Land overtook them, as it had him, they were going to be well prepared–far better than he'd ever been.

His wife patted his arm, bringing him out of his reverie and turned toward the family chapel. It was time for her to pray.

"Armand, won't you pray with me?"

"I want to talk to our sons. I promise I will pray with you tonight. Mother will keep you company."

She smiled. It was a smile that he had held in his heart during the almost unbearable days of the crusade. They were long years, during which time his aristocratic hands became callous and a corner of his heart forever cold.

Unbelievably, she'd waited for him. Her devotion was unbreakable, her heart pure. When he'd returned to France he never wanted to see a sword or even a horse ever again. Alas, he was a nobleman and horses were part of the picture, along with his hunting dogs, servants and all the trappings of a wealthy landowner.

Truly he loved his family estate. When he smelled the rose garden, tears glimmered in his eyes. He thought it unmanly to cry but in those moments he felt divinely blessed, not when he'd help defeat the infidels, first saw the Holy Land nor when he knew he was returning home. It was his daily walks in the rose garden, his marriage to Angelica and the birth of his sons that helped his war-torn soul.

He kept constantly busy. In his moments of rest the flashbacks would come. Sometimes something he saw would trigger them. Once he entered the kitchen just as the cook chopped off a chicken's head. He left abruptly and ran to the gardens as fast as his boots would take him. Sweet smelling fragrance was the antidote to his bad memories. It calmed and soothed him. His aging mother always smelled of lavender, a plant he was determined to raise. Loud noise would bring the screams of men and horses or shouts and the clanging of swords into his mind. Then there were the nightmares when he called out and woke in a sweat. Over time they'd become less intense and fewer.

In the mornings after a dark episode he tried to count his blessings. Often he remembered the time he first saw Angelica.

She was fourteen, he eighteen when they met. She contemplated becoming a nun but the order wouldn't take anyone so young. He had two years to win her heart.

Then Pope Urban made his decree–heaven guaranteed to those who fought in the name of God. But only if they won back the Holy Land. Of course he must go. He had the most beautiful stallion, the best livery and the most devoted servants. He was a natural leader. Angelica promised to wait for him. It was impossible to hope that she had.

Upon his return he'd made inquiries and found that, in two weeks time, there was a grand ball being held at a neighboring estate and she would be there. His mother could not recall if Angelica had married or not. His usually fiercely devoted mother had that hallow look of someone who no longer took care of herself or her surroundings. The estate was slightly run down, gardens needed tending and the surrounding walls newly rocked. They needed more servants, but his mother didn't seem to notice.

On the day of the ball, Armand took great care with his toilette. He trimmed his beard, bathed in warm water scented with rose and carefully combed his hair. His boots shone and his clothes were immaculate. When he entered the mansion the ball was in full swing. Many lovely women danced with their partners in the middle of the room. When the music stopped, a tall, slender woman walked up to him. She was stylishly dressed in azure-colored silk yet wore simple jewelry, unlike the other women.

"Armand," she said. He looked into familiar sparkling blue eyes. His breath caught and he couldn't speak. He held out his arm. She placed her arm on his and he led her out the door, down the stone steps and into the fragrant garden. He breathed in the rose and lavender. They walked in silence until they reached a waist-high, stone wall, made of grey rock.

During those long, dusty, heart-wrenching years he'd dreamed of seeing her again, knew exactly what he'd ask; yet now when he could see her beauty and feel her warmth his throat constricted.

He searched his mind for something meaningful to say that would impress her.

She said softly, "I attended your father's funeral. There were many candles lit. I helped your mother give alms to the poor." She looked away over the stone wall as if embarrassed. Or remembering.

Armand was overcome. His senses sharpened. He saw her in a softly glowing light: Her skin was luminous, garden roses scented the air, his body seemed to vibrate and his well-rehearsed speech vanished.

"Uh, I have many ideas for the estate," he heard himself say, as if from a great distance. "I plan on planting grape vines, many of them ..."

She looked up at him. "I like grapes," she interrupted.

He cleared his throat. "Eventually, I will make fine French wine out of them instead of the bitter slosh they serve now."

"I like grape juice," she said. "The nuns would like it for their communion. Maybe our Lord Jesus really turned water into grape juice. What do you think?" Her eyes twinkled and she was smiling.

Armand gave himself a brief mental talk–you've faced many dangers, fought valiantly, defeated the Muslims, you can ask her this. Instead of answering her teasing question he asked softly, "Did you marry?"

"Too busy," she said lightly.

He exhaled. "Doing what?"

"Attending chapel three times a day praying for your safe return."

He smiled. Suddenly he was back to himself. He brought her hand to his lips and kissed it. "I can see where that might discourage any suitors."

She nodded staring at him with an amused look. "God blesses the devout."

He cleared his throat. "It did indeed work. Here I am."

"Yes."

They stood in silence for a moment. He was aware that the

moon was up, the crickets were chirping and she, too, smelled of roses. "Is your father still living?"

She nodded.

"In the morning I will ask him for your hand in marriage."

She smiled, blushed and nodded. His heart touched the stars. As they walked back to the chateau, he spoke briefly of the plans he had for the estate: a modern workshop, fields of lavender, bees for honey, small gardens for vegetables and flowers, especially roses. Of course, grapes—lots of grapes. He'd name the vineyard after her. He wanted to make the place magnificent again and profitable.

One month later the two virgins married.

During the crusade, he'd kept his vow of chastity before marriage. He took his pent-up energy and discharged it through battle. After battle he fasted and prayed. He remembered their wedding day in the estate chapel. He was nervous and emotional but the ceremony went well. It was the feast afterword where he almost spoiled the day. It had been the fish. Or rather the sight of the fish when it was brought in on a platter with it's dead staring eyes. He suddenly saw the dead eyes of men who had been cut down in battle. He quickly pushed his chair back and walked outside.

Perhaps it wouldn't have been noticed by the celebrating guests if, when he took his place at the head of the table again, Angelica hadn't been cutting the head off the fish. The memory was so strong that he had to grab onto the arms of the chair and look down. Both sides of those fighting in the crusade had made sure that heads were separated from the shoulders of opposing forces. Then paraded them on poles.

"Take it away," he mumbled.

"But Armand this is the main ..."

"Take it away *now*," he'd gasped.

Angelica, seeing his white face, ordered the confused servant to take it away. Their cook quickly filleted the fish, added a sauce and heaps of vegetables and the meal went on. Armand never explained and Angelica never asked. She never served a whole fish again.

On their wedding night, when they first made love she was nervous and scared, which excited him. Her skin was fragrant and soft under his calloused hands. Fortunately, he knew that the way men and women had sex was different than the animals in the stables had sex. The many servants and crusaders did as they pleased when it came to the pleasures of the flesh. Many nights during the campaign Armand heard the ecstatic groans and moans coming from neighboring tents, or, when the evenings were hot, as they often were, the camp followers and servants would have sex openly outside under the bright moon. Armand couldn't help but watch and think of Angelica. Nine months after their wedding night she delivered Reginald; a year later Goswin; and then Baldwin. Armand thought them perfect.

Secretly, the proud parent studied other religions and beliefs. He created a library in his house of ancient manuscripts along with his detailed instructions on how to run a large estate. He was no longer sure that his beliefs were the only beliefs that counted, but he kept his opinions to himself. He was still devout, but he knew he'd already been to hell and dark demons were still with him. He tried not to be bitter. Sometimes when he was by himself he wept.

Angelica lived her life by the mandates of the church. She prayed three times a day. Armand found when he tried this too many thoughts crowded out most of his prayers. Or he was so exhausted from being busy that he'd fall asleep. But she never scolded him for his laxity in his devotion. He'd brought her a relic from the Holy Land of a saint's small cross, which was tied on a cord. He'd taken it from a private chapel, which had been ransacked by both Christians and Muslims. She wore it around her neck. He'd brought back several small items from Jerusalem. A six-inch, jewel-encrusted cup was his favorite.

When he wasn't reliving episodes from the crusade, Armand felt moments of happiness and satisfaction. He had a reputation as a fair and honest man, which grew as he aged. He instilled his morals and insights into his sons, knowing one day their reputations as forthright, honest and pious men would serve them well in these troubling times.

While Angelica taught the boys piety and religion, Armand made sure they were well educated but tough. No easy country squire lives for them. He did have hopes that Baldwin would be the one to take over the running of the vineyards. Baldwin had a natural way with plants and was the most dutiful of the three sons—devoted to his mother and religion. However, Reginald as the oldest son would inherit everything. But first he wanted to formally learn accounting and see more of the world. Goswin wanted to go to sea.

However the reality was, taking Jerusalem back from the Muslims did not stop the fighting. Battles were constantly taking place and Armand knew that one day another Pope would start another crusade if the Muslims prevailed. All three of his sons were taught how to hunt game both big and small; how to ride with and without a saddle; how to mend and sew (much to Angelica's amusement); and how to skin a small animal and cook over an open fire. He taught them everything he knew they would need, just in case.

The devoted father had hired a tutor who was skilled in teaching languages. The tutor, Rajeev, Armand met while he was returning from the Holy Land. He'd seen the small, neatly dressed man seated atop a wagon filled with people on the muddy road to Paris. Armand had ridden up just in time to thwart some marauders, who, upon seeing him, decided to gallop by and leave the travelers alone. He'd escorted the group to Paris, chatting with the foreigner along the way. Rajeev was a new convert to Christianity and surprisingly to Armand he knew Latin, French, English, Greek and Hindi. He's been hired by a wealthy French family to educate their children. At first wary of his dark skin and the foreign ways of India, Armand found he liked the man's intelligence and enthusiasm for his future.

Several years later while on a trip to Paris, Armand met a less enthusiastic and jobless Rajeev. The family he'd worked for no longer needed him and had fired him without compensation. Armand hired him immediately and brought him home to tutor his two sons and the one on the way. Over the years they had become friends. Rajeev also taught Angelica Latin, which greatly pleased her. Now she understood the Latin prayers that she recited every day by heart.

As a way of identifying and unifying themselves as a family, Armand, with the help of Rajeev, Angelica and their sons, suggested a family motto. "It should convey the very ideals of our family," he said, which was met with much debate and enthusiasm.

Eventually, *By Faith We Live* was decided upon. Baldwin thought it should be on their shields and got to work on a simple design. Angelica decided it should be embroidered above their hearts and she set to work on each of their tunics. She decided on blue thread that matched the color of the Virgin's robes.

Armand showed his enthusiastic sons how to use all the weapons that he had seen in the crusade: the sword, mace, spear, lance, bow and arrow and the axe. He advised them to keep daggers with them even in France where criminals could attack anyone on city streets. He showed them his chainmail and how to put padding under it to help keep the chain from chaffing and the enemy's arrows from penetrating. He advised them to carry water at all times and told them how honey was used to help heal wounds after battle. He also tried to explain camels.

"You're telling tales," Reginald scoffed when he heard his father's description of the ungainly beast.

"They have humps on their backs?" Goswin asked, sounding skeptical.

"They spit?" Baldwin asked, sounding intrigued.

"There are beasts in the world like nothing in France," their father said. "People, plants, animals, clothes, buildings, are all different," he stated. "Beyond anything you can imagine."

The boys looked at each other and shook their heads not

knowing if they should believe their father or not. They loved his stories. He was a great hero in their eyes although he tried to dissuade them of that notion. They took after him and thrived in the outdoors and were taller and more robust than any of the other neighbor boys.

They each had an affinity for animals: the oldest a falcon, the second a lizard and the third a dog. Reginald's falcon and Baldwin's dog were always trying to catch the lizard. But it was fast and knew every escape hole on the estate. Although the falcon and dog were local, Armand had no idea where Goswin had gotten hold of a desert creature like the lizard. Probably from a peasant who'd brought it from the Holy Land. Having brought a few things back himself, Armand couldn't very well scold his son for acquiring it. Goswin was fascinated by the scaly creature and didn't seem to mind that the other pets took a dislike to it.

Armand didn't mention that if they took their animals with them into any kind of battle, the animals more than likely wouldn't survive. They'd be killed and eaten. There were other things he needed to tell them though. Things in their devotion to their religion they would find hard to believe.

CHAPTER TWO

MOTHER AND SONS

1119 A.D.
Marets, France

Shaking his dark head in exasperation, Rajeev was doing his best to give Reginald some advice but failing in his task. They were gathered in the lower-level library fondly called by the family, The Everything Room. One day Goswin had looked around and stated that the shelves held "everything you'd ever want to know." Baldwin promptly named it The Everything Room. From then on the boys always called it that.

"Rajeev," Reginald said in his usual serious tone, "you're better than any monastic school."

Rajeev smiled and put his hands together and bowed over them. "I am humbled by your praise young master."

"Young!" Reginald exclaimed as he smoothed his short brown beard. "Look at my fine, manly beard. It's far better than those of my two immature brothers."

A small, blue decorative pillow came flying toward his head followed by protests from both of his younger brothers. Reginald caught the pillow in mid-air, grinned at his brothers, tossed the pillow up and caught it. "I will retaliate when you least expect it," he said as he slowly walked around the room taking one step for each toss. His brothers watched him slowly toss the pillow a bit higher each time. He was good at this–building up some wariness before he struck back.

The trio stood in the vaulted-ceiling room along with Rajeev examining some manuscripts and leather-bound books carefully laid out on a long, oak table. Two blue and gold brocade couches with carved legs and clawed lions feet flanked it. Beautifully stitched burgundy, blue and green pillows with nature scenes of birds and flowers were lined along the couch backs. From the lack of wear it was obvious the couches weren't often used.

Between Armand's thirst for knowledge and Rajeev's extensive grasp of languages this was a build-up of one of the finest, if not *the* finest, manor libraries in their region of France. The two men liked traveling to monasteries to look at the latest works of monks or some recently found volume on the lives of saints. More often than not they would negotiate with the abbot of a monastery or abbess of a prominent abbey for an elaborately illustrated manuscript or leather-bound book. The holy ones were always in need of money and were not the best of negotiators. The pair also hunted for poets and writers of secular works who were always willing to sell their artistic endeavors.

The three lanky young men, tall as their father, looked warily at each other. Their much shorter tutor tried not to smile at their playfulness. The pillow throw had been from Baldwin, whose beard was just starting to show. Goswin had shaped his beard and kept his long hair in a ponytail.

"I think I have a precocious beard because I am precocious," he stated.

"How can your beard be precocious?" Baldwin asked as he sat down on one long couch. His dog, Bhaiya, sat on the floor beside him.

"Ah," Rajeev broke in, "because it has developed early."

"Exactly, full and magnificent, too." Goswin said.

"This is your fault Rajeev," Reginald stated. "He's now too smart for us. You've taught us many languages and filled our heads with the knowledge of all these words," Reginald said.

"Yes. We're overflowing," Baldwin added. Reginald threw the pillow and made a direct hit in Baldwin's face. "You've got to be quicker, Dog Face," Reginald said. Goswin snickered.

"I do *not* have a dog face," Baldwin said as he launched the pillow in Goswin's direction. "Bhaiya likes my face," he said grinning. "Don't you boy? Handsome. Smart and charming, too." The longhaired dog by his side stared up at him and thumped his tail against the floor. Baldwin reached down and patted the auburn colored head.

"I'm going to be clean shaven and people will think I'm a monk," Baldwin said. Bhaiya barked.

"Baby Face then," Goswin said as he aimed the pillow at his younger brother.

Just then Angelina walked through the archway and immediately saw her favorite pillow being launched across the room. She stepped forward and caught it. "Your grandmother made this! It's not a ball to be tossed around!" She set it on the couch and patted it. "Rajeev I'm afraid they will not be able to leave your care until they learn to be civilized."

Rajeev smiled. "I have tried milady but it has not sunk in. I have let them read all the scrolls and manuscripts in every language that I know, but," and he bowed his head to hide his smile, "they have not heard the words clearly. As the great sages of my country say, "Words do not teach. Only experience.""

"Exactly!" Reginald said loudly. "We'll be the greatest scholars only if we go out and get experience."

The boys looked expectantly at their mother. Angelica looked back at her grown sons and sighed. "Come on upstairs where there's light and air. We have much to discuss."

With their mother leading the way the foursome climbed the narrow stairs, which opened into the bright solarium. Rajeev stayed behind to put the precious reading materials away. Due to the lack of light in the vaulted ceiling room, the persons studying the materials would choose one or two and take them up a flight of stone steps to the sunny solarium, although they were careful

16

not to expose the illuminated illustrations to too much light, as the bright colors of the illustrations would fade.

The solarium was everyone's favorite room in the manor. It had floor-to-ceiling windows on one side and comfortable, much used, beautifully carved and upholstered couches and chairs. Large pots held luxurious plants that were the pride of both Armand and Angelica. The entire manor had a thick wall around it, which gave the occupants a feeling of protection from the frequent wanderings of beggars and brigands.

Angelica walked to the long windows and looked into the well-tended garden—one of several gardens within the manor walls, all with the same square-bed design. The fragrant herb garden was filled with healing herbs of chamomile, several types of mint, fenugreek, rosemary, rue, sage, bergamot, lovage and fennel. Armand had planted angelica—he said one day he would make something sweet and delicious out of it. "Like you, my dear," he'd said.

She noticed that the mint was spilling over its borders again and she would have to pick and dry some. The nuns had taught her the best herbs to plant. Her young sons had been eager to learn about them, too. They could all heal minor insect bites and scrapes—useful since they had a lot of them. A fountain had been built into one side of the wall with water spilling out of a lion's mouth. She remembered when she'd first seen the fountain. It had been when she and Armand were young teenagers just getting to know each other. Thoughtfully she watched the water pour from the lion's mouth into the scalloped basin below. Her eyes misted as she remembered.

Reginald's birth had been easier than she'd been told it would be. She'd ignored all the women who came to see her when she was expecting, seemingly just to tell her tales of woe and agony when having children. Fortunately, she was attended by the nuns who had no birth experience or agonizing stories. They knew about oils, herbs and teas to soothe her pain.

When the baby boy was put into her arms she'd named him

Reginald after Armand's late father. The look that Armand gave her when he saw the baby and she suggested the name was so soft and tender that she knew she would go through any pain if he would look at her that way again. That tender moment made the small birthing room just off their bedchamber bright with light and love. Armand was overjoyed that he had a healthy, squalling baby boy. Together the parents showered the child with love and affection. Armand would get tough with the boy later, but for now he was a hands-on father.

For the first several months they didn't hire a nursemaid. Then Angelica became pregnant again. Angelica's maid recommended her own sister to help. Armand interviewed her with Angelica looking on. He determined that she was down-to-earth and sensible. With a nod of approval from Angelica, Rosza was hired on the spot. She was a great help to Angelica and stayed with the family for all three children.

At first when Rajeev arrived Rosza didn't know what to make of him. She'd never heard or seen anyone like the short, brown-skinned man who seemed to make every sentence a question. But they soon found out what was best about each other. Rosza listened in class right along with the boys and was now a fairly well-educated woman.

Angelica was pulled out of her reverie by a soft bark from Bhaiya. She smiled. With his intelligent, dark eyes, and direct stare Bhaiya seemed always to know what she was thinking. She turned toward her three grown sons and their tutor who had just entered the room. What was she going to do without them?

"I know what you're implying Reginald," she said. "That you've absorbed all the words these scrolls have and yet ..." she sighed, "words don't teach. It's time to go out into the world and learn true knowledge through life experiences." Her sons looked at each other and grinned. "It's time to pray. You can bring your pets this time. Our Lord Jesus was born in a manger so I'm sure he doesn't mind that you have pets watch over you."

"Thanks, mother, they'll behave," Reginald said as he went to get his falcon, Guruda.

Rajeev was a practicing Christian yet he couldn't help but teach his charges the tenets of Hinduism, the predominant religion of his region. The young boys were fascinated by the many stories that Rajeev told. Reginald and Baldwin had decided to name their pets with Hindu names, just to amuse themselves. In Hindu mythology, Guruda was a mixture of eagle and human features. Snakes feared him. Goswin's lizard wasn't very fond of him either. Reginald thought it the perfect name for his pet falcon.

Reginald trained Guruda to hunt, sit on his gloved hand and wear a cloth cover over his eyes when being carried. The bird was smart and took his training well. Since he and Bhaiya were raised together almost from birth, they knew each other thoroughly and would often pair up to play and hunt. Guruda would soar far above Bhaiya, spot a small prey–often a fox or a rabbit–and suddenly dive. Bhaiya took this as a challenge and although he couldn't see what Guruda saw, he often sensed where the bird was going or smelled the prey. He'd take off. Rarely could he beat his falcon friend but he would bark and run circles around the prey as Guruda went in for the conquest. It seemed to their human owners that the two were playing more than hunting.

Baldwin's faithful dog's name, Bhaiya, was Hindi for "brother." The dog was Baldwin's companion, protector and confidant–the boy swore that Bhaiya understood everything he said to him. When his father had first suggested a dog for Baldwin and had taken him to several kennels where shorthaired hunting dogs were trained, Baldwin didn't want any of them. On the way home, Armand stopped to look in on one of his serfs and Baldwin had spotted recently born pups. The bitch had long auburn hair, a friendly face (at least Baldwin thought so) and was licking and pushing her fat, wiggling pups around with her nose.

"One of these, father," Baldwin said and looked at each closely. One of the pups turned in a circle, as if chasing his tiny tail before latching onto his mother's tit and sucking. "That one," he said pointing.

Armand, looking amused, offered a token sum to his surprised peasant. Being Armand's property, everything the serf had was also Armand's. The serf put his hands up in refusal of the money.

"So you can feed the bitch properly and she'll provide my son's pup with plenty of milk," Armand said gruffly and laid the coins on the table.

"He'll be weaned in about three weeks," the peasant said. He wasn't fooled by Armand's gruff tone. His lord had quietly done other unnecessarily kind things for his serfs. Other peasants knew of this and wanted to be part of the DesMaret's landholdings but those already working on the lands made sure they worked hard and steady so there was no room for anyone new. The serfs were proud of their owners and kept close watch on the boys and their mother. Their cottages were tidy and their reputations orderly so no ill treatment would befall them as had the peasants of less honorable lords.

"May I come and see him before he's weaned?" Baldwin asked.

"Of course, young master!" the man said. His wife stepped up beside him.

"You are always welcome to come anytime." She would tell all the other serfs of what had happened and solidify the DesMaret's honest and fair reputation.

"Thank you," Baldwin said as he was mounting his horse. The husband and wife looked at each other. They knew they were lucky to have such polite and generous owners.

After a few minutes of riding his father said, "I'm proud of you son for treating our serfs with respect. Always remember, even if we do own them, and we do, they are human with emotions and needs just as all of God's children have desires. Always be firm but fair."

Baldwin smiled at his father. "I noticed you paid a sum for the dog and I know you didn't have to. We could have just taken it. Isn't that so?"

His father nodded. "Yes. I am his lord, which gives me power over him, his family and possessions. Our society is basically divided into three categories: clergy, nobility and serfs. As you know, many of the sons of nobility become knights. When I was a knight, I in effect protected him. However, so many peasants went to free Jerusalem from the Muslims and got cut down for their efforts I'm surprised we have any. No doubt he lost grandparents or other relatives in that prolonged fight. The pope promised all who heard his call-to-arms speech that their sins would be forgiven and they would go straight to heaven if they killed the infidels and took back the Holy Land ..."

"You, too, yes father?" Baldwin interrupted eagerly.

"Oh yes. Guaranteed. Straight up," Armand answered and pointed upward. "I don't think Pope Urban realized that the peasants, including women and children, would start marching immediately and eventually get slaughtered for their eagerness and efforts. We sons of nobility and some of our fathers, too, organized first. We had a tournament at Anchin to prepare us as knights and we, therefore, actually reached the Holy Land." He looked away and shook his head.

"They're all in heaven now," Baldwin stated.

Armand looked at this son and nodded. "If the pope was correct."

"Father!" Baldwin exclaimed. "The pope speaks directly to God. He is his mouthpiece. Of course you're all going to heaven!"

Armand smiled at his youngest son. "I know for a fact that your saintly mother will be in heaven with me. No one is better than she. You will notice that she treats the serfs like humans, also."

"Yes," Baldwin said. "Leaving them food outside the chapel and visiting the sick and those having babies."

"She has the qualities of the Blessed Mother of Jesus."

Baldwin looked thoughtful. After a moment he said, "Father you still have nightmares about the Holy war, do you not?"

"Not as many as before. There are good things in my life now that keep the remembrances away." He looked over at his son. "Why do you mention this?"

"I'm having dreams," Baldwin said shyly.

"Of?"

"Women."

Armand laughed so loudly his horse snorted and tossed its head. "I should think so at your age. If I hadn't gone galloping off to save a city I'd never seen before, I'd have married your mother at the age you are now. It was God's blessing that she waited for me. Who is the lucky lady?"

"Um," Baldwin sighed. "I don't know."

His father looked at him curiously.

"What I mean is, I think she must be an angel or ..." he lowered his voice, "Mother Mary, maybe."

Armand rubbed his chin and thought for a moment. "This is something you have to discuss with your mother. It's possible you're having holy visions. If so, you're mother will be overjoyed."

"Thanks father," Baldwin said sounding relieved. His father glanced at him. "For not making jest of me," Baldwin continued.

Armand smiled. "In a family such as ours where your mother prays three times a day and strives to be as perfect as Mary the Mother of Jesus, while I have a free pass to heaven, I would think it strange if you didn't have visions." They laughed and urged their horses into a trot, not mentioning it again.

Armand thought his sons old enough and strong enough now to learn some jousting with unwieldy lances as he had at the Tournoi d'Anchin. Over 300 knights had participated, then the ones who still had arms and legs signed an oath to go on the crusade. Such devotion and ambition. He would start their lessons soon.

The middle son Goswin had waited several months after the others before getting a pet. Angelica thought it might be a cat, but they didn't interest him. Then one day he came home with an ugly, scaly lizard. At first Armand questioned him about where he'd obtained such a creature, thinking that perhaps it was brought in unwisely from the Holy Land where heat and sand were common. He was sure it would die in the lush lands of France. But Goswin took good care of his odd looking creature and named his lizard Monster. His brothers thought that was an appropriate name.

Angelica felt great comfort as she knelt inside the chapel with her three sons on either side of her to pray. Bhaiya was on the floor beside Baldwin. Monster had scampered up the wall and could barely be seen against the green background. Guruda was tethered on the back of a chair because everyone knew he could see Monster perfectly well. The pets were well behaved indeed.

The chapel had been added to the small manor in the 10th century. It was simple rather than the elaborate chapels in the monasteries that dotted France. It had plain glass in the arch over the wooden doors with a curved wood design. Angelica always admired how something so simple could look so beautiful. The walls were painted a dark green with gold wreaths lovingly hand painted in a beautiful design. The green gave the chapel a somber feeling while the gold design added a touch of richness. Angelica thought it perfect. A statue of Mary, mother of Jesus, dressed in azure blue robes was in an alcove behind the dark brown, wooden alter. One white candle was in front of the statue, which Angelica lit.

One winter Armand had gifted her with a small brilliantly illuminated bible written in Latin. She always carried it with her to pray and blessed her thoughtful husband for giving her such a gift. He was truly a devoted husband. Even though she had learned basic Latin from the abbey nuns and because he was an expert translator–more knowledgeable than she–Rajeev often read the Latin passages to her in French. She then gave impassioned sermons to the serfs who came to the chapel, knowing that the French translation would be perfect. Her favorite passages were about Mary, how pure she was and how devoted. If only all the Christian women of France could be so devoted, then what a blessed world it would be. She also owned a beautifully stitched and illustrated devotional book, also written in Latin, which she read nightly. The nuns had given it to her as a wedding gift and Rajeev and taught her how to read it properly.

Angelica sat in the front of the chapel on a red velvet covered chair and held hands with Reginald on her right and Baldwin on her left. Goswin sat on the other side of Baldwin. Angelica reached over Baldwin and patted Goswin's folded hands. Baldwin then held his brother's hand and his mother's. Together, mother and children quietly finished the brief prayer of devotion. The peace and quiet joy of the moment settled into their mother's heart. The one thing she allowed herself to be proud of, even knowing pride was a sin, was how much her sons loved each other. They had been rambunctious but also caring and had more fun together than fights. As Reginald and Goswin got up to leave, Baldwin remained seated holding his mother's hand.

"Mother, I've something to tell you," he whispered.

She nodded at her other two sons as they quietly left but remained seated with her youngest son at her side.

"I may be having visions," Baldwin whispered. "Do saints eyes glow?"

"Yes, I suppose they do," his mother said gently as she fingered the cross around her neck.

"I saw a sparkling angel in the corner. Its eyes glowed. She was saying something to me. Either 'no' or 'go'. I couldn't be sure."

His mother put her hand over her heart. "Was it Mother Mary?" she asked softly. Tears suddenly sprang to her eyes and they glimmered in the soft light.

"Maybe," Baldwin answered. "I've seen her before. She wears a robe just like that statue of Mary only brown colored. She doesn't look the same. Sometimes there's another one, younger and thinner. She's always barefoot and surrounded by a forest."

"A forest?"

Baldwin nodded. He wanted to ask if demons' eyes glowed, too. But he dared not upset his mother. If she thought he saw demons … He loved his mother deeply but he didn't know how she'd react if she ever knew he saw a shadow beckoning him to come into a dark pit. He was glad he saw angels, too.

"You are blessed to see these angels. Your father and I are blessed to have you as our son." His mother leaned over and kissed him on the cheek.

"Thank you mother," Baldwin said squeezing her hand. "You are always such a comfort to me." He felt something tugging on the end of his tunic. He looked down at Bhaiya wagging his tail. "Ah, my master calls," he said smiling.

His mother reached down and gave Bhaiya a pat. "He takes such good care of you. He will always stay by your side."

Baldwin stood up and reached out his hand to help his mother up.

"Not just yet," she said. "I need to speak to the Virgin."

Baldwin kissed her cheek and left with his faithful companion trotting by his side.

In the quiet chapel, Angelica sank into thoughts of her past. She knew her children would soon leave her to start their own journeys. She wanted to keep them as close as possible in the little time she had left. As lord of the manor, Armand had prepared them as best he could for what she considered "the outside world." It was a world she knew little of. As she remembered it, her husband had seemed so young when he left her to serve God in battle. When he came back he was definitely a man, battle weary and yet able to love and provide for her. Together they had prospered on their country estate and the children had thrived along with the Kingdom of France ruled by the House of Capet.

Angelica couldn't believe how quickly her boys had grown to manhood, or how different their personalities were. When he was very young Reginald loved to count everything–over and over. He'd hide his wooden toy soldiers in the house or bury them outside. Her second son Goswin loved his soldiers, too, but he took them down to the pond or floated them on small bits of wood in the fountain in front of the manor. Of the three boys, he was the one who couldn't wait to take a bath. It seemed to Angelica and

Rosza that he liked to take a bath just to splash all of the water out of the basin. That always made Armand laugh.

"It's good to take baths now," Armand said. "You might not like them so much when you're grown up."

"You like them," Angelica pointed out. Armand smiled.

"When you've lived in hot desert sand for awhile you'll understand the effect just watching water can have on the soul." He'd lift the squirming boy up and swing him around until the baby either screamed or giggled.

The name Goswin was a combination of the names of Armand's two loyal servants—Goshen and Godwin—both of whom had died valiantly in the crusade serving Armand, giving up their lives to protect him. Angelica hoped Goswin would have the loyal qualities of those loving men. He was sturdier than Reginald and liked to strut instead of walk. He also had a quick temper but seemed to calm down when little Baldwin came to play with him.

Baldwin was always questioning but also the peacemaker between the boys. At a young age he had dreams of angels and saints. Their youngest had been named after Baldwin of Boulogne, king of the Crusader state of Jerusalem, whom Armand considered one of the greatest commanders of the crusader army. Although, like the other crusader nobles, Armand at first opposed Baldwin be made king—after all his brother, Godfrey of Bouillon, had refused to be crowned king in favor of the title Defender of the Holy Sepulcher. But Baldwin of Boulogne with his shear force of character and outstanding leadership abilities had persuaded them and he was made king of Jerusalem in December of 1100.

Angelica and her husband hoped that each of their sons would live up to their names. They were trained as knights of nobility, skilled as warriors and yet still so young and loving. They could make each other laugh and, as yet, had no real burdens of responsibility, yet she knew whatever they did they would do it to the best of their abilities. They were always challenging each other to invent something, just as Armand loved to make new things in his woodworking shop.

She smiled as she remembered Goswin's idea to build a small castle in the middle of the pond so he could sail his toy boats up to it. She had no idea where he came up with the plan but all three boys got into the design of the thing. There was already a buildup of mud and silt in the middle of the pond. She thought it was Reginald who figured out a way to drain the pond low enough to let the trio transport rocks by walking next to a raft to the middle and stack the rocks. Eventually, they made a small island. Naturally, she had to stop them from entering the manor with their muddy feet. But they laughed and had fun.

One day they invited Armand and herself to come to the pond and then excitedly ran ahead. When the parents looked out into the middle of the pond Goswin was walking in a circle on the water!

"He's Jesus and we're his disciples!" Baldwin shouted with Reginald laughing by his side.

Angelica was too astonished to either laugh or admonish her sons for their reckless blasphemy. Armand, however, saw how the trick was done and smiled and clapped at the boy's cleverness.

"It's a miracle!" Armand had shouted good-naturedly.

Angelica gave him a shove saying, "Those boys!"

They smiled at each other.

Reginald and Baldwin walked up to their parents, smiling.

"What's next?" Armand asked.

"Next is to build the island above the waterline and build a miniature castle."

"It already has a good-sized moat," their father said and grinned. "I have an idea for some training. You can put a target on the island, make your horses go into the water and shoot your arrows with them swimming around it."

The boys nodded and smiled.

"We'll go tell Goswin of the new plan," Baldwin said enthusiastically.

They spent so much time on their horses sloshing in the pond while shooting the straw man they'd fixed to the center of their man-made island that they never built the castle.

Realizing it was getting late, Angelica made haste to the manor to give the cook instructions for tomorrow's guest. Hugues DesMarets, the priest at the Benedictine Abbey of Valbenoite and distant cousin, was honoring them with a visit. He would arrive in the early evening.

For such an important man, he arrived the next day with little fanfare, which impressed the devout Angelica. After praying in their chapel and enjoying a simple dinner, which naturally included wine from their own vineyard, he told them the latest news from Jerusalem.

"Baldwin the Second is fighting the Muslims and holding his own. They could use more good knights," he said looking at the three young men at the table with him.

"Father has made sure that we are well-trained," said Reginald proudly, "but I will manage the estate."

Armand smiled. "Not quiet finished with the training."

"Father?" the aging priest asked with a slight frown. "Oh, you mean Armand. Sorry I'm addressed as Father as well. Titles cause such confusion."

They all smiled.

"*Father,* do you remember the tournament at Anchin?" Armand asked.

"Indeed, I do," the priest answered. "You had to show bravery and then swear allegiance to go to be a crusader. You knocked a few off their horses as I remember."

"We're going to have a mini-tournament tomorrow with the boys, if you care to watch."

"Absolutely. Wouldn't miss it!"

CHAPTER THREE

KNIGHTS TO BE

1119 A.D.
Marets, France

Early the next morning, the DesMarets family was sitting in the chapel's front row. With them were Rajeev, Rosza and her sister, the cook and another servant girl. They all listened attentively as Father Hugues DesMarets spoke eloquently in French about Mary's love for her son Jesus. Baldwin was sure the statue of the virgin was listening also and crying. He was.

The priest, dressed in blue and gold vestments, vividly painted a picture of suffering and heartbreak as he told the story of Mary seeing her son slowly dying on the cross. Sniffs and low murmurings could be heard in the chapel among the serfs who had come dressed in their finest to hear the great priest.

While the women and children sat in chairs the men stood in back shuffling their feet and blowing their noses. Even the brawny blacksmith was seen to pull out a black rag and wipe his runny nose.

"Can you imagine," the priest asked quietly, "seeing your son crucified before you? *Can you?*" he said slightly lifting his voice. "Blood dripping from his side, his soul in agony and his life draining away." He paused, clenched his fists and raised his voice so that it boomed off the rafters.

"Our Lord Jesus sacrificed himself to save our sinful souls! Who among us has not sinned? Who among us could make such a sacrifice?" He stared around the room, which had plunged into silence. Then, in a whisper that could be heard by everyone he said, "Blessed are they who love the Son of God with all their hearts and all their souls so his sacrifice was not in vain."

Soft sobs broke out followed by whispered words of comfort.

"Let us pray."

The group as one bowed their heads as the priest intoned a prayer of might to the righteous and death to all who did not believe. Having not as yet translated it, the prayer was in Latin so only the family and Rajeev understood his message. "Amen." He walked straight to the back of the chapel and out the door with the DesMarets and their household following him. The peasants followed after.

"Remarkable that you let your serfs come to the family chapel," the priest said to Angelica who stood beside him in front of the chapel door. She was handing fruit out to the peasants as they walked by. "You are truly a daughter of the divine Mary."

Baldwin hugged his mother's waist. His brothers were standing beside him nodding and greeting the serfs by name, while Armand stood on the other side of the priest. Bhaiya sat patiently beside Baldwin.

"I'm glad you gave the sermon in French so the peasants could understand," Angelica said.

"Ah, yes. I believe our Lord Jesus wanted his message of suffering and redemption to be told to everyone. One can't do that in Latin," he said and winked at Angelica who nodded her approval. "Some day," he whispered, "all will hear God's word in their own language." He put his finger to his lips, "But don't say I said so. The pope likes Latin and that's that."

Suddenly Bhaiya stood and wagged his tail in recognition as one serf in particular walked up.

"He was a wise choice for you master Baldwin," the man said, turning a brown battered hat in his hands. "He's a fine dog indeed."

Baldwin patted Bhaiya's head. "Claude, where is your lovely wife Josephine today?" Baldwin asked politely.

"She's feeling poorly, I'm afraid. She so wanted to hear the priest but couldn't make it out of her bed."

Angelica overhearing said, "I will visit her today and see what ails her."

"I also," Baldwin said. "I'm fairly good with herbs you know."

"I've heard that you are especially good," the peasant said. "You helped cure the blacksmith's wife of the cough. I heard that, yes."

"I did," Baldwin said and looked over at his mother. "With the help of my good mother, naturally."

"We'll come with you now and see what herbs she might need," Angelica said.

The priest looked between mother and son. "I will also accompany you. Good healers are rare even among the nuns and monks. I'd like to see what you do. We do attend to many people who come to us."

Angelica noticed the serf had paled. She smiled. "Ah, my dear Father, the arrival of a priest may scare our poor Josephine so badly that she might faint at the sight of you."

For a moment the priest just stared at her, then laughed heartily. "Oh, yes I see. Yes, yes, go ahead of me and tell her of my coming. Better say to offer her a blessing for better health."

"Thank you Father," Claude said putting on his hat and bowing slightly to the priest. I'll warn her, I mean *tell* her that visitors are coming." With a flushed face he quickly strolled away.

The priest turned to Rajeev who was standing behind Angelica. "Rajeev come help me put away these vestments," he said and strolled back into the chapel.

Because the chapel was a small family one there had been nowhere for the priest to change into his vestments. Rajeev had volunteered to help the great man with his special holy garments and while doing so they discussed religion. Rajeev admitted that it was his deep desire to visit the holy city of Jerusalem and, "See where our Savior Lord the Jesus lived, was crucified and born again." The priest was much impressed with the humble man's devotion and desire.

With the tutor reverently carrying the vestments they walked back to the manor engaged in conversation.

"Did you know," Father DesMarets asked, "that there is a cave, a grotto actually, in southern France where it's thought that Mary Magdalene once lived and died?"

Rajeev raised his eyebrows. "She was the woman who anointed Our Lord Savior with oil."

"You really know your scripture," Father DesMarets stated sounding pleased as they entered the room to break their fast.

The smell of freshly baked bread was mouth watering. Along with the bread, the servants had laid out honey, pheasant and, of course, the DesMarets' juice from freshly pressed grapes, and wine. After a brief prayer Father DesMarets reached for the wine.

"Why?" Rajeev asked.

Father DesMarets looked at him curiously. "Pardon, my son?"

"Why did she use oil on his feet?"

Everyone looked at the Father as if they all wanted to know.

"Interesting you should ask Rajeev as the oil used, Spikenard, grows in India."

"Really?" Baldwin asked. "Rajeev did you know?"

"The Himalayas. A healing oil, the color of amber with a lovely scent."

"Yes, indeed," the priest said. "As you can imagine, very expensive. But she was so devoted, you see. She wiped off the oil with her hair. Can you imagine such humility and love?"

"Mother is devoted," Baldwin said.

"Very devoted," Armand said. "But not to change the subject, is it really necessary you go to the sick woman's bed now? The tournament starts at 11:00."

"The servants have everything in hand as I'm sure you, Reginald and Goswin do. Baldwin will hurry back as soon as we've helped the poor woman."

"Don't worry father," Baldwin said.

The priest turned to look at Baldwin, then said, "Oh," and pointed to Armand. "*That* father. So confusing."

The family smiled at the white-haired priest.

"We'll take precautions. Mother and I will wear garlands of the herb Angelica to ward off any disease."

"Angelica wards of disease! How fitting," Father DesMarets exclaimed.

Armand looked fondly at his wife. "My children, myself and my wife have all studied the works of Avicenna: *The Canon of Medicine* and *The Book of Healing*," Armand said.

"Ah, yes," Father DesMarets said. "Herbs are the natural creation of God, which aid the spiritual and physical healing of the sick. Very, good. Very good."

A half hour later, Father DesMarets' black carriage was pulled around by his driver—a somber man who'd slept and ate in the stables. The priest had explained that the man was mute and preferred his own company. With the priest's help, Angelica stepped into the carriage and the cleric followed her in. She was carrying a small covered bowl.

"Something to help the woman?" the priest asked.

"Yes Father it's honey," Angelica replied. "Armand has beekeepers so we always have a fresh supply. It's very healthy for you."

"Indeed. Your family is robust with fresh complexions and glowing cheeks. Armand amazes me with everything he raises and the amazing things he makes in his woodworking shop."

"Yes, we're kept busy all the time. I'll send you back to the monastery with some honey and, of course, several bottles of our wine."

The priest clapped his hands and then held them together as if praying. "That would be most welcomed. I'm sure I shall be healthier than ever."

Angelica smiled at the appreciative priest. "I have to say, I'm very impressed with your staff. That Rajeev knows more about Christianity than some of my monks. We had a divine conversation as he was helping me this morning before and after the service. How long has he been with you?"

"Armand brought him home to tutor the boys when they were young. He was at Baldwin's birth. I guess he's been with us 18 years or so. He's like part of the family. He gets along especially well with Armand. They have a great many deep conversations, I can tell you."

"He told me he has a desire to see Jerusalem."

"Oh?"

"Did I tell you I'm on my way to see the monks who guard a grotto in southern France? It's little known but some say they are there because Mary Magdalene lived and died there."

"Here in France? Oh my no. I'm afraid Father I haven't traveled far and wide like my husband has. Like my sons will soon do." She sighed.

"Oh dear. You must come with me then and let the monks tell us the story. Someone close to Jesus who heard him preach, it must be a very holy place. Do you know the story?"

"No. The nuns spoke of Mary the mother of Jesus but not Mary Magdalene. Although, I do know she was part of the group of people who followed him and that she was the first one to see him after the resurrection."

"Mathew, Mark, Luke *and* John all say that she was indeed the first one. How blessed. Let me tell you the tale and why the monks think that Saint-Baume is where her blessed body is buried." Angelica sat back, delighted to hear the story.

As the priest and Angelica talked, Baldwin rode alongside on his well-built chestnut-colored Ardennes stallion. Bhaiya trotted behind. Baldwin's father favored the breed Ardennais from the Ardennes region because Godfrey of Bouillon and his knights had ridden them into battle.

"You want stamina and strength in a horse," Armand had advised. Baldwin was going to use it for the tournament that afternoon and was glad to be giving it some exercise beforehand.

He'd wanted to name all the horses in the stable but his father advised him not to.

"It's not good to get attached to your horse in case he gets cut down from under you in battle," his father had said. "You'll have no time to mourn. I lost three horses during the crusade and couldn't find another one to obtain money for the trip home. I found a camel."

Baldwin knew of at least one war hero who had named his horse—Alexander the Great had ridden the massive Bucephalus in all his battles. However, taking his father's advice, Baldwin tried to not favor any of their horses in particular. Sometimes he jokingly called all of them Bucephalus.

The serf greeted Baldwin, his mother and the priest at the door of the tidy cottage. As they entered they could hear coughing behind a faded, brown cotton curtain in the corner. Angelica immediately disappeared behind it. The men could hear a mumbled conversation and something about milady's beautifully embroidered clothes. The priest looked around the room while Baldwin looked out the window at Bhaiya and his birth mother greeting each other with jumping, barks and a great deal of sniffing.

After some moments, Angelica reappeared and asked Baldwin to step outside and pick some peppermint. The priest followed him to the little herb garden to the right of the cottage. As Baldwin picked the green herb he explained to the priest that it was for a dry cough. It would be mixed with honey and help relieve the woman's sore throat. If the peasant had a wet cough with mucus then Angelica would make her a tea of thyme, ginger and marshmallow root. Or anise, horehound, fennel root, radish and wild celery. Whatever was in their garden or surrounding area. A big spoonful of honey would also be recommended. "But obviously it's a dry cough," Baldwin said.

"What do you think she has?" the priest asked.

"Hard to say exactly," Baldwin answered, "unless I look at her. Mother will ask her permission. Sometimes the women are sensitive to having a male around when they are sick and feeling poorly. But they know me. I'm fairly harmless," he said and smiled at the priest.

The priest raised his eyebrows. "Oh well then, I'll pray for you during the tournament that you have at least enough harm in you to win over your opponents in swordplay."

Baldwin laughed. "Archery is my game," he said as he walked back into the cottage.

The woman gave Angelica permission to let Baldwin put some herb infused oil on her throat. Josephine smiled at Baldwin's warm and gentle touch.

"Young lord if my man touched me that way I'd be well in a moment." She smiled, then had a brief fit of coughing. Baldwin patted her back while Angelica waited out the cough, then offered her more soothing tea.

"Yes," Angelica said. "Sometimes the proper attention is all you need." She left the room to speak to the woman's husband as Baldwin continued to rub the oil in.

As he helped Josephine sit up to sip the peppermint tea her husband pulled back the curtain and walked into the small space with Angelica and the priest hovering in the background.

"Here now let me help you …" he paused for a moment as if trying to think what he could help her with, then said, "plump up the pillows."

Baldwin sat back and smiled over at his mother. He knew she'd instructed the serf to give his wife some loving attention. He heard Bhaiya bark, excused himself and left the room as the priest stepped forward to offer his blessing. Baldwin walked out and patted his dog still frisking around his birth mother. He popped his head back inside and told the group, "I'm off. The tournament starts soon."

As Baldwin mounted his horse, Bhaiya ran forward then looked back at his mother who wagged her tail. Bhaiya ran back and touched her nose with his then ran after his master. Baldwin smiled and set off at a trot toward home. Bhaiya barked and shot out in front of him as if eager to get there first.

As the two of them raced up to the manor Baldwin saw that local villagers, serfs and others from nearby towns were already gathering to see the events. The DesMarets–father and his three sons–had been training with their horses for weeks, as had the sons of their noble neighbors.

Serfs had even come to help set up the Baldwin designed DesMarets' blue and white flags with the new family motto *By Faith We Live*. The serfs also covered straw bales in cloth where people could sit. It wouldn't be grand like a full-blown tournament with stands, or anywhere near the size of the Tournament of Anchin held in 1096, which Armand had attended, but it would be entertaining.

Baldwin thought Armand was eager to show off his son's skills at martial arts. There would be a bit of jousting, sword fights and trying to hit a target with arrows while riding horseback. The blacksmith and his assistants had been kept busy making chainmail to Armand's specifications. Baldwin thought his father also wanted to show off his skilled horses. Although their manor wasn't as big or elaborate as a castle, which usually included many servants and knights for protection, their lands were extensive and their stables excellent. Armand kept a variety of horses, including Ardennais, Camargue and Boulonnais.

He told his sons, "Look at how nature likes to mix it up. If you see just one type of tree growing in a forest, you know that man has planted that forest. That's why I like to grow a collection of various herbs, flowers and fruits because nature knows best."

"Bees, too," Reginald pointed out. "They're all dependent on each other."

"Very good Reginald," his father said.

"But horses father?" Goswin asked. "How does that work with horses?"

"Should one type of horse become sick often the whole herd goes down, but a mix of animals keeps them safer. One breed could be ill but that sickness may not affect the others. Also, each breed has it's own qualities. The Camargue are particularly good with wet conditions such as marshes. And, apparently," he grinned, "good with tutors."

They all grinned back. Rajeev's horse was the shorter, gray Camargue horse. Although the Indian was not raised on horseback, the sturdy Carmargue made him feel somewhat secure. The horse showed remarkable intelligence and patience with his rider. He lead Rajeev rather than the man directing him.

Baldwin was greeted by his brothers on horseback. The tallest of the three, Reginald, carrying a wooden lance, sat magestically on his gray Boulonnais, which had some braids and ribbons in its mane. The elegant horse was a favorite among the sons.

Baldwin laughed. "Been busy, I note," he said, nodding to the sturdy steed's mane.

"Mother's influence," Reginald said. "If I hadn't stopped her the poor horse would have a complete costume. I'm glad she's busy nursing the serf."

Goswin patted his not-yet-decorated Ardennais. "Mother is as elated about this little event as we are."

Two riders came galloping up laughing with excitement. Baldwin recognized them as being from the Champagne region. One young knight-in-training hailed him.

"DesMarets! Ready to be beaten in every game?" It was Thierry the nephew of Hugues de Payens, a knight who had ridden with their father during the crusade and was still in Jeresulum. With Thierry was a young boy. He looked to be about twelve and was riding a black stallion that was stampng, snorting and obviously too large for the boy to handle.

"Baldwin! This is my cousin on my mother's side, Francis. He's ready to do battle with the strongest of you. As am I!"

Baldwin looked at the slight figure of Francis, smiled and shook his head. "Welcome. What is your skill, Francis?"

"I'm trying out for all of them," Francis said loudly, as if his voice could make him seem bigger.

Baldwin hid his smile as best he could by pretending to cough.

"The knights tent is at the far end of the field," he said raising out of his saddle and pointing. "Good luck to you both."

As the pair rode by Baldwin, Thierry leaned over and whispered, "I hope you have good healers here. He's not very experienced at anything." He urged his horse forward leaving Baldwin shaking his head and thinking that it was going to be an intersting day. Perhaps it was good they had a priest on hand.

"Urm, Baldwin," Goswin said as he nodded to Baldwin's neck, "you've still got that herb hanging around you."

Baldwin looked down. "I'm leaving it on. I hope it acts as protection."

"I hope it acts to staunch the flow of blood," his brother replied.

A field just beyond the manor had been set up as the sporting area. Horses were tied outside a large tent, which was made of linen and rope, where the combatants were gathering. The tent was already covered by a light dusting of dirt that was being kicked up by the excited horses. The young men were milling about, checking out the food, settling down the horses and greeting each other.

Armand was waiting until they all arrived before giving them their instructions, which he had carefully researched. One of the many manuscripts in the vast family library was written by a self-defense instructor in 1102. It concerned everyone's favorite sport, sword fighting.

The basic rules were:
Never stand still.
Always be on the attack.
Thrusting, cutting and grappling are all allowed.

Armand decided to go by the rules but tone it down a great deal or they would be dead nobles on the ground instead of newly minted knights. Although he knew this was not going to be a popular decision, Armand would remind his guests that this was sword *play* and if they drew too much blood from their opponents, they would lose. But to make the games more interesting, he also decided all three events—swordplay, shooting arrows at a target and jousting—would take place on horseback. Since he'd been in battle, he knew that the real skill was keeping your horse in line and under you. In the end, Armand wanted a sword tagging game with little blood drawn, but he also knew that the lads coming to "fight" at the tournament were trying to win and show off. A dangerous combination.

With Armand's permission, some of the more ambitious serfs had set up boards placed on two four-legged trestles, one trestle under each end of the board, for selling food at a nominal price; mostly bread, onions, pork pies made with rye flour, grapes and the DesMarets wine, which was kept in barrels. There were no cups or plates. The wine was poured into the "customers" own flasks. The food was eaten by hand. Several of the young participants had already filled their flasks more than once. The priest, having arrived with Angelica, also came by to bless the food and fill his own flask.

The field was overflowing with more people than the DesMarets had anticipated. The air was crackling with excitement.

"Oh Armand," Angelica said looking out at the field. "How wonderful."

"Yes. I'm glad we decided to do it." He mounted his horse and Angelica handed him her embroidered headscarf.

For her sons she had a colorful ribbon. "One color for each of you," she said as her three sons rode up. "They're to remind you the great faith we have in each of you and for good health, especially since your father is the only one wearing a helmet."

"Very clever and thoughtful of you mother," Baldwin said as he took his black ribbon and used it to make a ponytail out of his long, wavy hair. Reginald and Goswin did the same with their gold and blue ribbons. Armand laughed and tied her scarf to the back of his helmet, which Rajeev had handed him. Then he leaned over and kissed his wife on the top of her head. Rajeev handed

Armand his shield then hoisted the blue and white family flag and lead the way into the makeshift arena.

With blasts from several hunting horns and shouts from the crowd Armand, Reginald, Goswin and Baldwin rode in formation into the ring carrying their shields. Rajeev held the family flag high while the four men riding behind him held their swords high. As practiced, they rode slowly around in a circle. Armand, in a loud voice, announced that all the games would be on horseback. The crowd cheered.

The visiting young noblemen rode out to the middle. They had changed into linens and silks in the tent. Most of them had brought servants who now nervously walked by their master's horse with a banner. As the knight-in-training had not been into battle yet, most did not have a knight's coat-of-arms but banners of one or two bright colors. The exception, besides the DesMarets, was Thierry and his cousin Francis who did have battle worn knights in their family tree.

Armand raised himself up from his saddle and shouted out the rules of swordplay on horseback. At his signal hunting horns sounded and all the men started whacking away at each other. The more skilled horsemen could turn their horses and avert a blow. Cloths had been tied around each combatant's right arm, which was protected by chainmail. The object of the game was to cut the cloth away. The one left with a cloth, won.

However, some of the men did not wear chain mail. Others had wisely worn thick cotton long sleeved shirts. One or two had bare arms, a clothing choice they would soon regret. Francis had chain mail but was not a good horseman nor was he good with his aim. He tried to remove the armband from Reginald who just laughed and swatted Francis's horse on the rump. The horse jumped and kicked causing Francis to fall off. Everyone laughed as the boy dodged his way out from the stomping horses. Baldwin grabbed the rider-less horse by the reins, led him over to Francis and handed him over.

"I'm sure you'll do better at archery," he said.

Francis nodded, a determined look on his face.

As the mock battle continued, dust and blood flew everywhere—dust from the horses trampling feet and blood from many too eager thrusts of swords toward arms. Even minor cuts with sharp blades drew copious amounts of spewing blood. The crowd cheered equally as loudly for a knight who took an armband as for a knight who drew blood.

Armand, who had left his horse with Rajeev and was sitting next to his wife, watched proudly at his son's skill with their horses. He just shook his head while Angelica hurried off to help with the bleeding. Fortunately at Armand's bidding a tent had been set up for the wounded with bandages, herbs, water and straw bales for resting. The horses were not spared from the slashing blades and they were attended to as well.

After much shouting and clashing of swords only Reginald and Goswin were left with armbands. Baldwin had lost to Thierry. He wasn't disappointed as he knew his skill was with arrows so he watched proudly as his brothers battled. They circled left, then right, trying to out maneuver each other. At last Reginald lifted Goswin's armband by his sword tip and held it up to the cheering crowd. Goswin laughed good-naturedly and swatted Reginald's horse's rear with the flat side of his sword. The well-trained horse turned his head and snorted at Goswin. The crowd stamped and applauded.

Reginald heard someone shout directly behind him. "You might be good on a horse but I can outmaneuver you on the ground!"

Reginald turned and saw Thierry clashing swords with a husky-looking, young noble. With shouts almost everyone dismounted and started sword fights with each other. Squires were gallantly grabbing horses and moving them away. Horses started munching on the straw bales and the peasants tried to grab their reins and move them off. Reginald and Goswin backed up their horses a safe distance and laughed at the chaos. The crowd cheered everyone on. The noise could be heard several miles away.

Dust flew, swords clanged and young nobles tried to out fight each other. Thierry got the better of his opponent by tripping him. He raised his sword hilt over the fallen fellow, changed his mind, leaned over and helped him up. Grinning they turned toward Armand and Angelica, raised their sword and bowed. The other knights-to-be stopped, raised their swords in salute to each other and bowed toward the stands. The crowd went wild with stamping, cheering and throwing straw into the air.

After a moment, Reginald dismounted and walked to where his parents sat. Armand stood and presented his son with his own helmet for winning. Reginald put it on, mounted his steed and took a victory lap around the arena waving his sword to the delight of the crowd.

Armand left his seat, mounted his horse and trotted to the middle of the field.

"My friends!" he shouted, "next the young warriors will shoot arrows at the targets now being set up. They will do so from horseback!"

Serfs were setting up five targets on stacked straw bales. The targets, which had been drawn by children, looked like stick figures of unknown origin. They had been drawn on cloth, which was then sewn as best as possible into the straw.

Once again the young men, some now wearing cloth bandages, galloped onto the field with full quivers on their backs and bows in their hands. They galloped by one after the other shooting at the targets. All of them hit at least one except for Francis. His first shot went wild, almost hitting a serf who fortunately ducked. Some watchers laughed, whooped or called out insults.

Back at his seat, Armand had to stand and quiet them down. Each of the young knights had five passes. Baldwin stopped Francis after three passes, as none of his arrows got even close. To the excitement and astonishment of the crowd, Baldwin hit all five targets in the center. Everyone stood and cheered, even the other knights were impressed.

For his prize, Baldwin won a new handcrafted harness with

two blue sapphires embedded in the leather. He kissed his mother who had returned to her seat and shook his father's hand then waved to the crowd as he walked his horse back toward the tent.

Armand stood and announced the rules for jousting. The knights would ride toward each other with long poles and try to touch their opponent's chest. They were not to try and knock each other off or harm the horses in any way. The tournament goers listened intently as most had never seen jousting and didn't know how it would be played.

"I've seen it, of course," the priest said to Angelica. He turned to Armand. "Are those long poles used in battle?"

"Too unwieldy. Mostly in combat the men are on foot marching in formation. It's frightening to see a wall of long sharp sticks and shields coming toward you in battle," Armand answered. "In this tournament the poles they are using are blunt. Still they can do some harm if the horses are charging too fast."

Rajeev too was very interested in the game. He knew little about tournaments or jousting, which was a fairly new and minor sport. Swordplay and shooting arrows were far more major events and went on longer. But he felt jousting was more difficult as the wooden lances were heavy, unwieldy and difficult to control while on horseback, especially in a crowd of galloping horsemen. He knew the object of the game was to touch your opponent's chest with your blunted lance. If you hit his horse you lost points. The one with the most points won the prize. Rajeev wasn't sure what the prize was but he hoped that at least one of his noble charges was the winner.

For months he'd watched in fascination as Armand and sons practiced with their horses; stopping, turning and galloping with just pressure from their legs. Making his horse move forward was all he'd mastered and not that well. He knew none of the other "knights in waiting" as he thought of them, would be as skilled.

He sat bareback on his gray Camargue at the end of the turnaround where the jousting knights turned their horses. He had just a rope for a harness and was using the horse as an elevated place to sit and watch the games. This was the last game of the day. Being a new sport, not too many knights were taking it on.

Reginald was going to represent the DesMarets and was just mounting his horse in front of Rajeev. At the far end was the young Francis whose sleek, black stallion was prancing nervously, not use to the crowds. Rajeev didn't think the slightly built man, who couldn't be more than twelve if that, had much control over his steed.

Angelica dropped a bright red cloth and the horses charged toward each other at a full gallop, dust rising under their hooves. About midway they raised their lances. Immediately Rajeev could see that the young boy had little control over his weapon. As they met, Reginald knocked his opponent's lance upward, which caused the boy to let go of his reins and grab the lance with both hands. The out-of-control horse kept galloping, directly at Rajeev!

The uncontrollable lance swayed sideways and caught Rajeev in his middle. With an "oof" he went flying into nearby spectators sitting on the bales of straw while the horses collided knocking Rajeev's Camargue to the ground. The boy's black stallion bucked and kicked but much to the young man's credit he stayed on.

The Carmarge did not get up. He lay on his side screaming, wildly kicking and then trying to stand but failing. Armand pulled out his sword and ran toward the flailing horse. All three of his sons ran after him. Baldwin got there first, turned and blocked his father.

"Son I have to put the animal out of his misery. His leg is broken."

"No! Please father, wait. Please," Baldwin said putting his hand over his father's sword hand. "Reginald, Goswin, Rajeev see if you can gentle him so he stops kicking."

Rajeev jumped from the ample woman's lap where he'd fortunately landed. The three of them tried to get close to the horse but it kept kicking.

"Son," Armand said stepping around Baldwin but too close

to the horse. A violently kicking leg caught Armand in the right ankle and he fell.

"Father!" All three sons yelled at the same time. Reginald and Goswin rushed to Armand and helped him up.

"It's not broken but it hurts like …"

Angelica rushed up. From her seat, she hadn't been able to see what was happening. She quickly took it all in and went to support the injured Armand.

"Father let me do something. Just for a moment," Baldwin pleaded.

"Baldwin obey your father and step away."

"Mother please. I can see …" He paused for a moment and patted the horse's head. The horse quieted.

"Rajeev say soothing words to the horse."

As Rajeev mumbled something in Hindi, Baldwin took hold of the injured leg at the knee, then rested his hand at the joint. He pulled. There was a pop, a moment of silence then the horse jumped up. Everyone who could scattered away from it's prancing hooves.

Armand and Angleica stared in disbelief. The horse turned in a circle and took off. Rajeev followed, trying to catch the rope harness. The crowd, which hadn't been able to see exactly what happened, saw Rajeev chasing his horse and roared with laughter and applause.

Armand stared at his son. "How did you know to do that?" he asked quietly.

"It was a miracle," Angelica said. She held her husband's waist as tears dripped down her face.

"No mother," Baldwin said. "Not a miracle but an observation. I knew what the horse looked like normally, in it's completeness. I could see where his leg had come away from its natural placement. The leg wasn't broken just out of place. I put it back where it belonged."

"You made him whole again," Angelica said softly.

Reginald and Goswin looked at each other and then at their younger brother.

"You're going to have to teach us that trick little brother," Reginald said.

Armand rubbed his hand over his eyes and shook his head. "It's a talent that could be used on the battlefield."

Baldwin shrugged. "Maybe so."

Angelica stepped up to her son. She was touching the cross that she always wore, the one that Armand had given her so long ago. She kissed Baldwin on the cheek.

"You are truly a blessing," she said. Then she turned to her other sons. "You are all so precious." By now she was crying so heavily that all three young men brought out cotton cloths, which they normally used to wipe sweat off their foreheads. She took Reginald's and smiled.

"Well my dears," Armand said solemnly. "We need to finish this tournament with a procession of champions."

"Father you need to stay off of that ankle," Baldwin said. "Let mother put some of her healing oil on it. I'll make a splint."

"I may not be able to walk well," Armand said. "But I can ride."

He heard Angelica "Tsk" and smiled down at her. "My love you have to give all the young knights prizes. Do you have more ribbons?" he asked hopefully.

Angleica laughed. "Don't worry dear. They'll all be rewarded."

"Come on mount up sons. We have a tournament to finish." Stoicaly he swung up into his saddle and led his sons back to finish the game.

CHAPTER FOUR

SEEKING THE DIVINE FEMININE

1120 A.D.
On the Road to Saint-Maximin-la-Sainte-Baume, France

The morning sun saw Armand sprawled on a dark blue velvet covered couch in the solarium. His linen-wrapped right ankle was propped up on an ottoman topped by three embroidered pillows. Father DesMarets sat across from him in a matching blue velvet plush chair wearing a mud-colored cassock.

"It really was a fine tournament Armand," the priest said as he set down his dainty cup containing a special DesMarets blend of herbal tea. "Hardly any major injuries, comparatively. Wouldn't it be a blessing if actual wars were that way? Just a few cuts and scrapes here and there, a flag raised by the victors and the spoils distributed wisely."

Armand nodded, an amused look on his face. The serfs and servants were still cleaning up the blood. "Angelica tells me you're on your way to visit some of your fellow monks. It's rumored that they guard the grotto of Mary Magdalene."

"Yes, it's one of those secrets that everyone knows," Father DesMarets said as he polished off a piece of bread spread with the famous DesMarets rose petal jam. "Absolutely astonishing."

"What is?"

"For one thing that you make your own blend of tea and this delicious rose petal jam. It's better than anything I get in the monastery."

"The whole family is involved. The boys have a great deal of fun developing new recipes for us. But you said that was for one thing. What is the second?"

"That Mary Magdalene came to France and died here. People have been climbing up to the grotto for centuries to experience the silence and reverence of the place. Maximinus of Aix, who traveled with Mary here and brought us the teachings of Christ, is buried there but most say that is where Mary Magdalene spent out her final days."

Armand shook his head and adjusted his leg. "I've heard that but didn't pay much attention to it. Do you think it's true that Mary Magdalene came here and preached?"

"Oh yes," the priest said quietly. "Can you imagine? One of Jesus' great saves—from a sinner to a devoted follower. I am led by the Spirit to go."

The priest was so taken away with the idea that Armand thought the old man was going to swoon.

"Steady Father," Armand said.

"It will be the highlight of my life before I go to my heavenly home to be with the Lord. I want your lovingly devoted wife to accompany me."

Armand looked alarmed. "To be with the Lord?"

Father DesMarets smiled. "To visit the cave. Angelica is so devout. I know she'll be ecstatic to visit such a holy place."

Just then Angelica, the three sons and their friends Thierry and Francis, along with Rajeev and Rosza entered the solarium on their way to the downstairs library.

"What's this I hear about a holy place Father?" Angelica asked innocently.

Armand looked at her. He thought she sounded a little *too* innocent. He realized she must have known where the priest was going and wanted to go, too. But she would have to get permission from her lord and master. Armand smiled at the thought. Lord and master? Him? The women–wife and female servants–ruled the roost in the DesMarets' family. Now the sons were under the impression they knew more about absolutely everything than he did. His eyes twinkled.

Angelica seated herself next to her husband. Reginald sat on the arm of the couch, Baldwin with the ever-present Bhaiya sat on the floor, while Goswin pulled up a side chair. Rajeev and Rosza stood.

"Sons," Armand said, "your mother wants to travel to the grotto where Mary Magdalene lived and died in the mountains of Sainte Baume. As knights you may go along to guard her."

"The room erupted as all three boys started talking at once. Reginald was the loudest.

"Father! What about the discussion we had at breakfast? I'm off to a new monastery school in Paris to learn about modern computation, writing and speaking."

"I'm going to apprentice on a sailing ship," Goswin said.

They all looked over at Baldwin. "Thierry tells me his uncle has assembled knights who are taking the holy vows in Jeresulem."

"They call themselves The Poor Fellow Soldiers of Christ and the Temple of Solomon," Theirry said. "They've been sanctioned by King Baldwin II. I'm going to join them as soon as I can."

"Mother, you know I want to go!" Baldwin pleaded. Angelica touched her heart then fingered her cross.

"A monk? Oh Baldwin how …" She choked for a moment and teared up, "How wonderful. I'm so proud of you, of all of you, of course."

"What about your mother, boys?" Armand asked quietly.

Silence met his question.

Father DesMarets cleared his throat. "It won't be easy climbing the mountain to the grotto. It's possible the monks won't let us through although I do have an in with one in particular since he's my brother."

Everyone stared at him.

"You mean he's your brother as in a fellow monk devoted to Christ?" Rajeev asked tentatively. "Or your actual relative?"

The priest smiled broadly. "My step-brother actually. My father had two sons when he married my mother. One of my stepbrothers, both were much older than me, went into another order. We correspond regularly and I asked if I may visit the holy site. Can you imagine what praying at such a glorified place can do for your soul?"

Angelica crossed herself and everyone else followed her gesture.

Armand looked at each of his sons. "Due to my injury I can't go to protect your mother and the good Father here." He looked at each son in turn.

The reverend pressed on. "The grotto itself is Saint-Maximin-la-Sainte-Baume. It's not widely known what's up there but I can tell you the story at the noon meal."

"I'll go with you mother," Baldwin suddenly blurted out.

"But what about …" Thierry started to say but Baldwin interrupted.

"My mother is more precious to me than myself. I would give my life for her."

Reginald and Goswin looked at their father, then down at the floor.

"Of course. Mother is the most precious woman on earth," Reginald said. "We'll all go."

Armand smiled and held up his hand. "No, your words have proved your devotion but Baldwin can handle any marauders that come his way. Don't be of concern. It's only a one-day trip."

"Ah!" Both the shame-faced boys said at the same time.

"I was thinking it was a long pilgrimage," Goswin said.

Armand smiled. "She will be back to see you both off. Reginald you won't miss the start of your school and Goswin will have plenty of time to find his ship. Baldwin will start off to Jerusalem."

The sons looked relieved.

Angelica shook her head. "Do you really think I would go off and let my three precious sons ride away without me being there? Do you consider me a bad mother?"

Once again the room erupted, this time louder than before. "Never mother!" Baldwin shouted. All three young men jumped up and then knelt before their mother.

"Mother, we are your devoted sons but also selfish sinners," Reginald said.

"Forgive us please mother. We would be lost without you," Goswin said.

"Please give us your blessing Mother," Baldwin said quietly.

At this Angelica reached out her hand and touched each of her sons on the head. She smiled. "May my little sinners realize that they are as precious to me as saints."

The three young men looked up into their mother's smiling blue eyes. They hugged her each in turn. The servants stood in the background wiping away tears. After a moment, Rajeev cleared his throat and they turned toward him.

"Sire, if I may, I would like to accompany milady and the Holy Father."

"Me, too," Rosza said.

Angelica laughed. "Who will take care of Armand? We can't leave him all alone."

Armand cleared his throat. "The cook will be more than happy to serve me. Rosza's other sister can come in to help tidy and her sister Claire will go with you, as you will need your maid. I'm sure our tenant serfs will keep me busy with their petitions for this or that."

"But Armand ..." Angelica started to protest.

"You are going," Armand stated in a tone that was a command. "The question is, who rides with whom?"

"Your dear wife will ride in my carriage and my mute monk will be the driver," the reverend said.

"I will ride alongside them," Baldwin said.

"Rajeev, Rosza and Claire will go also," Armand said.

"Armand, why do I need a maid for such a journey?" Angelica asked.

Her husband held up his hand to stop her speaking.

"It's appropriate that you take your lady's maid," he stated in no uncertain terms. "You are a lady and you travel with a maid."

"Of course," Father DesMarets said. "The more the merrier. Although perhaps *merrier* isn't quite the right tone for the visit."

He stared off into space as if trying to find the appropriate wording for the holy journey. He mumbled something under his breath that sounded like *spiritual* or *celestial* and nodded.

"Rajeev will ride on the Camargue, of course," Baldwin said, trying to get the conversation back on track.

"If you don't mind," Rosza said quietly, "Claire and I will share a horse. I'm not too good on my own."

"They can't ride in the carriage with you?" Armand asked the priest.

"It's much too small," he answered.

"We'll have to take provisions," Angelica said. Then she looked around at Thierry and Francis. "I guess I'll be seeing you both off before I go."

She teared up. Their visit to the library was forgotten as each son hugged her again.

At Baldwin's turn he whispered, "I had another dream I'd like to tell you about."

His mother sniffed, nodded and stood up. "I'm going to the chapel to thank the Virgin for this gift."

Armand swung his leg off the ottoman. "I'm going to my woodworking shop and fashion myself a walking cane that will be the envy of all."

Reginald walked over to help his father stand. "I want to see that and maybe learn a bit more before I'm off to Paris."

"We'd like to see inside your shop, too," Thierry said as he and Francis stood also.

"You're most welcome to join me. Perhaps you can inform us more about this new company of knights that your uncle is forming," Armand said as he limped toward the door leading outside.

The priest stood. "I'll tell my squire the plans. Shall we have more of a discussion over the noon meal?"

"That sounds good to me," Goswin said over his shoulder as he headed downstairs followed by Rajeev.

Angelica turned to Rosza. "Please tell cook that we'll all have our refreshments in two hours and we plan on leaving tomorrow morning for the grotto so we'll want some food and drink for our journey, too."

Rosza nodded and headed toward the kitchen. Angelica turned toward her youngest son and put out her hand. He smiled, lightly squeezed her fingers and escorted her to the chapel, Bhaiya trotting behind. After lighting candles and saying a prayer, Angelica asked her son what was on his mind.

"Mother," Baldwin whispered. "I had a dream last night of a beautiful woman wearing clothes from the time of Jesus. She was surrounded by golden light."

Angelica put her hand up to her cross. "Who do you think it was?"

"I thought it might be Mother Mary but now I think it could be Mary Magdalene."

Angelica's eyes shone as she looked at her youngest son. "Calling you to her grotto perhaps, or calling you to recognize her virtue after she was saved by our Lord. It's a good omen for our trip."

"I hope so," Baldwin said uneasily. Angelica didn't notice his hesitation. She got up and held out her hand but Baldwin shook his head. "I will stay for awhile and pray for a safe journey."

His mother smiled and kissed him. "I am so blessed. So very blessed."

Baldwin waited until he heard the heavy, wooden chapel door close before he shut his eyes tightly. He'd had more than one dream last night. The second one didn't have golden light but blackness. He remembered it vividly. At first he heard a dog whimpering. His mind said it was Bhaiya but then he realized he was asleep and dreaming. He remembered when he was young and a mysterious shadow had crawled across the wall and then beckoned him with a bony finger. But in this dream it moved out of the window and Baldwin followed.

The scene changed and now he was in a city full of people wearing strange clothes. He realized there was a mixture of foreigners speaking in multi languages while shopping at an outdoor market. The air was scented with odors that he could not identify. A brown robe tied with a rope belt covered his body and even though sweat trickled down his back he had his hood up. Dust layered the air and he coughed.

No one noticed Baldwin as he saw the shadow racing across a far wall. He pushed through the crowd to chase it. As he got near, the shadow detached itself from the wall and jumped at him. Its eyes burned fiery red as black talons sunk deep into his shoulder and darkness seeped into his bones.

Baldwin sat up in his bed and shouted, "No!" Both his brothers groaned from their beds, pulled their blankets over their heads and went back to sleep. They were use to their youngest brother sometimes shouting in the night.

After a moment Baldwin felt the coolness of his room, which was once again quiet and the same as usual. He swallowed but his throat was not dry. He felt his shoulders but no skin was broken and there was no pain. He lay back and fell into a dreamless sleep.

In the morning, he woke to Bhaiya licking his hand. As he patted his faithful companion's head he thought about the dream. Just a dream and yet he shivered at the realness of it and the thought that somewhere there was a dark demon and it was coming for him.

He sat up and smiled at Bhaiya, glad the dog was there to take away his troubled thoughts. Bhaiya was the bravest yet calmest dog Baldwin had ever known. He was a mix of retriever and mountain dog, the latter bred to hunt bear, mountain lion and wild boar.

If Bhaiya faced a demon, Baldwin thought, but he shook his

head–it was just a nightmare, a childhood fantasy relived. He grabbed Bhaiya's head and gently pulled his ears.

"No bad old demon would bother you, would it boy?" Bhaiya barked in response and wagged his tail.

Perhaps it was fortunate that he'd escort his mother to the holy cave of Mary Magdalene. He was sure that the beloved follower of Christ could take away his nightmares. Then he could travel to Jerusalem in safety, which was his deepest desire. He was certain that the outdoor market was in Jerusalem and that's where the demon was waiting. *But it's a fantasy*, he reminded himself. *A fairytale.*

A rumbling stomach brought Baldwin out of his dark thoughts and back to the reality that he was sitting by himself in his family's chapel. He looked down. No, not by himself. Bhaiya was looking up at him with his intelligent brown eyes as if saying *time to go*. What would he do without Bhaiya?

In the dining room large platters of filleted fish, meat, fruit and bread were being placed on the long wooden table. Armand was sitting at the head with Angelica on his right and Father DesMarets on his left. The old knight was glad he had fashioned such a long table so long ago in his woodworking shop. It was made of a light and fragrant pine but fortunately covered with a cotton cloth for meals. Meals with as many people as this one could bring all kinds of spills and sometimes burns from tipped candles. Once there was a friend who stabbed his meat with his dagger, missed, and the tip of the blade lodged into the table. None too pleased, Armand had sanded out the mark after his guest left.

Altogether nine people were gathered around the table: Armand, Angelia, Reginald, Goswin, Baldwin, Father DesMarets, Rajeev, Thierry and Francis. Rosza was eating in the kitchen with her sister and lady's maid Claire, the cook and one other servant. The priest's coachman, whom everyone thought of as the mute monk, was eating in the stables.

The priest bowed his head to bless the meal. "May this great meal and everyone here be covered with the blessed blood of our Lord Jesus. Amen."

Baldwin looked up. Both Armand and Francis had coughed behind their hands and Baldwin was sure he heard Francis say some word like "bleck." He noticed that his father had turned slightly pale, his mother touched her cross and Goswin had bit his lip. All others assiduously kept their heads bowed as they said their *amens*.

Baldwin smiled inwardly. The holy man certainly had a way of painting a picture with words. Whether he intended that particular picture Baldwin wasn't sure.

After raising his glass to the host, the priest started in on the fillet of white fish—covered with a parsley, sage and mint sauce—and his story of Mary Magdalene at the same time.

"You know Mary Magdalene's story, of course," he started. "She was a woman of ill repute, a terrible sinner in God's eyes, who later became a disciple and devoted follower. Our Lord Jesus pointed a finger at her and commanded that the demons which possessed her be driven out!" The man waved his fork in the air for emphasis. He raised his voice as if preaching from the pulpit. "Not one but *seven* demons flew out of the sinner's mouth!" He slapped his hand on the table.

Rajeev nodded. "Seven."

Baldwin shuddered. He wondered if one of the seven was still around.

Warming to his subject, Father DesMarets sipped his beverage, raised his goblet and said, "Our Lord Jesus saved the sinner and all sinners are saved because of Him!" Armand winched as the priest brought down the heavy goblet on his lovingly crafted table. He wondered if it'd made a mark.

"But how did she get to France?" Francis asked impatiently. Since the young, awkward knight rarely spoke, everyone looked at him.

The reverend picked up his fork and pointed the tines at Francis. "By Divine guidance," he said flicking the fork three times at Francis in the same way that he sprinkled holy water in a blessing. Several of the group nodded as if this was obvious. The priest continued, "You see the story passed down through the centuries tells us of Mary's journey."

"I'm sure it must have been embellished along the way," Francis said stubbornly.

Once again everyone looked at him. Father DesMarets smiled. "May I tell the story?" he asked impatiently.

Francis nodded. Father DesMarets stabbed a piece of fish, popped it into his mouth and slowly savored the taste. All eyes were on him once again.

"When our Lord was crucified it was Mary Magdalene, the Blessed Virgin Mary and Lazarus who witnessed his resurrection along with other devoted followers."

"It was Lazarus' tomb, was it not, that Jesus was laid to rest in?" Reginald asked.

"No. Jesus had raised Lazarus from the dead. After our Savior's crucifixion, which Mary Magdalene also witnessed, his body was taken to Joseph of Aramathia's tomb. I think we all know the story of what happened."

Everyone nodded having heard the story dozens of times. Angelica put her hand over her cross.

Francis piped up. "I wonder how much a tomb cost? They say Joseph of Aramathia was a rich man so he must have bought himself a very nice tomb. Wonder if tombs come in different sizes."

Father DesMarets shook his head while the others smiled, smirked or stared at Francis.

"But," the priest pressed on, "the disciples were in danger. The Romans made note of anyone who was at the crucifixion and vowed to get rid of them."

"Heartless," Angelica murmured.

"But they either didn't want to crucify the onlookers or the law wouldn't allow it, so they gathered up Jesus' mother Mary and her sister Martha, Mary Magdalene, the disciple Maximin, Lazarus, his sister, an Egyptian servant named Sarah and a few others depending on which version of the story you've heard."

Francis leaned forward, "I heard there were many Mary's. He ticked them off on his fingers: one, Mary Magdalene; two, Mary Salomé; three, Mary Jacobé and of course Mary Mother of Jesus."

"Who are Mary Salomé and Mary Jacobé?" Goswin asked.

"Mary Jacobé was Mary Magdalene's mother," Francis answered, "and Mary Salomé was the mother of the disciples James and John, or so the story I heard goes."

"Not too original in their names back then were they?" Baldwin observed grinning as his father gave him a crooked smile but then pretended he was wiping his mouth when Angelica looked his way.

Realizing that he'd lost his audience for a minute, Father DesMarets cleared his throat and spoke louder. "It's not clear who all came but that's not the point. The point is the Romans put our Lord's followers on a rudderless boat with no sails and no oars, thinking that they would all perish at sea. But instead it landed in Provence."

"A miracle," Angelica said quietly crossing herself. Seeing her, they all crossed themselves.

"From there they split up and some went all around France to preach the gospel. Mary Magdalene paired up with Maximin. Eventually, Lazarus became the first bishop of Marseille and Maximin became the first bishop of Aix-en-Provence. While Maximin lived on the plain, Mary climbed the mountain and lived in the grotto."

"A grotto?" Rajeev asked. "What is that?"

"A small cave usually with a spring nearby for drinking. I've heard though that Mary's was bigger than usual. Still people call it a cave or a grotto."

"This is where we're going?" Rajeev asked. The priest sipped his beverage, nodded and then took a big bite of fish. He inhaled to speak, sputtered and choked. Everyone stared at him. Bhaiya, who had been sitting quietly under the table at Baldwin's feet waiting for someone to drop a scrap of food, jumped up, barked and put his paws on the Father's back, then looked at Baldwin. Baldwin looked back at him perplexed but then jumped up and hit the reverend in the upper back. Everyone gasped as a small fishbone dropped out of the priest's mouth and onto the table. Gasping, he gulped his drink, coughed and sputtered.

"How did Bhaiya know to do that?" Goswin asked Baldwin.

Baldwin shook his head. "Sometimes I think he was once human."

"Oh yes," Rajeev said. "Perhaps a god in disguise."
Breathing heavily Father DesMarets wiped his brow. "There is only one God," he said gaining his composure.

"But obviously many miracles," Armand said.

"Yes indeed," Father DesMarets said quietly. "I think I will continue the story on our journey."

Baldwin patted his dog and sneaked him a piece of cheese.

Armand turned to his wife. "Will you, my dear, treat us to a song to settle the very delicious meal in our full stomachs."

Angelica smiled. "If you will all accompany me into the drawing room I will sing you a song of love and cheer. Her sons stood then disappeared toward their rooms while the others settled into chairs in the drawing room. Like all good noblemen's sons, the three young men were trained in musical instruments: Reginald on the flute, Goswin on a small drum and Baldwin on the mandolin.

Angelica stood in the middle of the room with her sons behind her. She looked at Armand sitting in his comfortable chair as she sang:

Strip off your armor my lord
And throw it all into the sea.
Give up your shield and glittering sword
And stand naked in front of me.

Come take me away my beautiful knight
Ride hard under the darkening sky
Let your arms hold me tight

And your sword be the light
That lets our two souls be able to fly.

Give me your cares my lord
And let the world live as it be.
Let us ignore the gathering horde
And make quiet love to me.

Come take me away my beautiful knight
Ride hard under the darkening sky
Let your arms hold me tight
And your sword be the light
That lets our two souls be able to fly.

Come take my hand my lord
And kiss me until you feel free.
Let us leave nothing that is unexplored
We'll live together in eternity.

Come take me away my beautiful knight
Ride hard under the darkening sky
Let your arms hold me tight
And your sword be the light
That lets our two souls be able to fly.

Armand clapped loudly followed by everyone else. "My favorite. Thank you my love."

Angelica walked over and kissed his cheek. "I wish you were coming with us."

"As do I. But you're in capable hands with our youngest. Now away with you all and ready your traveling clothes for tomorrow. You'll start before dawn so you won't be on the road in the hot sun. We'll have a light supper, uneventful I hope," he said looking over at the reverend, "and retire early."

Several hours before sunrise as the stars still shown brightly and the birds were sound asleep, the servants held candles and lanterns in the crisp cold air as Angelica and Father DesMarets climbed into the carriage. Baldwin, sword strapped to his side, rode before it on his stallion with Rosza and her sister following behind on the shorter Camargue that Rajeev usually rode.

After much discussion it had been decided that the tutor should ride inside the carriage so he and Father DesMarets could discuss religion. After he helped Rosza and her sister onto the horse and loosely tied it with one loop of the rope to the back of the carriage, Rajeev climbed in. Baskets of food were tied on the back and tucked inside the conveyance. The journey would take many hours. The plan was to arrive while it was still cool, eat an early meal and walk up the trail to the grotto.

Armand limped up and kissed Angelica on the palm of her hand and folded it. "Stay safe," he whispered. Reginald and Goswin kissed her on the cheek. Thierry and Francis stood behind them and put up hands in farewell. They would be leaving for home at sunrise.

"Safe journey!" Goswin called as the party started off.

With Bhaiya trotting to the left of Baldwin's horse the group departed the confines of the walled chateau and out toward the main road. As he rode, Baldwin could just make out snatches of lively conversation between his mother, Father DesMarets and Rajeev. It wasn't long before the stars were hidden by the rising sun and Baldwin was filled with thoughts of an enjoyable day ahead. Several hours passed pleasantly.

Behind the carriage, Rosza and Claire chatted quietly.

"Rosza," Claire said urgently, "I have to *go*. Loose the reins and let's ride into the trees. It won't take long."

With a slight tug the rope unloosed and Rosza guided their horse into the trees. They both hopped down and found a clear area to relieve themselves, giggling as they hiked up their dresses and pulled down their pants. When they emerged from the trees they were startled to find two rough looking men standing by the horse.

"We thought we heard the sound of young ladies," one of the men said eyeing the women, "and with a fine horse, too."

Without warning the second man grabbed at Claire and she screamed.

Bhaiya got there first. Barking and snarling he had one of the thieves treed as Baldwin galloped up with sword in hand. But by that time, the ruffian had a large knife to Rosza's throat. Baldwin halted his horse.

"Sheath your sword," the man said gruffly while pressing the knife closer.

Slowly, Baldwin put his sword back in its scabbard. He looked at the man then jumped down from his horse. The man backed himself and Rosza closer to the tree.

"I'm unarmed," Baldwin said holding his arms wide.

Rosza stared at Baldwin, winked and kicked back at the man's knee as Baldwin launched himself at the bandit's arm before the knife could come down. The man was strong and they struggled while Rosza jumped out of their way. Then she gasped, but not at the two men struggling. She'd seen a large snake slithering down the tree above the men's heads. Without thinking she grabbed the snake behind it's neck and threw it at the thief's head. It was his turn to scream as he grabbed for the snake. Baldwin smirked as he quickly put his sword to the man's throat and handed the knife to Rosza.

"Bhaiya let the vile man down from the tree." Bhaiya looked at Baldwin and then slowly backed off the second thief. Baldwin motioned with his sword for the two men to stand together.

"Are either of you hurt?" he asked the two women. They both scowled at the men but shook their heads. "What shall we do with them?"

Bhaiya growled low. Rosza patted him. "Perhaps Bhaiya can tear them apart," she said sweetly.

Both men turned pale and took off running. Claire picked up a stick and threw it at the backs of the hastily retreating men.

Bhaiya thought the stick was for him and ran after it, grabbed it and returned it to Claire. They all laughed.

"Good boy, Bhaiya," Claire said and hugged him.

Rosza hugged him, too. "What a good dog."

"Hey, what about me?" Baldwin asked feigning a hurt look. "I'm the knight here."

Both women patted him on the shoulder as they walked by and back to the road where their horse was unconcernedly munching grass.

Father DesMarets was leaning out the carriage. "What's going on?" he asked.

Baldwin shook his head. "Seems like I forgot about a rear guard. Bhaiya looks like the ladies need you more than me. Stay with them."

Baldwin rode up and briefly told the trio in the carriage what had happened. He then told the driver to move on. He smiled as he remembered the look on the bandit's face when Rosza had thrown the snake. She saved me, he realized. Women were the strong ones, at least in the DesMarets' household. He grinned again as he spurred his horse onward.

The rest of the trip was uneventful. At the bottom of the mountain they stopped to have a light meal. The climb up the mountain would be a long one and fairly steep. The day had turned out cool and low hanging clouds made the mountain look mysterious and mystical. There were few other pilgrims making the visit to the holy site. After a meal of pheasant, bread and fruit with the usual wine the group started off on foot.

"Bhaiya," Baldwin said petting his dog. "Stay and guard the horses and carriage."

After his master took a few steps on the narrow path, Bhaiya followed.

Father DesMarets laughed. "My driver will stay," he said nodding to the man sitting under a tree whom Baldwin had forgotten about, much to his embarrassment.

Baldwin nodded to the monk who nodded back. Wagging his

tail Bhaiya, trotted to the mute servant and licked the man's hand. Baldwin laughed at his crazy yet smart dog.

The mountain was filled with fragrances of pine, cypress and olive trees. Baldwin felt the breeze cool his face as he breathed in the scents. Suddenly, Bhaiya growled and started running.

"Bhaiya!" Baldwin yelled, skirted the travelers and ran after him up the steep mountain grade. Clearing the rise, he saw a brown groundhog frantically trying to climb a tree with Bhaiya less than a foot away, blocking any safe exit for the hapless creature.

"Good boy, let it go," Baldwin said laughing at the scene. With a few more barks to remind his prey who ruled, Bhaiya stepped back and allowed the groundhog his escape. They both watched as it disappeared down a creek bank.

"Come on boy," Baldwin called. "That nasty old groundhog won't bother us anymore."

He shook his head and patted his dog. Bhaiya was so protective and courageous without being aggressive. Just his presence would discourage a threat, human or otherwise. He was bred to hunt the bigger animals but never got a chance to. Baldwin was sure a more intelligent companion he would never find.

They turned and headed back down the hill to meet up with their group who were slowly climbing up. The grotto was in sight. He could see his mother's eyes shining with anticipation, the reverend muttering a prayer, and the household staff chatting with each other, eager to see the resting place of the honored saint. Father DesMarets and Angelica stopped for a moment to catch their breaths. They stepped to the side to let the others walk past. In the next moment a shrill scream shattered the air.

Bhaiya shot off as Baldwin saw his mother and Father DesMarets lose their footing and disappear over the cliff. As Baldwin rushed up, Rosza and the rest of the group were leaning over the cliff yelling and crying.

"Move back!" Baldwin shouted pushing his way through them. He leaned over and saw Father DesMarets several feet down crawling up the rock cliff with Bhaiya pulling at his cassock sleeve.

Angelica was several more feet below him hanging onto some shrubbery. Small rocks rolled down around her as the reverend slowly climbed up.

A gnarled tree was growing horizontally out the side of the mountain and Baldwin hastily unbuckled his sword, climbed the tree and carefully shimmed out to a thick branch that overhung the pair. Bhaiya tugged and pulled at the priest until he got him safely over the ledge and back onto the trail. The dog turned to go back down the cliff but Baldwin realized it was too steep and the animal might start a landslide.

"Bhaiya, no!" he shouted. The dog stopped and stared at Baldwin hanging out on the branch, then started whimpering and pacing. A frightened-looking Angelica was staring up at Baldwin who was now hanging off the branch by his knees and stretching his arms out toward her.

"Mother you have to reach toward me. Can you climb up a bit?" He saw his mother take a deep breath and slowly exhale. She was barely hanging on.

"Just reach up with one hand if you can," Baldwin said as he stretched himself as far as possible. His head was hanging down almost vertical over the deep canyon below. "Mother I will count one, two, three and you lift your arm."

Angelica shook her head. "No Baldwin, we'll both fall."

"Have faith child!" Father DesMarets shouted from the ledge. The group was looking over and causing small rocks, sand and pebbles to slide into Angelica. Bhaiya barked and with his body moved the party back away from the cliff edge.

"Trust me," Baldwin said as he stared into his mother's frightened eyes. Angelica nodded.

"One, two, three." Angelica swung up her arm, Baldwin stretched farther than he thought possible, grabbed her forearm with this left hand and with a powerful pull got his right hand under her left armpit. Then he realized he had to swing her instead of pull her and he lifted and swung her out over the ravine and into the tree.

They stared into each other's eyes. "Son," she said quietly. She hugged the tree as tears rolled down her dusty cheeks.

"Mother, I will always protect you."

"My son, my precious son."

Carefully he climbed around her and she kissed his cheek. He tried brushing away her tears but his position was precarious and all he managed to do was leave dirt streaks on her face. Giving them some moments to catch their breaths, he lifted her to the branch and helped her scoot toward the waiting Father DesMarets and the others who were all reaching toward her. When she was safely back onto solid ground Baldwin sighed with relief. He carefully climbed back onto the branch.

With a loud "crack" it broke off plunging him into the deep, dark forest below.

CHAPTER FIVE

RESURRECTION

1120 A.D.
Saint-Maximin-la-Sainte-Baume, France

Bhaiya howled and peered over the ledge. After a frantic back and forth movement toward the edge he shot down the trail, barking furiously.

"My son, my son!" Angelica wailed and raised her hands. "Holy Mary Magdalene please help him!"

The priest crossed himself. The rest of the group crossed themselves, too, as Father DesMarets pulled Angelica away from the edge fearing she would fall again. She embraced him as her tears welled over. Rajeev, Rosza and Claire gathered around them. All were in shock.

"What can we do?" Rosza cried.

"Pray," Father DesMarets said as he patted Angelica's back.

"Bhaiya will find him," Rajeev said reassuringly. "I will follow his barks."

While the rest of the party comforted each other, Rajeev started running down the path, listening for the dog's distant sounds.

Far below Baldwin's body had tumbled through the forest painfully hitting large tree limbs on the way. As he thought his fall would never stop it did suddenly, knocking the air out of his lungs. He lay on decaying ground feeling stiff and, *God please no*, broken. After a moment he inhaled. Then slowly exhaled trying to gather his thoughts.

All was dark, damp and smelled of earth and decomposing leaves. His thoughts were scattered, his body bruised but ... there was something just outside his consciousness that was calling to him. Maybe it was a hallucination. No, he was sure a voice was calling him. His vision blurred but his body relaxed. His mind flooded with visions.

A younger, strangely dressed version of himself–thirteen or fourteen years old, he couldn't tell–was standing in a small, well appointed room staring at a child–she must have been ten–who was dressed in a fine silk dress with a large blue satin bow. She was sitting at a dressing table brushing her long, shiny brown hair. She turned to him and smiled.

"What does betrothed mean?" she asked him. Her large brown eyes stared innocently at him.

"It means, milady, when you get old enough you'll marry the czar of Rus," he said and looked down at his brightly polished, black boots.

She shrugged. She was too young to understand, he thought. Too young to realize that they would be separated and he could not see her anymore. Love her anymore.

The scene changed and Baldwin was a young man of sixteen wearing the chainmail and sword of a knight. He escorted the young girl, Christina, as she boarded a ship bound for distance shores. He realized he was relieved that he would be with her to protect her and disappointed that she would never be his.

The image changed once again and Baldwin found himself standing at attention inside a vast cathedral as the beautiful child bride entered dressed in flowing white satin with a floor-length veil that covered her from head to toe. Slowly she walked up to the alter where a heavily bearded man in full military dress waited for her. He was at least 30 years older than Christina.

Baldwin silently wept when she said, "I do." She would become czarina and change her name to Anastasia, as was the custom. The name meant resurrection. She would add new life to the cold country they now called home. Baldwin knew he could never kiss, hold or make passionate, devoted love to her. His longing would never be quenched. She was lost to him forever. He felt a chill run down his body as his soul ached with loss and sorrow. Tears fell silently as the image faded.

On the ground at the foot of the mountain in France blackness swirled inside his head and filled him with bone-chilling dread. The demon had arrived. It was blacker than the darkness and no longer a shadow. Baldwin shivered as it started toward him. A sound emanated from its throat that sounded like a scratchy growl combined with screeching wind. "I am nameless, formless yet known to you and my influence is vast. I have come from inside the earth to take you down." Fear paralyzed Baldwin. The evil came toward him, reached out and touched him.

Suddenly a light glowed and a woman's voice said, "Be gone demon. He has come to me and you are not wanted here."

Warmth filled Baldwin's soul, his heart lifted and a wave of love washed over him. In his mind's eye, he saw a beautiful woman dressed in white and blue and knew it was Mary Magdalene.

"Baldwin," she said softly, "thank you for your faith in me. I indeed lived and died in the grotto but my whole story has not been revealed. Centuries will pass before it will be told. The love you have for your mother and the love you still hold in your heart for Anastasia allows me to give you my Divine guidance throughout your life. You will be going on your life's adventure soon and will have much help along the way. Know that I love you. Also know this Baldwin, evil is but an illusion. Only love is truth. All is possible within the power of unconditional love." Her voice faded away.

Baldwin woke. He was lying among green and gray foliage on hard earth and small rocks. The air felt dense with dew. The side of his face was slimed with bits of bark and mud. His bruised and battered body ached but his heart felt light. Sounds of the forest came rushing back. Birds were cawing to each other. A lark was singing as a squirrel skitted up a tree. He turned his head and saw the opening to a small cave. He had the urge to go in but felt there was something ominous standing in the shadows waiting for him. Then, somewhere in the distance he heard people calling his name.

"I'm here," he called hoarsely. Slowly and painfully he pulled himself into a sitting position and called again. "I'm here! I'm all right!"

He heard Father DesMarets' distant voice say, "Oh, thank God," as Bhaiya jumped over a bush, landed almost on top of him and stuck a cold, wet nose in his ear. Baldwin hugged him and sighed. The cave was ignored as he let his dog nudge and shove. Then a rough hand reached down. Baldwin looked up. A young man was standing there wearing monk's robes. The thought flitted through Baldwin's mind that the brown of the robes matched the color of the surroundings. Maybe the man was some kind of forest nymph. No, that couldn't be right. Perhaps he was one of the monks who guarded the grotto. Baldwin shook his head and then recognized him. It was Father DesMarets' mute driver.

He helped Baldwin up, brushed leaves off his shoulders, motioned him to turn around and brushed his back. He took out a faded cloth and patted Baldwin's bleeding cheek. He placed Baldwin's hand over the cloth indicating that he should hold it there until the bleeding stopped.

"Thank you," Baldwin said realizing that he didn't know the man's name. He was about to ask when he remembered that the man was unable to answer. Taking Baldwin's arm the mute helped him through the thick woods until they found a small deer trail. They walked down it single file, Baldwin in front and the mute behind. Bhaiya bounded ahead while occasionally turning his burnished-colored head to see if the men followed. The narrow trail came out at the bottom of the mountain where the carriage and horses were tied.

More pilgrims had arrived and were just starting up the path to the grotto. They looked at Baldwin's clothes, which were fit for nobility but torn. His face was scratched and his boots scuffed. Although he was physically functional Baldwin's hips felt sore and he limped. He felt for his sword and remembered he'd taken it off to climb the tree to save his mother. Thank God he'd done so or he might have fallen on it. He shook his head. What a knight.

One old woman separated herself from her fellow travelers and spoke to him.

"Sir knight, the Blessed Mary will help heal you." At this Baldwin grinned at the mute servant who grinned back.

"Thank you. May I escort you up the mountain?" Baldwin asked the crinkled-faced woman. She was finely dressed and Baldwin thought she must be nobility or perhaps royalty.

"Very kind son,' the woman said, "but I don't want to slow you down. You look like death warmed over so you better hurry."

Just then Rajeev rushed out of the woods. "My lord! Bhaiya stopped barking and I couldn't find you!" Bending, he put his hands on his knees and tried to catch his breath.

Startled, the old woman pressed her hand over the cross around her neck and exclaimed, "Protect me Jesus from people jumping out of the woods!" She looked Rajeev up and down. "Are you one of those dark-skinned heathens I hear so much about?" Rajeev peered up at her and said nothing. Baldwin shook his head.

"Madame, he is no heathen but a true believer in Christ. And, a respected member of my household. Now, since you don't want my assistance I will allow my dear friend to walk with me so we may have an intelligent discussion along the way. Peace to you."

The woman shook her head and Rajeev's eyes twinkled as he gave his former student a sideways smile and winked.

"A question," the woman said giving Rajeev a piercing look. "How did you become a Christian?"

"I was taught to believe it and so I believe it. Not many people think for themselves," Rajeev answered.

"He knows a lot about a lot," Baldwin put in, tiring of the woman's questions.

With the Indian by his side, he turned to the mute and motioned him to walk with them but the man silently shook his head and sat down inside the carriage. Baldwin nodded. Bhaiya trotted up, allowed Rajeev to pet him, butted Baldwin in the knee, then shot up the path. With Rajeev holding his arm, Baldwin slowly followed. He left the mute to his duty of guarding the carriage and horses and the curious old woman to walk with her friends.

As he walked painfully onward, Baldwin thought, was the dark figure he'd seen Death? Who was Anastasia to him? He's never met an Anastasia. How could he love her? What had Mary Magdalene said? Something about illusion. Baldwin shook his head trying to understand. He couldn't remember it all clearly.

Everyone was overjoyed when Bhaiya ran up, stopped, spun around three times then wagged his tail furiously as they all turned to look down the path. Impatiently, Angelica rushed down it until she saw her tattered son and Rajeev walking slowly up. Overcome with emotion she burst into tears, grabbed Baldwin and hugged him. He winced. After many questions about his fall and assurances that he was still in one piece they made their way to the little group waiting for them.

Father DesMarets handed Baldwin his scabbard with sword and patted him on the back saying, "Thank God, thank God."

Rosza and Claire kissed his cheeks. He blushed. Then once again the little group started up the steep path, this time more slowly.

While protectively holding her son's arm, Angelica asked Father DesMarets, "Please tell us more of the story of the cave."

The priest cleared his throat. "Yes, of course. Now where was I?"

Coming up from behind, the old woman and her group spotted Father DesMarets and greeted him as if she knew him.

"Hello again," Baldwin said. "Father DesMarets was just going to tell us the history of the cave."

"I know some of it," the woman said sharply.

Baldwin saw his mother put her hand up to cover her disapproval. She hated arrogance. Baldwin smiled.

The woman continued, "I also know there are many versions. All of them tell about the rudder-less boat and about Mary landing in Marseille where she and Maximin began teaching Christianity. Am I right so far Father?"

"Yes, Madame …?" Father DesMarets was confused by this stranger's interruption.

"My friends call me Constance," the woman said. "I am patroness of the Saint Victor Abbey of Marseilles," she said importantly.

Father DesMarets bowed. "Oh yes, of course."

Rajeev whispered to Baldwin, "Are we her friends?"

Baldwin answered, "A woman rich enough to give money to monks in Marseilles is always considered our friend."

Rajeev nodded and grinned.

Father DesMarets continued, "After finishing her ministry Mary Magdalene came to this grotto we are about to see and is reported to have lived here for 30 years."

"What a hardship that must have been," Constance said.

"Indeed," Father DesMarets said. "But it must be true that she lived here because the monastery was built around 415 AD, established by Jean Cassian. "You must know this madam as you are a patron of his abbey."

"Jean Cassian was the patriarch of the monks of Saint Victor Abbey, yes," Constance said. "He was a devout man."

"Yes," Father DesMarets said. "I am privileged to know one of the holy Cassianist friars who guard the grotto from unintentional destruction by the many pilgrims who come here."

"I understand that two popes have visited the holy site," Constance stated.

"Oh yes," Father DesMarets acknowledged, "Pope Stephen VI in 816 *Anno Domini* and in 878 it was Pope John VIII."

Baldwin thought they were trying to one up each other with their knowledge of the grotto.

"At the Monastery of Saint Victor we are privileged to have Saint Jean Cassian's relics," Constance said proudly.

Rajeev gently nudged Baldwin and raised his eyebrows. "Um, yes," he whispered. "Very important indeed."

"What relics are those?" Angelica asked.

"His head and right hand," Constance said.

Every person crossed themselves.

As the small group came around a bend in the steep trail a brown-robed Cassianist friar stepped out to meet them. He put his hand to his lips and whispered that from this point on they would be in silence. He put a hand on Father DesMarets' sleeve to stop him and passed him something, then bowed, stepped back and let them all pass.

Although the opening to the cliff cave was spoken of as narrow, Baldwin found it was a little wider than he had imagined. A few other travelers were already inside, sitting on pillows or blankets facing a coffin. He knew it wasn't the Blessed Mary Magdalene's coffin but Maximin, the first bishop of Aix-en-Provence, whose bones lay inside. He remembered the words from his dream that evidence of Mary living there would be found later. He wondered when that would be.

From the First Century people had been visiting this holy place where Mary Magdalene lived and died. Although the basic story had stayed the same the details of her life had become embellished with visitations from angels who'd fed her and transported her to heaven and back. After thirty years, she'd come down from her grotto and died in Maximin's arms. Why his coffin was there Baldwin wasn't sure except that the monks watched over him, perhaps because he was the bishop. History was full of details that didn't make sense.

Baldwin silently settled his mother and the priest on cushions they'd brought with them. Both the priest and Angelica had shawls–she put hers over her head and he wrapped his around his shoulders. It was cold in the grotto. Few candles were lit for light but not for warmth. The watching monks wore thick wool cloaks with the hoods pulled up.

Rajeev, Rosza and Claire sat on folded blankets. Rajeev sat cross-legged, which he'd taught his three pupils to do when they were young. He said it was a balanced way to sit. With his hips hurting, Baldwin didn't even try to get into the sitting position, although normally he enjoyed sitting that way. Not today. Stiffness was taking over.

With Bhaiya lying quietly beside him, Baldwin sat on a small cushion with his back to the cold rock, eyes shut listening to some far off water dripping. He heard Rajeev take in a deep breath and let it out slowly. He did it several times and Baldwin followed suit. As Baldwin slowly breathed in, and out, in and out, the drip, drip, drip soothed and settled him. His mind quieted. After a few moments he heard nothing at all.

He remembered Mary's words and felt comforted … and curious. Why was there dripping in this small grotto? Was it warmer in the far reaches of the grotto where no one went? Wasn't this supposed to be just a small cave? It seemed bigger.

He breathed in and … he was walking in darkness, away from the candles and the quietly praying strangers toward the back of the cave. Then he saw a wall of darkness. He walked through it. He was awestruck when he saw a formation of ice stalactites dripping from the ceiling and their corresponding stalagmites rising like spikes from the floor. It was wondrous, like an enchanted forest of water.

As Baldwin stared at his surroundings he noticed a narrow trail winding toward the back wall of what now seemed a much larger cave then he first entered. How curious. If he was careful, he thought, he could walk on the trail, see where it went. Cautiously, he faced the spikes of water and, with his back scraping along the cold wall, walked sideways around the back of the cave. At the very back his eyes blurred or perhaps it was a fog or gray shadows floating around him. *No*, not in Mary's cave. Then he felt the warmth and suddenly … he was no longer in a grotto, but in a massive cavern with high rock walls dotted with cave-like openings.

Baldwin looked up but couldn't see the ceiling. He thought he saw something large and shiny flying high in the dark. For some reason his brother's lizard, Monster, sprang into his mind. A flying lizard? Crazy. As he looked at the many caves he saw a small flame shooting out from one of them. Curious. If it were a fire, the flames would be contained not shooting out sideways as if thrown. What was this place?

Baldwin didn't know if he was up or down. Had he gone down into the depths or up inside the mountain? After a moment he realized someone was speaking to him. It was the gentle voice of Mary Magdalene.

"Baldwin, there is more to life than most people know and more creatures above and below us than you can imagine. Know this, there is an interconnectedness of all life and the separation between our inner and outer worlds is but an illusion."

Baldwin slowly opened his eyes and found himself still sitting on the cushion with his back against cold rock. He saw Father DesMarets lips moving in a silent prayer; his mother touching her cross with a look of ecstasy; Rajeev sitting straight-backed in his cross-legged position with his eyes tightly shut; and Claire, Rosza and most of the other travelers slumped with heads nodding. He smiled at that. So much for the deeply pious. More like the travel weary.

Painfully, he heaved himself up and carefully walked to the cave entrance and looked out over the valley. An eager Bhaiya wagged his tail and started down the path. Baldwin saw one of the Cassianist monks and, although they looked identical to each other, thought it was the one who'd handed Father DesMarets something. Baldwin assumed it was the priest's half brother.

After a moment Father DesMarets, escorting Angelica, walked up beside him. He waved at the monk and the three of them walked over to him.

"How do you find the holy place?" the monk asked quietly.

"It's more profound than even I thought it might be," Father DesMarets answered.

Angelica sighed. "I could feel Her presence. I'm so deeply moved to be able to sit in the same cave where She spent all those years. Such a holy, holy place."

"And you?" the monk asked Baldwin.

Baldwin thought about his vision.

"Is there a cave behind this grotto?"

"Not that I know of," the monk answered. "We Cassianists have been guarding this holy place for centuries. I'm sure, however, that there is much more to this cave than meets the eye."

There was something about the way he said it that made Baldwin think the monk knew more than he was telling.

"I will walk with you brother and we can talk about things great and small," the monk said to Father DesMarets. They started down the hill in deep conversation.

Baldwin looked back into the grotto and saw that Rajeev, Rosza and Claire were still sitting undisturbed. Angelica glanced back.

"My son," she said putting her hand on Baldwin's arm. "I thought I'd lost you." Her voice caught and her eyes glistened with tears. Baldwin hugged her but she pulled away. Reaching around her neck she unfastened the cross that Armand had given her so long ago.

"Soon you'll be going off to become a full-fledged knight fighting for the true believers of faith. I think now is the time to give you this." She held out the cross to him.

"Mother, your precious cross," Baldwin whispered shaking his head and pushing her hand away.

"Baldwin you are the precious one. I want you to wear this for protection and to always remind you of your family and our Lord's sacrifice. Will you do that?"

Baldwin took the cross and fastened it around his neck. He then held his mother in his strong arms.

"Mother I will never forsake you."

"I have faith in you son. By faith we live."

At the entrance of the sacred grotto of Mary Magdalene the wind was whispering through the trees either as a blessing or a warning to the two who held each other for a long while.

CHAPTER SIX

THE JOURNEY BEGINS

1120 A.D.
Marets, France

Before dawn a week later, the DesMarets were in the family chapel holding hands and praying. Angelica told the servants that it would only be the immediate family for the morning prayer. Even Rajeev and Rosza, who considered themselves part of the family, had understood the need for privacy and respected it.

Neither parent had wanted this day to come—all three of their children were leaving at the same time. Reginald to attend the modern monastery school in Paris; Goswin to be an apprentice on a sailing ship: and Baldwin to join a new religious military order of knights in Jerusalem calling themselves the Poor Knights of Christ and of the Temple of Solomon.

Although chomping at the bit to leave, Baldwin's older brothers had waited for him to heal enough to ride. After his fall at the grotto Angelica and Father DesMarets had forced him to ride back in their carriage. Rajeev simply held the reins of the big black stallion and let the horse trot along beside them. Rosza and Claire took pity on him and rode alongside chatting gaily.

At first Bhaiya had jumped inside the carriage behind Baldwin, but it had proved too crowded. Instead he played guard dog and trotted behind the group making sure no bandits bothered them on the journey home. None did.

The next day Baldwin couldn't get out of bed. His entire mid-section, along with his arms and legs, were black, blue and purple with bruises. His brothers came into his bedroom and made fun of him but then gently helped him into a copper tub of hot water filled with healing herbs that Angelia had instructed be brought in.

"This is for our own good, not yours," Reginald joked as he playfully poured water over Baldwin's head.

"We're leaving together so hurry up and heal," Goswin admonished. "And count your blessings that we all know how to use herbs to heal banged up knights. Good thing you didn't break any bones or we'd leave you." Goswin grinned as he said it. Baldwin splashed water on both of them but then groaned as they retaliated. When his bruises started to turn yellow and greenish and he could walk around, although rather stiffly, they decided he was good enough to ride.

After making fun of him for walking bent over like an old man, Baldwin's brothers casually and slowly sauntered with him to the stables where the stable boy put on the stallion's saddle—Baldwin was sure he couldn't do it yet—and helped him up. Armand came out to watch.

Baldwin groaned, closed his eyes for a moment then nudged his horse into a slow walk. He tried sitting up straight but his ribs hurt causing him to gasp, which naturally resulted in more "ribbing" by his siblings. Still, he was up in the saddle and knew in a few days time he'd be off, if not at a gallop perhaps at a slow trot. His brothers and father applauded when he awkwardly dismounted took a painful bow and announced he was ready for the journey.

Armand smiled and escorted everyone back inside. With all three sons leaving at once the dent in the family fortune would be substantial. However, Armand had planned for at least two of his sons to journey off and had saved accordingly. He'd thought his oldest son would stay to run the estate, as was the custom. One day Reginald would inherit it all, but first he wanted to satisfy his intellect and learn modern estate-running techniques. The monastery school in Paris not only had an up-to-date library but allowed experts to relay their hands-on experience in demonstrations and speeches. It was an exciting time to expand one's knowledge. Plus, he didn't have to become a monk.

Armand understood and respected Reginald's decision. Besides, he wasn't ready to sit by and let others run all that he'd taken a lifetime to build. Fortunately, the spring harvest had been a good one. All his serfs were productive and his own innovative ideas on estate management had paid off. Each of his sons would have more than sufficient funds for their travels.

Goswin's parents had always known he'd head to sea. From a young age he'd loved his toy boats: constructing, sailing and repairing them. He played all the roles he could think of: including but not limited to, deck hand, captain and cutlass-carrying pirate. He'd taught his pet lizard Monster to walk a tiny plank and made him a captain's hat out of a nut's shell. Surprisingly, Monster liked playing in water and, at least in Goswin's mind, liked running around in his hat. The little lizard ran fast, could balance on anything and camouflage himself by changing color.

Goswin had memorized all the seafaring terms, studied maps and ran outside to look at cloud formations and make drawings of them. No one was surprised by the middle son's decision. His parents were glad he hadn't run off at a much younger age to become a cabin boy.

Baldwin's journey would be the longest and most arduous. Even though the crusade had made it safer for pilgrims to travel over land, lately many more travelers were being robbed and murdered along the way by bandits. Another hazard was greedy landowners charging a large toll to cross their land. If not paid the pilgrims would often disappear. As a knight Baldwin could protect himself, still, and with Goswin's urging, he decided to travel by sea, which was slightly safer but not without peril. Rajeev, of course, would go with him along with the beloved Bhaiya.

First they would travel to Venice and buy passage on a ship for about sixty Italian ducats each. They'd sail to Acre, the chief port of the Kingdom of Jerusalem on the eastern Mediterranean. They'd stop at various islands along the way for provisions. At sea, pirates would be a threat and unscrupulous merchants in the seaside cities would overcharge the innocent pilgrims. Baldwin knew the hazards but thought it worth the risk. His father, who'd made the journey by land almost two decades ago but had returned by sea, had taught each of his sons how to defend themselves against the most dangerous of attackers. Eventually as a Poor Knight of Christ, he'd be defending the pilgrims and leading an exemplary life devoted to God.

Now outside the family chapel in the early morning light, Armand quietly drew Baldwin aside. "Son," he said seriously, "you're going to a different land—a dangerous land, yet holy and worth defending. Rajeev will be a good companion along the way. But ..." he paused, "you cannot take your dog with you."

"What? No! Not take Bhaiya? Why not?" Baldwin's raised voice startled swifts out of a nearby tree.

Armand raised his hands to quiet him. "There will be battles, bloodshed and horses stamping around," he explained. Bhaiya would be an easy target and in the way. No, the commanders will not let you have him. He'd be in danger of being killed by them if not by the infidels. They wouldn't hesitate. Leave him behind. That's an order."

Baldwin put his head down as he walked to his room knowing that he could not disobey his father. His heart fell to the floor. He sat on the edge of his bed and ruffled his dog's long reddish-brown coat, running his hands down his best friend's back and scratching under his chin. Then he took the dog's big head in his hands.

"Bhaiya, while I'm away you take good care of the household. With all three of us gone you'll be the main protector. Understand?"

Bhaiya's big black eyes stared at his master then he put his shaggy head on Baldwin's knee. He was petted for a long time.

Everyone spent the rest of the morning quietly packing, sadness hanging over the household like a festering deep wound. No one ate much at the noon meal. Seeing that everyone was pretending

83

to eat but not actually doing so, Armand put down his knife, stood up and cleared his throat. All eyes turned toward him.

"Sons," he said, "you are nobility and you are knights. For the next journey of your lives where you may have to defend yourselves against the devil, each of you will receive new chainmail, swords, and helmets–except Reginald who already has my helmet."

"I won it fairly and I will wear it proudly," Reginald said.

Armand smiled and continued. "The design on the hilt of the sword has my favorite friend, the bee, and your devoted mother has chosen a small gem for each of you. These gems are embedded in your swords." He nodded to Angelica.

Angelica, looking more composed than she felt, stood and walked over to the sideboard, which was covered with a plain cotton cloth.

"Reginald, I chose for you a yellow citrine because you shine brightly like the sun." She pulled the cloth back and took out a sword sheathed in a hand-tooled scabbard. It was heavy and she held it with both hands allowing the tip to touch the floor. Reginald stood up, took it and raised it over his head. He kissed her on the cheek.

"Thank you, mother," he said as he pulled the sword out of the scabbard and looked at the hilt and the yellow jewel embedded there. He carried it back to his seat and put it across his lap, admiring it.

"For you Goswin, a blue sapphire that represents the sea."

Goswin stood and Angelica handed him his new sword. He smiled and exuberantly kissed both her cheeks, making everyone laugh. He, too, drew out the sword and admired it.

"Thank you, mother. It's beautiful. I'll be the envy of all the sailors on the ocean blue."

He nodded and returned to his seat. Angelica looked at Baldwin, who stood.

"For you my most devout son, a red ruby, which represents the blood of Christ."

Baldwin's eyes watered as he crossed himself, took the sword then kissed his mother and sat down. He ran his fingers down the scabbard but didn't look at the jewel. He'd look at it later when his vision had cleared. Tears slipped down Angelica's cheeks as she seated herself. Once again Armand stood and cleared his throat.

"As DesMarets, your mother and I, well mostly your mother," he glanced fondly at his wife, "have encouraged in each of you to hold acts of charity in the highest esteem. To be spiritually united in the praise of God, even in the most difficult of times–to abstain from gluttony, drunkenness and debauchery of any kind. You are knights but above all you are as stars shining above pettiness and greed."

He held his goblet high and everyone at the table followed. "May God and the saints protect our noble knights!"

As one the three sons stood, raised their goblets and cheered, "To father!" Took a gulp and turned to their mother, "To mother!"

They finished their drinks smiling and feeling lighter than they had earlier in the day.

After retrieving their belongings they all walked outside where the stable boy brought up seven horses. Baldwin and Rajeev would ride together to Venice, Reginald to Paris and Goswin to the port of Sete. Each one had an extra packhorse for their belongings. The cook had packed the leftovers for travel, which was divided between the packhorses.

Even though they were not expecting any trouble along the route, the two older sons were dressed in chainmail with swords fastened at their hips. Their helmets were tied securely to their saddles. Baldwin looked at them with envy. Although it was typical to wear a padded cotton shirt under the chainmail to protect the skin, Baldwin's bruises were still too sensitive to wear the ring armor. He was dressed in light silks and had his battle gear in a pack on the back of his horse. His sword, however, was by his side. Not to be outdone, Rajeev had a dagger clearly seen on his belt.

All three boys hugged their father and kissed and hugged their mother. Baldwin patted Bhaiya and told him to stay. Mounting their horses and waving at the sorrowful staff they trotted away.

Customarily, many relatives and servants walked several miles with journeying members of their domicile. However, Armand had decided not to travel part of the way with his sons but to stay with Angelia and the remaining household followed suit.

Armand called Bhaiya to come, kissed a tearful Angelica and arm-in-arm they walked back inside the walled estate. Bhaiya did not follow. Unnoticed, he trotted out after his master.

After a mile or so all four men started feeling the excitement and adventure of their journeys. They chatted amicably until the crossroad appeared where Reginald would turn toward Paris, Goswin toward Sete and Baldwin and Rajeev toward Italy. With Rajeev looking on and smiling, the three young men pulled out their swords, raised them and touched points.

Reginald shouted, "To adventure!"

Then all three shouted, "By faith we live!"

They turned their horses away and trotted off. As they turned, Rajeev noticed a small lizard peeking out of the pack on the back of Goswin's horse. Instinctively, he looked up and saw a falcon flying far overhead. Smiling, he shook his head and caught up to his young charge.

After some miles Rajeev asked if Baldwin wanted to stay in a tavern overnight but they decided to put down blankets and sleep under the massive display of stars. They unwrapped the cheese and bread sent by the cook and ate it as if they hadn't eaten for a month. They were quietly talking when Baldwin had a feeling that someone was staring at him. He looked at Rajeev who was looking over Baldwin's shoulder grinning at something. Baldwin turned. About three feet away Bhaiya was sitting with a dead rabbit in his mouth.

"Bhaiya, no! Go home!" Baldwin shouted and pointed down the road.

Bhaiya dropped the rabbit, put his head down on his paws and stared at Baldwin.

"Ah sir, let's not turn away the peace offering," Rajeev said. "It will make a wonderful stew. Bhaiya can have the bones and

I can dry the fur and make a hat. All will be used to nourish us. Nothing wasted."

Baldwin gave Rajeev a quizzical look. "A fur hat? For Jerusalem?"

"It might be cold on the ship," Rajeev said smiling.

A picture flashed in Baldwin's mind of a brown fur hat sitting on a young girl's head. It wasn't rabbit, but sable, as befitted a czarina. She was looking sad as if walking to her doom. He shook the sight from his mind.

Rajeev and Bhaiya stared at him, obviously waiting.

"All right take the rabbit," Baldwin said as he picked it up and handed it to Rajeev. "Come on Bhaiya you bad dog."

But he was smiling as Bhaiya thumped his tail on the ground.

As Rajeev built a small fire, Baldwin searched his surroundings for fresh herbs while Bhaiya rolled in the road.

"You better not be rolling in horse dung," Baldwin said over his shoulder. He suspected the dog was.

Baldwin found wild onions, various roots and sage. Rajeev added them to a small amount of wine and some pepper he'd packed for the journey. They threw the bones in the road for Bhaiya, as he was too dirty and smelly to sit with them. After stirring the stew, Rajeev recited a brief prayer thanking the earth for this great gift. Not expecting much in the way of taste they breathed in the stew's aroma, jokingly smacked their lips and spooned in a mouthful. Their eyes lit. The meager, side-of-the road meal was delicious.

Baldwin watched his matted-hair dirty dog gnaw hungrily on a small bone. "Bhaiya seems to enjoy horse dung for some reason."

"In India," Rajeev said, "they make many uses out of cow dung."

He pulled a water pouch from his side, poured a little over Baldwin's folded hands, then handed him a cloth for drying. He poured a small amount of water on his own hands and Baldwin handed him back the cloth. "Maybe the horses are holy to him," Rajeev added.

"I don't know what you mean," Baldwin said poking the fire with a small stick.

Rajeev sat back. "I will explain," he said. "The ancient texts, called the *Vedas*, say that the cow is divine and sacred. The holy beast is protected and many offerings are made to it. It gives milk for us to drink. Our mother's give milk. How can such natural beneficence not be sacred?"

"I hadn't thought about it before," Baldwin said. "I know my mother is very sacred to me yet it was the woman, Eve, who caused Adam to be tempted and fall into sin."

Rajeev shrugged. "A mistake to say woman is the cause of sin. That is Old Testament thinking. You should not feel guilty about your very origins. Your birth is not impure. Do you think your parents are impure?"

"My parents are the most spiritual, devoted and loving people I know! But only God is pure. We humans are fallen sinners."

"It does not seem logical that we who are created in God's image should be so low."

"The bible tells us that we are so I'm going by that. As low as cow dung apparently, which is what we were discussing." Baldwin frowned.

Rajeev smiled at the perplexed look on his pupil's face. He knew from experience that Baldwin would be thinking on the topic of creation for a while–trying to get clarity.

"Back to the uses of cow dung," Rajeev said. "We in India have been using cow dung for our cooking fires for centuries. It's natural, abundant and easy to use when dried. It's also makes good soil for growing things."

"Horse manure is good for growing things, too," Baldwin said. "But you can't pile it on the garden or field as it's too hot. A small amount works and it needs to be turned. The worms love it."

Rajeev nodded. "In India we like to make incense out of it and burn it in our temples. It's an ancient tradition. It helps cleanse the air of disease and gets rid of mosquitoes. Frankincense is popular in the Catholic Church, but I think sandalwood is most popular in India. At least I remember it that way."

"How do you add spices to it?" Baldwin asked. "That's intriguing,"

"Before I was found by my Christian parents, I was just a small boy working for a very bad man making incense. He had oxen, cows and animals of all kinds. He was good to them, not so good to most of us. But that is the past. I do know about cow dung though," Rajeev laughed. "It's a long process. First I would gather up the dung and spread it out to dry. Fresh air is the best. You can imagine the smell though. Anyway, three-to-five years of drying are what is preferred for the most excellent dung."

Baldwin nodded and smiled. "A process that requires a lot of patience."

"I don't remember it exactly, there was some always drying when it was hot, and the man was very secretive about everything he did. But, basically you use thin sticks and add the paste. You crush the cow dung with a binding material, add spices, perfumes, resins, and other things and some water or honey to help mold it into various shapes: balls, cones, sticks, blocks and even coils. Sticks are the most popular. All I can really remember is that I was very good at rolling the sticks in the spices."

"How old were you?"

"I think I was with him from about ages 3-to-5 years. I'm not sure of my age."

Just then Bhaiya ran up and tried to lick Baldwin who pushed the stinking dog away.

"Get back!" Bhaiya wagged his tail.

Baldwin stood. "The stars are bright and I'm not the least bit tired."

"Let's travel on then," Rajeev suggested. "We can clearly see the road by moonlight."

"Good. I can't wait to get to Venice so I can give Bhaiya a bath," Baldwin said.

They put out the fire, packed up and rode on side-by-side.

Bhaiya frisked about happily running in and out of the woods, chasing small animals and scaring sleeping birds out of trees.

"Tell me more reasons the cow is sacred," Baldwin finally asked.

"It truly has to do with women giving us life and nurturing us," Rajeev said and grinned.

"It can't be all about women," Baldwin said stubbornly.

Rajeev smiled inwardly. He paused for a moment to gather his thoughts.

"As you know, I was not raised a Hindu but a Christian by a couple who saved me from my life as a child worker to one of education and religion. I was very, very fortunate."

He crossed himself and so did Baldwin who murmured, "Thank the Lord," and touched the cross around his neck.

"However, one cannot live in India without learning the concepts of Hinduism as well as other belief systems. My new parents were also very learned people, scholars, in fact. I read many manuscripts, the spiritually minded would visit and I was taught many things about how to read the sky–both day and night. I can tell your fortune and your future from the planets and stars." He smiled. "I can tell the weather from the clouds, or as tonight, the lack of them. No rain in sight and we should be in Venice soon."

Baldwin looked at him quizzically. "My future? Good, I trust."

Rajeev smiled and nodded. "Of course, as good as a cow's in India."

Baldwin laughed, "Go on tell me more about the sacred cow."

"If I had known when you were growing up that you'd be so interested in cows I would have told you earlier in your education." Rajeev sighed. "So much you would learn about the divineness of all things if you came to India where gods and goddesses are everywhere."

"I believe my mother is divine," Baldwin said thoughtfully.

"She definitely has the spirit of Lakshmi, the mother-goddess who nurtures and nourishes all life."

"I don't know how she'd take it if I compared her to a cow though," Baldwin said and grinned.

"If she understood my culture she would be very pleased."

"Before we go off to India, let's get to the Holy Land first," Baldwin said smiling. "We're going to Venice and I'm not even taking the time to visit Rome. I'd like to one day go to pay homage to St. Peter's grave at the Basilica."

"As would I," Rajeev said. "Perhaps we can find ancient manuscripts in Rome on the early teachings of Christianity."

"Father would love that. Although I've heard their wine is terrible." Baldwin's eyes twinkled.

Rajeev smiled, shook his head and continued. "India itself has many holy people and places with much ancient knowledge. The slaughter of milk-producing cows is forbidden in parts of the *Mahabharata*, a great story of India. You'd gain a greater education there."

"As long as I don't harm a cow I would be welcome?" Baldwin asked smiling.

"As long as you were open minded to learning new life lessons," Rajeev countered.

Suddenly their horses shied as a large light brown deer bolted across the road followed by a barking Bhaiya.

"Holy cow!" Baldwin yelled while getting his horse under control.

Rajeev stared at him. They burst out laughing.

After getting *themselves* under control, Baldwin called for Bhaiya to come, then they hurried along at a trot to get to their destination before tiring from their long journey. It wasn't too long before they could smell the sea. They hurried their horses faster.

Two miles separated Venice from the mainland. After a brief logistical discussion, the travelers decided that Baldwin and Bhaiya would take the stallion and one packhorse on one boat and Rajeev would take his horse and the other packhorse on the next. The boats were not large but Baldwin had enough funds to hire two completely for themselves. Before leaving Baldwin picked Bhaiya up and threw him in the water.

"It won't help much but maybe enough that I can stand getting in this boat with him," Baldwin said to Rajeev. Bhaiya swam around for a few minutes then came onshore and furiously shook the water off his coat making everyone move away quickly. Then he trotted onboard as if it was the most natural thing in the world. The two men shook their heads and laughed.

The horses were well trained and didn't balk at standing at attention and making the crossing. Even the packhorses barely flicked their tails when the boat moved from the dock. Rajeev and Baldwin looked more nervous than the horses. Both men stood ramrod straight the entire distance, staring straight ahead while holding their horse's reins.

Venice was bustling with activity and more boats than either man had ever seen. Excitement permeated the air. Multitudes of pilgrims of every description, from peasants to priests, were lined up to purchase the limited passage on sailing ships or buy food for their overland journey. Groups of others were being guided to churches to see holy relics of the saints—heads to hands—teeth, bones and ashes. Even one of Goliath's molars was on display.

People jostled them from all sides as they lead their horses through the crowded, noisy streets. Bhaiya weaved in and out of the crowds, sniffing at the many food stalls and occasionally darting down a dark alley, then running to catch up. As a nobleman and knight Baldwin was allowed to purchase a small cabin for the three of them. There were two cabins in the aft of the ship they were taking. One belonged to the captain and Baldwin purchased the second one. Everyone else would make due in the hold with the cargo. Sadly, they would have to give up their horses, saddles and all, as the fare was exorbitant.

After sampling various delicious Italian foods at the bazaar and haggling over the sale of the horses, Baldwin and Rajeev boarded the gangway to the ship *Starburst*. Bhaiya trotted right behind them sniffing the salt air and enjoying the bustle. The weary travelers boarding the ship ignored him.

When Baldwin entered the cabin he could barely turn around. It contained one single cot-like bed under which was tucked a long, lop-sided whicker basket. Baldwin claimed the bed without hesitation. Rajeev unfurled his bedroll next to the opposite wall. There was about 3 feet of space between them. Bhaiya thoroughly sniffed around, then stretched out on the floor squarely in the middle.

The sparse amenities included a porcelain basin inset into a wooden stand with a "slop" pot under it. A small mirror hung above it. Rajeev looked at the mirror.

"Such luxury," he said.

Baldwin pressed his lips together and said nothing.

One small window was open, letting in the salty smell of the sea. Rajeev busied himself organizing their clothes, using the long whicker basket for storage. Then exhausted from the long trip, the noisy crowds and the strange food, all three closed their eyes. The motion of the ship quickly lulled them to sleep.

In his dream Baldwin was standing in front of a door holding a pointed staff like a spear. He knew where he was, when and why. He was guarding the bedchamber of the Czar of Rus and his new bride Anastasia was waiting inside. Baldwin wondered if she was fearful of what was about to happen on her wedding night. He could hear the Czar and some of his men loudly singing a bawdy song as they approached. The men laughed and patted the Czar on the back as he drunkenly opened the door and stumbled into the room. No one acknowledged the knight standing by. He was invisible to them.

Baldwin tensed as he heard the muffled sounds from the bedchamber. The Czar sounded loud and gruff. Sweat trickled down Baldwin's face. He realized he was holding his breath and exhaled then … Anastasia's scream shattered his heart. He knew the Czar had thrust inside her without care, without love. He groaned and swayed. All went black.

"Wake, wake." Baldwin woke to Rajeev's voice.

"What is it?" Baldwin asked hoarsely.

"You were having a bad dream," Rajeev said. "You moaned so loudly I thought a demon had you by the throat."

Baldwin sat up. "In a way," he said quietly. "I need some water."

Bhaiya put his head on Baldwin's knee and received a distracted pat from his master.

"Drink but a little," Rajeev advised. "Boiling it on this ship may be precarious."

"How much longer until we get to land?" Baldwin asked although he knew the answer. He was trying to sound normal but his mind was still back at his dream and his emotions were raw. Rajeev sensed his friend was troubled and distant and tried to bring up mundane things until Baldwin was fully present again.

"Bhaiya would make a good sea dog," Rajeev said. "He doesn't seem to mind the ship at all."

"No doesn't seem to mind at all." Baldwin said distractedly.

"Let me tell you what we can expect when we get to the first port," Rajeev said.

Baldwin nodded.

"We have several stops to make before we arrive at our blessed destination," Rajeev explained. "The ports will be interesting but dangerous. We can stretch our legs but stay away from the bazaars. Carry your money pouch strapped around your middle under your shirt or leave most of it behind. The beggars and thieves will immediately see that you are a wealthy noble and try and come up to you and steal from you. I will walk on one side with my knife prominently displayed and Bhaiya will walk on the other with his teeth showing." Rajeev was glad to see Baldwin's faint smile as he said this.

But in spite of his friend's chattering, Baldwin's heart was still heavy with remembrance of Anastasia's painful scream. And what it meant.

CHAPTER SEVEN
THE VOYAGE

1120 A.D.
The Eastern Mediterranean

"Let's go out and I'll tell you the weather that's coming," Rajeev said while looking toward the sky. "Perhaps we'll meet some of our fellow travelers."

They ducked out of their cabin in single file Rajeev leading the way, then Bhaiya on a rope leash followed by a gloomy Baldwin. His spirits rose, however, as the frigid salt air hit his lungs. They were going to the Holy Land! Baldwin smiled as he watched Rajeev studying the gray clouds.

"Hum," Rajeev murmured. "A storm is …"

Just then a wave rolled the Starburst to one side, carried it up … and dropped it. Rain burst from above. Both men were thrown on their knees and slid to the wooden rail. Simultaneously, they pulled themselves up and retched over the side. Bhaiya, sliding and growling, furiously tried to claw his way back into their cabin.

"I think the storm came," Baldwin moaned while holding his stomach. He retched again, managing to get vomit back on himself in the violently blowing wind. His hair whipped his face while his legs kept sliding. He could barely hold onto the wet, wooden rail. Rajeev slid into him. As they collided the wind momentarily paused and he heard the screaming of frightened animals.

"Is that the animals or you?" Rajeev yelled. Baldwin shook his head and smiled. Even in the worst of times Rajeev kept his sense of humor.

As the wind blew and the waves swelled, rocked and pounded, sailors shouted, "Tie the sail! Lower the oars!"

With great effort Baldwin and Rajeev fought their way back inside their cabin with Bhaiya scooting in ahead of them. The drenched dog shook vigorously then headed straight for the bed, nudged the whicker basket aside and disappeared. The basket, thanks to Bhaiya, was now sliding back and forth across the wet floor. Everything else was either tied down or somehow constrained.

Rajeev pulled off his drenched clothes, curled himself tightly under his blankets, shoved himself as hard as he could into a corner and moaned. He was glad he'd emptied the chamber pot earlier. Baldwin stripped, crawled under his thin blanket and held onto both sides of his swaying bed. Bhaiya let out an occasional whimper.

Lightening flashed. The rain thundered down sounding like rocks hitting a tin roof. An enormous swell caught up the ship again, Baldwin's hands slipped and his head hit the bulkhead. The ship dropped and for the briefest of moments Baldwin was free floating above his bed. Then he thudded down. He rolled onto this stomach, laughed at the thought that he was for a second sitting in the air and then moaned. He was sure he would never again eat or drink. His insides ached. The storm lasted for two gut-wrenching hours.

"Bhaiya, get out from under the bed," Baldwin coaxed after the storm had abated. "A sea dog you're not." Baldwin looked over at Rajeev as he was uncurling and trying to sit up. His face ashen.

"Not one of us is sea worthy," Rajeev said. "I would never make a sailor."

"Hoist the sail!" they heard a crewman call.

"I bet the oarsmen are happy to hear that command," Baldwin said. "Let's go check below deck and meet our fellow passengers."

"Oh no. Some honey first to sooth our poor stomachs," Rajeev said.

He opened his leather bag and took out a small pot of honey. "Nothing better than honey from home. Take just a little," he said holding out a finger-sized flat stick.

Baldwin took it and dipped it into the honey pot. He scooped out a blob and popped it into his mouth. "Ummmm," he said as Rajeev did the same.

Bhaiya looked at them and barked. Baldwin dipped his finger into the pot, held it in front of Bhaiya's nose.

"Just a tiny bit for you."

The dog happily and thoroughly licked it clean. Rajeev wrapped a cloth around the pot and carefully tucked it away.

"I could easily eat the whole thing," Baldwin said sighing.

Bhaiya barked.

"Yes, but who knows what food they have on this ship or what we'll find on our journey. Best to be frugal, I think," Rajeev said. "We have bread, cheese, honey and some dried, salted fish. People have lived on less."

Baldwin nodded. Two swaying men and one carefully treading dog emerged from their closet-sized cabin trying to get their legs functioning. The sea was calm and the sun was shining as if nothing had happened.

As they slowly made their way toward the hold a young brown-skinned, dark haired couple started climbing the ladder up. The man took one look at Baldwin and stepped back pulling his wife behind him. The young man nodded at them.

"*Buenaos dias señors,*" he said and slightly bowed his head.

"Erm," Baldwin said not understanding the greeting.

The young man smiled. "English?"

"French," Baldwin answered.

"Ah," the young man said, mumbled something to his wife and switched to French. "Monsieur, you'd better put something over your nose and mouth as it is alarmingly smelly down there. I'm afraid no one handled the storm so well."

"Come up first," Baldwin said.

"No, no. It is improper to step ahead of a lord," the man said.

"I am hardly that!" Baldwin said.

"You are someone of importance," the man insisted. "Finely dressed, with a servant and a dog. You are someone special."

Baldwin laughed. "This someone special wishes you to come up so we can meet each other in the open air and not at the bottom of this ladder."

The man and woman slowly climbed the narrow, steep steps as Bhaiya, Baldwin and Rajeev waited for them at the top. The man had dark hair, a thin black mustache and used a thin, shiny black walking stick, although Baldwin noticed that he didn't seem to have difficulty climbing or walking. His wife, plainly dressed, stood behind him. The man once again bowed to Baldwin.

"I am Rodrigo Ortega and this is my wife Elena Maria. We are from Spain but have traveled to Italy to visit relatives before taking our pilgrimage to the birthplace of our faith."

"I am Baldwin DesMarets. This is Rajeev. Our four-footed friend is Bhaiya."

Rodrigo nodded at Rajeev. "Ah, I was correct. Baldwin of Marets. Your ancestral land, *si*?"

"Yes."

"Marets is a very spiritual word. The divine Mary."

"No. It means marsh or water," Baldwin corrected him.

"Think of all the meanings of water. It is life-giving is it not? And Mother Mary gave us the greatest life we have ever known."

Baldwin's eyes widened. "I've never heard that before. I mean about Marets meaning Mary."

"And Baldwin is a king's name."

"I did know that," Baldwin said smiling. "My father named me after King Baldwin the First of Jerusalem."

"We are pilgrims on the way to the Holy Land. You are nobility going to do a noble deed is that not true?"

"Yes. I'm going to join an order of holy knights," Baldwin answered.

"Very spiritual. It's in your blood and in your ancestor's blood. Baldwin DesMarets is a very good name."

Baldwin looked at Rajeev and shrugged.

"The oarsmen sleep below with the animals, goods and passengers. I suggest you cover your mouth and nose. My wife almost fainted at the smell."

"I did not know there were animals aboard until we heard them during the storm," Baldwin said.

"Baby pigs, chickens and some beasts I've never seen before are kept in small cages. There aren't many but enough to make a great deal of noise," Senior Ortega said.

"How many people are below?" Rajeev asked.

"I think maybe 30 altogether with the oarsmen and other crew. Taking a ship to the Holy Land takes less time but is just as dangerous."

"I hear that the pilgrims are being robbed, even killed," Baldwin stated. "A band of religious knights are banding together to protect them."

"You are joining them then. That is good."

All of a sudden Bhaiya's ears perked up and he bolted across the deck, jumped up on some barrels and looked over the stern. He started barking furiously.

Both Baldwin and Rajeev ran after him, sliding across the soaked deck until they were by his side. Baldwin grabbed the dog by the scruff and tried pulling him back but the dog kept barking and whining. Baldwin and Rajeev peered over the side just in time to see a huge Viking-styled ship sailing dangerously toward them. Then they saw something bobbing in the water. A man dove off the bow and swam toward it.

After a moment Baldwin and Rajeev realized it was a dog in the water and the man wasn't rescuing it but swimming with it as fast as they could go away from the ship. Just then a flag was unfurled on the approaching ship and it pulled close to the Starburst.

"Pirates!" Someone shouted and all hell exploded. Baldwin dashed back to the cabin and grabbed his sword. Senior Ortega pulled a thin rapier out of his cane and told his wife to hurry back into the hold. Rajeev, however, ran to starboard just as the pirates were trying to put a plank between their ship and the Starburst. When it landed on the railing Rajeev grabbed it with both hands and with a mighty heave flipped it over. A startled pirate had just stepped on it and was flipped into the sea. Then Rajeev let the plank fall.

By this time the Starburst sailors had grabbed their oars and were shoving at the side of the pirate ship to make it move away or knocking the pirates on their heads. The pirates fought back with their own oars. It quickly became a shoving and bashing match. The captain of the Starburst then stepped out, lit a torch and threw it with all his strength across the gap between ships. It landed on a sail, which caught fire.

Neither Baldwin nor Senior Ortega had gotten into the fight. There was still shouting and cursing going on when Baldwin thought he heard a splash on the leeward side of the Starburst. Bhaiya was frantically running up and down. Finding some boxes he jumped on them and was once again furiously barking. Baldwin skidded over, sword raised high. As he peered over the railing he saw the man who'd jumped in after his dog now taking the oars of the Starburst's rowboat. The dog was in the bow. Astonished at how the man had done this, Baldwin was even more startled to see that the man's legs were bound together at the ankles with thick rope. The man looked up and flashed a smile. Baldwin shook his head at the audacity *and* dexterity of the man … he'd stolen one of their rowboats while being tied at the ankles! Baldwin reached into his boot and pulled out the knife he always carried there.

Leaning over the rail he held it by its tip and, hoping it would miss the man and land in the boat, he let it drop. Incredibly, the man caught it by its handle in midair. He stuck it in the rope around his ankles, gave Baldwin a small salute and started rowing away. Baldwin grinned then pulled the whimpering Bhaiya as they heard two barks from the dog below.

"I think she's saying goodbye," Baldwin said to his excited dog. "There is no way they can row to land from here. Sorry pal I'm sure she was as adventurous as her owner."

The captain gave the order to set the sail and for the men to row hard. As the sail unfurled the wind picked up they were soon moving away from the shouting pirates who were busy putting out the fire.

"I told you it was dangerous," Senior Ortega said. Baldwin nodded toward the man's walking stick. "Good with a blade?"

"Not bad," Senior Ortega answered and grinned. "I put it to good use when I fought the Muslims in Spain." He looked away for a moment then directly at Baldwin. "You know I am a little disappointed that the pirates didn't get a taste of our swords."

Baldwin stared at him then laughed. "You know, me too."

"Perhaps we will encounter them again," Senior Ortega said wistfully.

"Don't tell the monk that," Rajeev said from their side. He nodded at the white robed man with a crucifix in his hand who'd just emerged from the hold followed by the rest of the weary and very odorous passengers. Elena Maria curtsied to the monk.

The monk quietly said *"Bonjour,"* and made the sign of the cross toward her. Rajeev put both of his hands together and bowed. The monk looked him up and down then walked to the rail opposite. Baldwin fingered the precious cross, which had been given to him by his mother. He frowned at the monk's snub of Rajeev.

Baldwin looked at his friend. "I *was* going to warn him he should not stroll around the markets holding any object of value. Now I don't think I will even though he seems to be a fellow countryman."

Rajeev shrugged. "It doesn't matter what he thinks of me. It doesn't matter what I think of him. It only matters what I think of me." He paused. "I think of me all the time."

Baldwin laughed. "Good things?"

"Always good, yes. Very, very good," Rajeev said. Bhaiya barked and wagged his tail. Baldwin stared at the monk.

"I wonder where his monastery is in France. He's wearing white instead of black."

"Your blessed mother would know, presumably," Rajeev said.

Baldwin nodded. "Perhaps we'll find out later. It's a long voyage."

Rodrigo Ortega turned to them. "I was going to suggest a good game of dice to settle our nerves. But perhaps we can wait until the good man retires." He nodded in the direction of the monk.

Baldwin smiled. "Yes, I will play with you."

Rajeev frowned. Dice playing had been a pastime of many of the young orphans in India. He knew how the game was played–and how the cheats could work the dice. He'd also met game players during his extensive travels. He was sure Senior Ortega was a player–probably addicted to the game. If a "small wager" was suggested Rajeev would step in. He secretly readied a few coins. One of the habits of unscrupulous travelers was to get an innocent fellow traveler to reveal where he carried his money. Rajeev was aware of that trick and would out fox anyone who tried to get the best of him or his young charge.

The Indian had studied many religions besides Christianity. He hadn't been exactly truthful when he'd told Armand and Baldwin the story of his upbringing. He hadn't been saved by a Christian couple. Far from it. But he did understand the tenants of many faiths and how they were connected. Too bad those most faithful were taught to look at the differences and not the underlying unity. After all, the Muslims, Jews and Christians all shared many of their most beloved teachers. Many of the ideas were the same: the importance of a pilgrimage being just one of them. Baldwin was going on a pilgrimage all right just not the one he thought he was on.

Rajeev shrugged and focused back on the two men about to

play against each other. He knew the story of the Sanskrit poem, *The Mahabharata*, where cousins the Pandavas and the Kauravas eventually fought against each other. At first, Yudhishthira, the king of Indraprastha, thought he was playing his cousin in a game of dice. Instead the cousin substituted a dice-playing champion who won every game. The Pandava King Yudhishthira gambled away his entire kingdom—and ended up exiled, only to later battle his cousins in an epic war.

Rajeev was not going to let anything even remotely close to that happen to young Baldwin. Just like in *The Mahabharata,* which by telling various stories described the history of the student/ teacher relationship, Rajeev was the *guru* or teacher and Baldwin was the *shishya* or student. This was an opportunity to teach Baldwin how to understand that not everyone along his life's path would have his best interests at heart. Baldwin needed to avert the danger even before danger was evident.

Senior Ortega and Baldwin pulled up boxes to a water barrel and made it their game board. Rajeev stood beside Baldwin and Maria Elena stood behind her husband. Ortega threw six dice. Much to his delight, Baldwin won the first few rolls. Senior Ortega and his wife shook their heads as if they were distressed while at the same time admiring Baldwin's luck.

After the young knight had won several more rolls of the dice, Senior Ortega said casually, "Shall we wager a small amount to make the game more fun?"

Rajeev noticed that Maria Elena let an eager smile flit across her face before resuming her stance behind her husband. Now he was certain it was time to step in.

Rajeev threw a few coins down, surprising both gambling men. "Let me try my luck *senior.*"

"But …" Baldwin started to protest but Rajeev put a gentle hand on his shoulder. Baldwin knew what that meant. Settle down and pay attention.

Baldwin stood. "What can I say? He has the coins." He stood aside and let Rajeev take his place.

"May I have the first throw?" Rajeev asked holding out his hand.

"Of course," Senior Ortega said handing him the dice.

Rajeev made a show of cupping them in his hand and shaking them by his ear. What he was really doing was getting the feel of them. Were they weighted? He put them in his other hand and shook them by his other ear. They didn't seem to be, but there was something. He put the closed hand with the dice against his forehead as if resting in thought. Their history flashed through his mind in multiple images. Ah, there it was—*one* of the dice was weighted. He knew exactly what to do. He threw them so hard that two of them skittered off the makeshift table onto the deck.

"I am too enthusiastic!" he said as Senior Ortega stooped over to pick them up. While all eyes were on Ortega, Rajeev quickly pocketed the weighted die. When they went to resume play there were only five dice. Everyone looked around the barrels and boxes. Bhaiya started to sniff Rajeev's pocket but the Indian quickly shoved the dog away and got on his knees pretending to look for the missing die. A swell rocked the ship and they all slid.

"Guess we better turn in," Rajeev said. "I have no idea where the coins went either," although he did.

Maria Elena had quickly snatched them up when the men were looking for the missing game piece. She spoke quietly in Spanish to her husband not realizing the Rajeev understood most of the words. He smiled innocently.

"Better luck next time everyone," Baldwin said, seemingly unaware as to what had happened.

"Good evening seniors," Rodrigo said. He held his arm out to his wife and they made their way to the narrow, wooden stairs going down.

"What just happened?" Baldwin asked as he sat on his bed and Rajeev sat crossed legged in the corner with Bhaiya's head on his knee ... the dog was waiting for a good rub.

"You must watch for the clues as to a man's character. A woman's, too," said Rajeev.

Baldwin raised his eyebrows and shook his head. "You mean the Spaniard and his wife? They were nice enough," he said sounding perplexed. "Rich landholders on the way to the Holy Land perhaps?"

"She was too plainly dressed. His clothes a little too frayed. The rapier in the cane a little too hidden. Did you know she stole the coins from the table?"

"What?"

"They may be religious but not so sure about pious," Rajeev smiled. "Plus their auras were a little off."

"Their what?"

"Auras. Everyone has an energy field surrounding him-or-her self. It's made up of colors which when you are trained properly you can see."

Baldwin stared at him. After a few moments he said, "People are made up of different colors? And …" he paused, "*you* can see them."

Rajeev smiled and nodded. Baldwin grinned.

"Bhaiya, too? Can he see them?"

Rajeev patted Bhaiya's head. "I think he can smell good and bad."

"Huh. I think so, too. But … so what were the colors of Rodrigo and Elena Maria?" He held up his hand. "No wait. What are *my* colors? Tell me about me first."

"Depends," Rajeev said.

"What?"

"Your colors depend on a lot of different aspects. You're mood, health or what astrology sign you were born under."

"Of course, a mysterious answer from my masterful tutor. Why doesn't that surprise me? I barely know what astrology is. But will knowing all this help me win at dice? I was winning, you know."

"You were about to lose. He was using your wins as bait to make you start betting. Once you did he'd take you for whatever he could. Most likely your money and sword."

"How do you know this?"

"I told you. His appearance, his aura. You, my young friend, think that what people speak is the truth. Most of the time it isn't. They say what they *think* you want to hear. Or they say what they *want* you to hear, which can be two different things. Neither is the truth. You have to get the truth by really looking at what they are vibrating. What kind of energy they have. Most of all use what your inner teacher is telling you."

"My inner teacher?"

"Intuition. It's what you feel about something rather than what you think about something."

Baldwin yawned. "Now you've completely lost me."

"We can start this lesson later. You have much to do before we get into all that," Rajeev said.

"Does that monk give off any colors? No, let me analyze first. He's traveling by himself instead of in a group of fellow monks. That in itself is strange."

Rajeev nodded. "What else?"

"He's on this ship instead of traveling cross country which would be less expensive for a monk. I conclude that he has money or comes from money. Perhaps a son of a noble family like me."

"Yes, I too come to that conclusion. But he's not hiding that fact that he's a monk …"

"Or!" Baldwin interrupted excitedly, "He's *pretending* to be a monk and is really out to rob us!"

"Except that he has a very pious aura," Rajeev countered.

"That aura thing again," Baldwin sighed. "I can *see* it comes in handy."

"Ah, but that is the problem. You can *not* see everything in front of you until you can read the world properly. It's a matter of refocusing on what you are looking at and seeing another's energy."

"Lessons and more lessons from you."

"Many more my young friend. Many, many more. But Senior Ortega and his wife are not bad people. I do not think either of them would kill you in the night to steal your money. No, they are needy people. Perhaps they had a fortune that is now lost to them or had to use most of it to travel to the land where Jesus walked. They are sincere in their quest for forgiveness for their sins and trust that the Holy Land will wash those sins away."

"The Pope Urban said it would," Baldwin said as he rummaged in his traveling bag.

"As for the monk. I perceive there is some confusion in his soul. He lives a strict life. With all the beautiful abundance in the world …" but Rajeev's voice trailed off. His young charge was about to embark on a strict life. Rajeev hoped it would be an enlightened life, too.

"You have no idea how lucky you are to have the parents that you do," Rajeev continued. "Your father may be a hard man but he is also a brilliant one. You *and* your brothers worked and trained hard but did not have to sell everything you had to make this journey. No doubt most of your fellow travelers did."

Baldwin nodded. As a boy he felt he was being scolded rather than being taught. He didn't understand it. He loved his parents and they loved him and his brothers. That was what mattered.

Baldwin shrugged and smiled. The sunlight was fading and there was one more thing he wanted to do. He took out some parchment and the quill that Reginald had made from one of his falcon's feathers. Carefully he unfolded some crushed charcoal and dipped in his quill. Then he sketched a picture of the pirates and the rowboat-stealing man and his dog. Curious, Rajeev crawled over the short distance on his hands and knees and studied the pictures. "The man is puzzling, is he not?'

"Very," Baldwin answered, "and probably drowned by now if not recaptured by the pirates."

"Perhaps," Rajeev said, "but I think that one is resourceful and lucky. He's made a mark in your mind, has he not?"

"Definitely," Baldwin answered. He looked down at Bhaiya who was making whimpering sounds in his sleep as he was stretched out on the floor. "Bhaiya is dreaming of the bitch, I think. He was impressed too."

Smiling and shaking their heads, the two men took to their beds. Lack of sleep from the thunderstorm the night before, they were soon asleep. Baldwin tossed as his mind raced through everything that had happened that day. The pirates, the man, the mysterious monk, the dice playing and Rajeev's ability to see through situations, and read auras. His mind flashed back to the many times Rajeev had been by his side, helping him see things clearly. The intelligent Indian had been hired by Armand to help tutor the boys just before Baldwin's birth. He'd held Baldwin on the first day he was born.

Baldwin sniffed in his sleep. He thought he could smell the distinct fragrance of frankincense in the air as he walked through a crowd of people in exotic dress. They were dark-skinned like Rajeev. The women were wrapped in colorful silks and the men had loose-fitting pants and shirts. They all wore dangling earrings and their arms were loaded with bracelets. They turned to him, bowed as if he was of some importance, then smiled seeming happy to see him. As if they recognized him as someone they knew.

"Come this way," he heard Rajeev say. "And learn what is reality." Baldwin followed with Bhaiya by his side.

Next the people were left behind and he, Bhaiya and Rajeev were walking by a rapidly flowing river. Someone familiar was walking ahead of him but Baldwin couldn't bring the man's name to mind. It was as if he knew him and yet didn't.

"Once you have enough experience and left your ego behind, you will come here and learn everything. Everything, everything," Rajeev was saying in a chanting singsong. "Once created, nothing ever dies. It simply changes form, as do we all. The city will not look as you once knew it. It may look abandoned but that is a deception. The knowledge is here, in the rocks, in the foundation. When you learn to meditate all will be revealed. Oh beautiful, beautiful *Takhkhasilā*."

Baldwin tossed, his mind perplexed. Where was he?

"But there's nothing here," the man in front of Baldwin said, starting to turn around. Then Baldwin noticed a dog by the man's side. Bhaiya barked and wagged his tail.

"You're not focusing clearly," Rajeev said. But he sounded far away.

Baldwin woke. He rubbed his eyes and realized that he was disappointed that he hadn't seen the man's face. And yet … Bhaiya had recognized the dog. But …

Baldwin sat up and looked around the small cabin. Bhaiya was still sniffling in his sleep and Rajeev was still curled into a ball in his corner, breathing steadily. Water was rhythmically slapping the ship. Baldwin tried to recall everything in the dream but it faded. He closed his eyes and slept deeply until dawn.

CHAPTER EIGHT

STARBURST

1120 A.D.
The Eastern Mediterranean

After two weeks, Baldwin and Rajeev had gotten to know the other passengers traveling with them fairly well: a Jewish couple from Germany; one Englishman; one Italian; two sisters from France; one Scotsman, the monk–who remained quiet and aloof–and the Spaniards Senior Ortega with Maria Elena. All were happy to speak in French with the boyish Baldwin and his knowledgeable friend. Below deck the curious passengers had discussed the young nobleman and his companion, whom they assumed was his servant.

"You can see how Rajeev watches over him," Senior Ortega told them. They all nodded.

"And the dog," the Englishman Rupert Connally said. "Who but nobility would dare take a dog on such a journey as this?" They nodded again.

The two young French women had introduced themselves as sisters–Mademoiselles Héloïse and Ava D'Argenteuil.

"Surely you aren't traveling alone," Rupert said acting more shocked than concerned.

"Obviously not," Héloïse answered. "We're together. You're alone."

The Scotsman laughed. "Well said. You must have some Scots blood in ya. I'm Fergus." He bowed and the ladies curtsied.

The Italian also bowed. "I am honored to travel with you. I am an Italian businessman and terrible sinner. I pray all will be forgiven when I gaze upon the many places blessed by our Lord's footsteps."

They turned toward the monk but he just raised the small cross he was holding, mumbled a name that sounded like Bernard then got on his knees to pray. After a moment some of the crew and all of the pilgrims prayed with him.

Later, when the passengers were gathered on deck for fresh air, Baldwin thought the German couple a delightful pair, although a bit hard to understand. *Frau* Berkowitz was a head taller and twice as large as her husband, *Herr* Berkowitz.

"*Ja*, we are going to visit our cousins who own a small stall at the bazaar in Jerusalem," Frau Markowitz told Baldwin. "They say there are so many pilgrims that the place is always packed."

Her husband gave her a nudge. She looked down at him. "Oh, *ja*, we want to see all the wonderful places, too." She thought for a moment. "My favorite story is about Queen Esther. She saved our people. I adore her."

Héloïse was about to say something when Baldwin interrupted. "I'm joining a group of knights who are the protectors of pilgrims. I offer my protection to you all."

The women curtsied. "I admire your noble cause and am honored to travel with you as a friend," Héloïse said, "although so far the only protection might be from the Scotsman and the Italian."

Rajeev smiled. Héloïse was a curvy woman with long brown hair and sparkling blue eyes. Ava was thinner and shorter with the same coloring as her sister and equally as pretty. He felt these women were a formidable pair and not to be talked down to. "May I ask why such young ladies are visiting the Holy Land? You are too young to have gathered many sins that need forgiving." He put his hands together and bowed hoping he hadn't provoked a rebuke for his straight–forwardness.

Héloïse smiled. "There is nothing more historic or fascinating than the Holy Land," she said while pushing her long hair out of her eyes. "I want to see it for myself."

Ava interrupted. "The wind is starting to pick up," she said and grabbed the railing. "I hope that means we get there faster. I want to see for *myself*, too."

Rajeev nodded. Knowledgeable women, he thought, brave and competitive.

"We are catholic and …" Ava's words were drowned out by the crew suddenly amassing on the deck to take advantage of the wind. Several scrambled up the strong hemp ropes and unfurled the sail. The rest of the crew stretched their legs and went about their jobs while eyeing the passengers. They were a mix of nationalities and mostly non-French speaking.

The pilgrims stood together discussing the voyage and watching the sailors do their jobs. The Frenchwomen explained to their fellow travelers that they had always wanted to see Jerusalem from the time they learned about it in school, which was run by nuns.

"The name itself–Jerusalem–means The Holy Sanctuary," Héloïse said.

"I have to admit," Baldwin said, "I know about Jesus and his disciples but not much about the city itself."

"Oh!" Ava exclaimed. "Allow us to give you some basic history. I think you'll find it fascinating."

"Perhaps helpful when you take your tour," Héloïse added. "You don't want to miss anything."

"No indeed," Rupert said. "Enlighten us."

Baldwin thought the Englishman sounded smug, as if he already knew it all. Perhaps he and the Italian were scholars. They seemed to be together or maybe just befriended each other.

"It's one of the oldest cities in the world!" she said enthusiastically.

Rajeev smiled. India, Africa and some far off lands he'd only heard about probably had older cities. He kept his opinion to himself and nodded with interest.

"If it's that old," said Alfonso the Italian—a handsome man with long coal black hair tied with a black ribbon and wearing well-made clothes. "Perhaps you should only relate to us about the time of Jesus as that is in what we are all interested." He looked around at the others for agreement.

Baldwin remembered what Rajeev had said about appearances and looked carefully at the man. A man of wealth he surmised, about 30 or 35 years old. Baldwin wondered what his sin was that drew him to Jerusalem. Ninety-nine percent of pilgrims were going to obtain forgiveness for their sins. Except, perhaps the German couple. They seemed more interested in the material side of things. The two Frenchwomen seemed like scholars or historians looking for the experience. Baldwin rubbed his chin. The phrase, *words don't teach*, ran through is mind. They were book learners first and now they were adventurers.

"It's an interesting combination of cultures and sites that are holy to all the pilgrims who come from everywhere," Ava said, ignoring Rupert and Alfonso. "What was once the Al-Aqsa Mosque is now part of the royal palace on the Temple Mount."

"What I find fascinating," Héloïse interrupted, "is the mosque called the Dome of the Rock is supposed to be built over the Foundation Stone."

"It's in the middle of the Temple Mount," Ava added. "That is where the Temple of Solomon was."

"That's all very interesting," Rupert said, "but really that is Muslim culture and I'm interested in Jesus."

Héloïse pursed her lips, "Culture is culture and I'm sure Jesus appreciated it all."

"And every *one*," Frau Berkowitz added, "rich and poor alike of every religion."

Baldwin glanced at Rajeev.

"The culture wars are about to start," Rajeev whispered.

Héloïse and Ava smiled at Frau Berkowitz while her husband patted her arm and nodded approvingly.

"Is the Temple Solomon where Queen Esther lived?" Frau Berkowitz asked.

"The palace of Shushan," Héloïse answered immediately, "is in Persia."

"Muslim," said Rupert. Several of the sailors glanced over.

"Oh," Frau Berkowitz said, clearly disappointed. Her husband gave her a sympathetic look.

"Tell us about the Dome of the Rock then and this Foundation Stone," he said.

Héloïse continued, "The Dome of the Rock is thought to be built over the very large stone where Abraham was going to sacrifice his son Isaac to God."

The Berkowitz' nodded. "Ah yes I know that story, too," Frau Berkowitz said.

"The two mosques are together you see," Ava said.

"Which two mosques?" Fergus asked.

"The Al-Aqsa mosque and the Dome of the Rock," Frau Berkowitz said.

Héloïse smiled and nodded.

Ava continued, "Then the Crusaders saved Jerusalem and took over the two ancient mosques making one into a church and the Al-Aqsa is being used as a palace."

Baldwin leaned closer to hear more of the conversation just as the ship's massive sail caught a strong wind and billowed out, pitching the ship forward. Every one of the pilgrims fell while the crew remained upright. The sailors laughed. The strong wind didn't bother them. They enjoyed it. Baldwin managed to grab the rail and help Héloïse to her feet as the other passengers helped each other up

Captain Marco grinned and lit a delicately carved fishbone pipe. The smell of the smoke was intoxicating. After puffing on his pipe for a few minutes he announced, "It looks, my friends, as if we are making good speed to our first port where we will gather some supplies. While you are enjoying the sites, take care that you keep your possessions and coins close. Beware of bandits in the bazaars."

The passengers looked at him solemnly.

"But tonight," he said waving his pipe, "the skies will be clear and the stars magnificent." He glanced up. "After a brief squall." Rain pelted down.

"You know your skies!" Héloïse exclaimed.

Captain Marco nodded and grinned as the passengers headed for shelter. Later that evening the sky was clear and the stars shown brightly in the heavens. The rain had left the air fresh; the wind was blowing steadily but not disturbing the sea. The ship was gently riding the waves.

Everyone looked up. "The stars say many things," the captain said. "They are God's entertainment."

Rajeev cleared his throat. "They tell about our past and future," he said. "You must know the names of some of them captain."

"To navigate I use fisherman's knowledge of currents, ocean colors, even the taste of saltwater changes. My astrolabe is new, I daresay I may be the first to have it. Of course I know about the star's movements," Captain Marco said. "How could you be a seaman and not. The planets, too, and how to read the pictures in the sky."

"What pictures? Frau Berkowitz asked. The captain stared at her for a moment.

"To read the sky is a skill that sailors possess. Many people possess," he said looking at Rajeev. "From a young boy I always found the stars fascinating. The way they move, the way they dance." Everyone was listening to him as they stared upward. "They are beautiful, are they not?"

"Stunning," the usually quiet Maria Elena said. "Too many to count. How do you manage to sail by just the light of the stars?"

"I know how to read them better than words on a scroll. I also have help with my astrolabe."

"Astrolabe is a fascinating word," Héloïse mused. "What does it mean?"

"Basically it means *star-taker*, Captain Marco said. "Astronomers have used it for centuries and but some of us have adapted it for the sea. It's especially handy for those who sail long distances. I'll show it to you."

He escorted the party of pilgrims to the ship's wheel where he showed them "the latest in modern design." It consisted of a wooden rod with graduated markings, a plumb line with a double chord and a perforated pointer.

"They have metal ones I hear, which are heavier than wood, less prone to warp but too heavy for navigation. I like mine well enough." He turned toward Rupert.

"Our friends the Muslims invented them long ago as a model of the universe." The Englishman shrugged and gazed upward as did several of the others. Captain Marco looked toward Rajeev. "They are used in the science of astrology, are they not?"

Rajeev stepped toward the instrument and nodded. "I've heard this is so but have not seen one such as this."

Just then a group of stars shot across the sky. "Oh," whispered Ava while the others murmured awe.

The captain pointed upward. "We sailors also navigate by *stella maris* which means star of the sea."

Rajeev added, "In my native culture it is known as Dhruva which means immovable or fixed."

Captain Marco nodded, "That is so and what makes it so valuable as a navigation tool. It is also called Our Lady, Star of the Sea being a title of the Blessed Virgin."

"Ah," the usually silent monk said softly, "a much better description than Dhruva."

Rajeev raised his eyebrows and Baldwin shook his head at the monk's rudeness.

The man continued staring at the starry heavens. "The guiding light of Jesus and therefore God. Pure and bright."

The sailors who understood French whispered this information to the other sailors who murmured approval at the monk's words.

"Yes," the captain nodded, "The Blessed Virgin who guides us."

"Guides us to the way of Christ," Bernard said as he nodded agreement. He lapsed into silence again and stared at the star as if in rapture. Rajeev thought this was not the moment to discuss astrology as the monk seemed fixated on relating everything to Jesus. He wasn't sure how the two were related. But then Christians could relate everything to Christ and Muslims could relate everything to Mohammed.

Captain Marco seemed to read Rajeev's thoughts. He said, "I would enjoy discussing the meaning of the planets with you." He looked over at the monk. "Perhaps later."

Rajeev smiled and nodded.

"Is it the same star that led the Wise Men to Bethlehem?" Ava asked.

Captain Marco shrugged. "Perhaps. It's a bright star which guides us so why not them?"

Everyone was staring at the heavenly bodies twinkling above. In the quiet that surrounded them they heard a splash. Several of the sailors crossed themselves.

"Why do they cross themselves?" Héloïse asked looking around.

"We can see the beauty of the stars and think it is heaven," Captain Marco said. "But we cannot see into the depths of the sea."

"Hell is below us," Fergus stated matter-of-factly. "Monsters and strange creatures. We Scots have our share of monsters in our lochs."

The captain nodded. "Some very strange and some tasty to eat." He grinned. "You'll see some mysterious fish-like creatures for sale to eat in the marketplace when we dock."

Frau Berkowitz made a face and held her stomach. "I can barely eat what we have on board." She shrugged. "But who knows?"

"How far do you think the ocean goes down?" Ava asked.

"Very far," the captain said. "They're many fascinating things that jump out of the water. Some sailors say they've seen fish people."

"Fish people?" Fergus asked.

"Half fish half people. Like centaurs and creatures in ancient stories," Ava answered.

"Hell is below us and heaven above," Captain Marco said and grinned. "Jerusalem itself is 3000 feet above sea level. If you can get past the bandits along the road you'll end up in heaven on earth."

"Bandits?" Frau Berkowitz and Herr Berkowitz exclaimed together.

"Most come to Jerusalem to repent of their sins, but God does not make it an easy journey," the captain said and puffed for a few moments on his pipe. "You'll get your instructions on how to get to the Holy City safely before departing this ship. But you have our young knight Baldwin to protect you," he said slapping Baldwin on the back. "I'll bet our Scotsman and our Spaniard can put up a good fight." He eyed Rupert and Alfonso but said nothing about them.

"God will protect us," Bernard said. "As Frau Berkowitz pointed out, Jesus was a friend to saints and sinners alike. The Son of God and his Holy Mother Mary will be at our sides." He kissed the small cross he always carried.

Baldwin thought this was the longest speech he'd heard the monk make. As a cold wind swept over them they heard more splashing. Almost everyone crossed themselves. The monk was the first to head down the ladder to their sleeping quarters below. Fatigue quickly overtook Rajeev, Baldwin and Bhaiya. Without much discussion the two men took to their sleeping places with the dog in the middle. Baldwin shivered. What did live in the darkness in the sea? Was it the dark demon he dreamed of or something more?

He tossed on his small bunk as the wind pushed the Starburst to top speed. After awhile he fell into troubled sleep, full of darkness, strange noises and starless space. Strange people were speaking to him, telling him all was not as it seemed. *You must find the door down,* they seemed to say. Solid is not solid. Another world is under your feet.

In the morning he felt tired but couldn't fathom where his dreams had taken him. Or what anything meant. Did Fergus speaking of hell make him dream about it? Yet wherever he was in his dream didn't seem bad. He felt he wanted to find it. He shook his head. The noise from the sailors readying the ship to dock drowned out his thoughts. Then excitement overcame his drowsiness as he opened the cabin door to the rising sun over the island called Cypress.

When they docked at their first port of call Bhaiya ran down the gangplank as if the ship was on fire. Everyone laughed as the dog tried to walk on land for the first time in two weeks. Even the solemn and silent monk, the first one off the ship after Bhaiya, smiled as the dog slipped and slid until he got his bearings.

Next, Senior Ortega and his wife, looking relieved and happy, held onto each other as they stepped on land. The rest of the pilgrims followed. The burly Portuguese ship's captain came next. Baldwin and Rajeev turned, smiled and quickly stepped out of the way as the crew ran past them.

"Straight to the taverns and buxom women for that lot," Captain Marco laughed. "Join us gentlemen?"

"Tempting," Baldwin said smiling. "But I have to find out where my dog went. I don't want him disappearing into a dark alley never to return."

"Later then," Captain Marco said striding off.

The marketplace wasn't as bright, cheery or international as the one they had seen in Venice. The stalls were more worn and the sellers less enthusiastic about the pilgrims who had disembarked from the ship. Many of the people on a pilgrimage had spent most of their money booking passage and weren't interested in buying trinkets along the way.

"They cater more to the seafaring men, I think," Rajeev said looking toward several women who had taken the sailors by their arms and were guiding them to who-knew-where. Baldwin was too distracted to look in their direction.

"Where has Bhaiya run off to?" he asked worriedly while looking through the throng. Small, shoeless, dirty children shoved passed them. Rajeev knew they had spotted Baldwin and were trying to find where he kept his money pouch. At Rajeev's advice, Baldwin didn't carry one.

Suddenly they heard a shout. Everyone turned to see the monk pointing at a retreating boy. Out of the corner of his eye Rajeev saw Bhaiya shoot out after the boy. Rajeev, too, gave chase and caught up to Bhaiya just as the dog cornered the little ruffian against a wall. The boy was staring at the canine growling and baring his teeth.

"I'm not afraid of you," the boy shouted boldly.

Bhaiya moved forward. The little thief stood still. Silently Rajeev reached out his hand. The boy shook his head. Bhaiya growled. Rajeev raised his eyebrows and stared silently at the young thief then glanced over at Bhaiya. The boy got the message, unfolded his hand and gave Rajeev the priest's small cross.

"With all this water surrounding you and yet you are filthy," said Rajeev. "Bhaiya, do something about that." The dog looked at Rajeev and then looked at the boy. Rajeev could swear the dog smiled. Rajeev's eyes twinkled. Bhaiya lifted his leg and peed on the boy's feet.

"Now go to the sea and wash the rest of you!" Rajeev said stepping back to let the child run past. A pack of small children ran beside the boy, laughing.

Rajeev patted the dog. "Good boy. Sometimes I think you can read minds." Bhaiya wagged his tail. Together the pair walked back to the monk and Rajeev handed him his cross.

"Oh blessed be," the monk said while holding the cross to his chest. "I am humbled by so worthy a gesture. May the adored Mother Mary Queen of Heaven bless you."

"Ah, he speaks," Baldwin joked as he walked up. "Besides

saying *bonjour* to Elena Maria and saying a few quiet phrases we wouldn't know you were a fellow countryman."

The monk looked toward the sky but smiled. "I am a man of prayer and silence. Perhaps that is not as good a method of one who tries to follow Christ's example as I thought."

"We know a lot about our fellow travelers but little about you," Baldwin said. "I am Baldwin DesMarets of Marets, France."

"Yes, Senior Ortega was telling everyone that your name means Mary, like the sainted Mother of Jesus. The monk's eyes sparkled with tears. Baldwin thought he was going to swoon at the very mention of Mary's name.

"I'm not so sure that is the meaning but perhaps a better meaning than marsh dweller," Baldwin laughed. "Or 'of the marsh.'"

"In my capacity as a monk I have helped turn marshland into a beautiful garden to honor the Virgin. In that way I think you have become spiritual yourself."

"Hum," Baldwin said. "I am about to devote my sword to God's justice. Perhaps that is so."

"I am Rajeev of Kashmir, India," Rajeev said, bowing with his two hands together.

"I am Bernard, originally of Burgundy, although at the moment I am the absent Abbot of Clairvaux. We call ourselves Cistercians. We are hard workers specializing in raising our own healthy food and drink. I am devoted to Mother Mary and Jesus."

"Ah," Rajeev said, "you wear white robes to distinguish yourselves from the Benedictines who wear black."

"Just so," Bernard said quietly. "For awhile now I've felt the Holy Land beckoning me. I am on my way to visit with my uncle André de Montbard and of course to see where the blessed Virgin lived with her Divine son."

"But I know him!" Baldwin blurted.

Bernard looked confused.

"André de Montbard! He started the order that I'm going to join, him and several men from France."

"He said in a letter to me that they are headquartered in the palace that the mademoiselles were speaking of. The palace that was once a mosque," Bernard said.

"An entire palace?" Rajeev asked in surprise.

"A wing of the palace on the Temple Mount was granted to my uncle, Hugues de Payens, Godfrey de Saint-Omer and several others, is my understanding from the letter. I believe it was built over what was thought to be Solomon's Temple."

Ava and Héloïse walked up next to Bernard. "I know a little about that if you're interested," Héloïse said.

"I'm very interested," Baldwin said.

"Come, let us stand under the shade of those trees and get away from the smell of the strange fish," Rajeev said. They laughed.

"We haven't seen the fish yet," Héloïse said. "We've been talking to the women in the marketplace and the ones leaning against the walls."

Rajeev raised his eyebrows but said, "Please, tell what you know about Solomon's Temple."

"As you know Jerusalem has been the site of many wars. Currently, the Christians have it thanks to the Crusaders."

"My father was a knight who helped take the city away from the Muslims," Baldwin stated.

"Being a knight is in your blood," Bernard said.

"Yes."

"The bible tells us King Solomon built his fabulous temple in Jerusalem but it was destroyed by Babylon's King Nebuchadnezzar II," Héloïse continued. "Eventually the Jews returned and built another temple in the same spot now known as the Second Temple, which was built in the 1st century."

"May I add something?" Bernard asked politely.

"About the Ark of the Covenant?" Héloïse guessed and smiled. "Please, it is a fascinating story."

"Before the First Temple was built, Solomon's father, the great King David, united the Israelites, captured Jerusalem and built the temple on what is called Temple Mount to house the Ark of the Covenant," Bernard said rather breathlessly. "The Ten Commandments are inside the Ark."

"Yes, but it was actually his son Solomon who ended up building the First temple with an inner room to house the holy artifact," Héloïse added. "It took the workers seven years to build the temple out of stone and cedar and cypress."

"Is the Ark now in the second temple?" Baldwin asked in surprise. "The Ark is still there?"

Ava, Bernard, Héloïse and Rajeev all shook their heads.

"No one has ever been able to find it," Héloïse said.

"I, too, have read about the Temple," Rajeev said. "In the Second Book of Kings in the Old Testament it states that Solomon's Temple was decorated with chariots of the sun. Worshipers would face east and bow to the sun."

"You mean they worshiped the sun?" Baldwin asked surprised.

"No. They honored it. We have the same custom in my country."

"There were many rituals going on in Solomon's time that the church would frown upon today," Héloïse stated. "You see the women who are with our sailor friends now would have been honored during sacred rites at the temple."

"Heresy," Bernard said clearly upset.

"Historical fact," Héloïse countered. Just then Bhaiya ran up with a fish in his mouth.

"Oh no!" Baldwin said. "You've become a thief!" Baldwin reached for the fish and Bhaiya took off running. Past some of the ship's passengers and down narrow alleys they ran. Bhaiya stopped at the end of an alley, turned and stared at his master. Baldwin kept running, waving his finger and shouting, "This is not funny!" But he was smiling none-the-less. He knew the dog was leading him a merry chase just for the fun of it.

As Baldwin stopped to catch his breath he caught sight of something dark moving past the building at the end of the narrow passage. It cast a large, black shadow again the wall. Suddenly, he stopped smiling. A chill ran down his body. He stared. He'd seen that shadow before. He stood still.

He shook his head trying to clear it. Was he having a dream in daylight? The shadow moved up the wall. Baldwin realized it was more than a shadow now. It was black robed and hooded. It leapt to the top of the wall. Baldwin looked around but no else was there to see the dark–what? Man? Creature? Demon? He wasn't sure. Then it turned and looked down at him with those horrible eyes he'd seen long ago. It beckoned with one bony finger. Baldwin ran toward it then suddenly Bhaiya started barking furiously and tried to jump up the wall.

"Bhaiya! No!" Baldwin screamed. The shadowy figure laughed a ghastly deep laugh and jumped away over the wall.

Baldwin took deep breaths, slowly gathered his thoughts, walked over to Bhaiya and patted him. "Good, good boy." He looked up but no one was on top of the wall. The fish forgotten, they walked out of the alley and back to the bazaar. Baldwin looked around. None of the busy buyers or sellers was looking his way. Everything was as usual–a bright, busy day. He didn't feel a part of it. He felt as if he and his beloved dog were isolated, unseen and unheard by anyone in the marketplace. He walked past some of the passengers from the ship, nodded at them and walked on. He didn't want to speak to anyone, not even Rajeev. He wanted to block out the whole incident, but Bhaiya had seen the demon. It must be real.

He would think about it later. Right now he felt too hollow inside to think at all.

CHAPTER NINE

FRIENDS, FANTASIES AND ROUGH SEAS

1120 A.D.
The Mediterranean

Deep in thought, Baldwin left Bhaiya with Rajeev and hurried back to the ship. He didn't want to be around anyone. As he crossed the deck to the rail, the sun glared and a light breeze blew salt water on his face. He inhaled deeply letting the wind blow hair into his eyes. Baldwin gazed over the railing and remembered the dream he had of a strange place where a man walked in front of him with a dog. Now he realized the man was the rowboat thief who had escaped the pirates with his animal friend. Why was he in that dream? Why were strange people and strange landscapes making him toss and turn? Worse, the demon was now real because Bhaiya had seen it, too. It truly was a person or a *thing* beckoning him. Taunting him. Blackening his soul.

"No! He won't get my soul!" Baldwin said aloud making the few sailors onboard stare at him for a moment before returning to their work. Baldwin whispered, "I belong to God."

As he stared out to sea the hung-over but happy sailors started returning. All of them had sacks of supplies on their shoulders, both for provisions and to sell when they disembarked at the next port. Then Captain Marco strode up the boarding plank alternately puffing on his pipe and whistling.

"Back already!" he shouted at Baldwin. "Didn't fancy the place?"

Baldwin shook his head. He was going to turn away but the sound of the pilgrim's lively chatter caught his ear. He could clearly hear Bernard and Héloïse arguing.

"Mary Magdalene was devoted to Jesus. The working women of Cypress are no less devoted to God," Héloïse said.

"Working women," Bernard scoffed. "I hardly think ..."

Héloïse interrupted, "They get paid for their services. That puts them on the same footing as men!"

"Women should follow the example of our blessed Virgin and ..."

"How do you know she didn't work?" Héloïse interrupted again. "I'll bet her life was a hard one."

"She certainly didn't do *that* kind of work!" Bernard shouted turning red in the face.

"You mean she didn't have relations with her husband?" Héloïse asked.

Baldwin was both tickled and shocked. He'd never heard anyone talk about the Virgin Mary except to call her a virgin. Of course that was *before* she was married. Baldwin shook his head. Héloïse was clearly getting under Bernard's skin.

In the next moment Baldwin wondered what his parents were doing. Was his father in his woodworking shop and his mother praying for their souls? He wondered if they were lonely with their three sons and Rajeev all leaving at once. What would his mother think of the passengers on board the ship? Of course she had visited the shrine of Mary Magdalene and she was equally devoted to the Virgin Mary. Would she be amused by Héloïse's opinions or take Bernard's side? What would she think of Bernard? As he watched some seagulls floating on the wind, sadness overtook Baldwin. He missed his parents. He sighed, deep in thought and touched the cross that lay under his tunic, close to his heart.

The rest of the travelers straggled up to the deck. No one seemed to have purchased anything at the bazaar except some sweets. Ava was walking up the gangplank with Rajeev and Bhaiya. Obviously they, too, were having a lively conversation but laughing instead of arguing and clearly enjoying each other's company.

Ava looked up, saw Baldwin, and smiled. The sun was shining on her pretty, laughing face. His heart jumped. Then Bhaiya made a beeline towards his master and Baldwin was able to bend over to pet his canine friend and hide his blush.

Before they could engage him in conversation Baldwin strode to the small cabin, leaving Bhaiya to roam around the deck. The deckhands were use to the friendly dog and often patted him or played small games with him. Inside his cabin, the young knight rummaged under the bed and took out his charcoal drawings, then got to work on some new ideas. After some thought, he decided to go outside and capture the sailors at work and the passengers in conversation with each other. He tried hiding quietly behind a pole and some barrels but Alfonso spotted him and walked over. Baldwin ignored him but Alfonso stopped directly in front of him blocking his view of the other passengers. Baldwin looked up.

"You're an artist?" Alfonso asked noticing the quill in Baldwin's hand. "May I look?"

Reluctantly, Baldwin showed him his beginning sketch of the Berkowitz' sharing something they had purchased at the bazaar. Baldwin thought it was perhaps a piece of fruit. Frau Berkowitz was holding something up to her husband's mouth and he was about to take a bite. It was an intimate, touching moment.

Alfonso smiled and nodded. "This is as good as I've seen in a while," he said. "I should know, I too am an artist, apprenticed to Alberto Sozio at the age of eight. He has taught me to illuminate manuscripts and write in elaborate script and decorate God's words with flowers. But I think that is for monks, no? I am too hot blooded to ever become a monk. Much to my *madre's* unhappiness."

Baldwin laughed and shook his head. "No, I cannot see you becoming a monk."

"No, I like to create on a larger scale. Where did you learn this technique? It is quite good."

"Um. I simply draw what I see. I use to draw the flowers and herbs in our gardens. Nature is fascinating. I've always drawn. My brother Reginald fashioned me this quill and I carry charcoal and parchment. But I haven't seen you draw."

"Ah, the ship's motion doesn't allow me to steady my hand, nor my stomach. But when I get to Jerusalem I will draw the great buildings. Maybe I will add some interesting people. Perhaps I can draw you after you join your group of knights."

Baldwin laughed. "That would please my parents if they ever saw it."

"Once I have been forgiven my sin of disobeying my *madre* ..." Alfonso glanced up toward the sky and shook his head, "amongst other sins ... I will travel and see the sites of the world. I am very tired of sitting behind a drawing table. But I shall not keep you from finishing the portrait of our German friends. Are you going to show it to them?"

"Probably not," Baldwin shrugged.

"No you're right, then everyone will want to pose. But then perhaps you want to impress the pretty *Mademoiselles* with your talent?"

Baldwin looked down and shook his head. For the second time that day he blushed. Alfonso laughed and walked away. Baldwin realized the sun was setting. He glanced up and saw Bernard saying something to Captain Marco who nodded.

Then the captain cleared his throat and shouted, "Everyone! The good Bernard here wants to lead us in evening prayer!"

The pilgrims gathered in a semicircle, as did all of the sailors except one. A burly, swarthy-looking sailor continued to coil the large hemp rope and kept his back to the monk standing beside the captain.

"Defarge!" the captain shouted, "join the others!"

"I'm finishing my job!" Defarge shouted. "I don't have time to pray to a God who may or may not exist."

Some gasped at this. The captain clearly was not pleased. Suddenly he had a whip in his hand and cracked it against the deck. At the same moment Bhaiya walked over to the captain, sat on his boots, wagged his tail and stared up at the captain's face. Captain Marco looked down at the dog, patted his head and smiled.

Then the dog stood and walked over to Defarge and licked his hand. He, too, patted the dog. Everyone roared their approval and some clapped. Bhaiya walked down the line of sailors and pilgrims and everyone reached out and patted him.

Héloïse whispered, "That's the spirit."

Then the dog stood next to Rajeev and looked over at Defarge. The sailor got in line with the others.

"Clearly a creature of God!" Bernard shouted. "Let us pray that the problems of the world can be solved with such insight as this faithful beast. Please bow your heads."

After Bernard said a thankfully short prayer Captain Marco shouted at his men to hurry below to start rowing. The pilgrims went down also but before returning to his cabin Baldwin stayed on deck to look out to sea. After awhile he opened the door to see Rajeev sitting cross-legged on the floor patting Bhaiya.

Rajeev looked up at Baldwin. "This dog has the best instincts of any animal I have ever seen," Rajeev said.

Baldwin nodded. "He's always been a smart one. He wasn't going to put up with any violence on board. No mistake."

Bhaiya thumped his tail on the floor and pushed his head under Rajeev's hand for more petting.

"What happened at the market today? Bhaiya's not talking," Rajeev joked.

Baldwin shrugged. "I guess I don't like crowds. What did you do?"

Rajeev realized Baldwin was trying to change the subject away from himself.

"I found that the *Mademoiselles* are very well educated. They speak almost as many languages as I do. They have studied Latin, Greek and Hebrew."

Baldwin shrugged, seemingly unimpressed. Rajeev continued the praise. "Ava is not closed off to other's opinions or religious beliefs but eager to learn. I believe her heart is as expansive as her intellect."

"Oh?" Baldwin said teasingly. "Interested in her are you?"

"Aren't you?" Rajeev asked pointedly.

Baldwin put his drawing things in the basket under the bed and then sat down not looking at Rajeev. He was determined not to blush for a third time in one day. When he looked up the Indian was looking at him, grinning.

"What?" Baldwin asked.

"We were talking about the very pretty and intelligent Ava," Rajeev said.

"No we weren't, you were. You were the one having such a great time."

Rajeev stared at his friend. Something else was going on here.

"Why did you come back to the ship so early, my friend?" Rajeev asked. "Why are you in a dark mood? Do you think something is wrong with befriending the ladies? Making friends is a positive thing. Their opinions can expand your thinking. Even the quiet Bernard has come out of his shell since Héloïse has challenged his beliefs about women. He is devoted to the Virgin Mary. But I think Héloïse wants him to see that she was a woman, not just a sainted virgin, perhaps having a more difficult life than women do now. It was after all long ago that she walked the earth."

"What does that have to do with Ava?" Baldwin asked.

"You are a man. She is a woman. You are about the same age, both from France, both Catholic journeying to the Holy Land. I would think you'd have a lot in common to talk about. That's all," Rajeev said smiling. "She and her sister will need protecting when they get off the ship to travel the last dangerous miles to Jerusalem."

"We'll all need protecting," Baldwin said as he stripped off his clothes to go to bed.

Bhaiya stood, took two steps to his regular resting place and lay down again. Rajeev curled up in his corner. He smiled. Ava was tempting and Baldwin would make a good husband, he thought. But he knew that wasn't going to be his destiny. He liked teasing him and testing him anyway.

Baldwin was trying not to think about Ava. He thought about the Berkowitz', Alfonso, the Spaniards, Bernard, Captain Marco and the incident with Defarge. He smiled. Good ol' Bhaiya. He knew things, he could see things. Oh no, no *no*, don't think about that.

Baldwin tossed, then tried focusing on the movement of the ship. The sailors were rowing away from the port. He could hear the piper setting the rowers' rhythm. He knew the helmsman was guiding the ship and other men were on the bow. He wondered if there was enough wind to unfurl the massive sail. Finally Baldwin sat up. It was hot and stuffy in the cabin. Rajeev seemed to be asleep but Bhaiya immediately lifted his head. Baldwin pulled on his breeches and tunic, opened the door to let Bhaiya out and walked onto the deck.

All the pilgrims were there spread out next to the railings. Some had clothes folded under their heads. Others were using their hands as pillows. Of course, he thought, it must be at least twice as hot below deck as it was in his cabin. They came up to try and get some cool air so they could sleep. He walked around until he saw her at the bow. The wind was lightly blowing the silk cover over her hair. She was staring at the stars.

"Can't sleep?" he asked, trying to sound interested rather than shy and stupid, which was what he was feeling.

"It's ghastly hot below," Ava said. "You?"

"Cooler out here." He looked up at the stars. "Do you believe your future is written in the stars as some say?"

"I suppose it's written somewhere, might as well be in the

heavens. At least it's a nice thought that we have some kind of destiny. Don't you think?"

He nodded keeping his eyes on the stars.

"Your destiny is obvious," she said. "A knight. You're committing yourself to keep the pilgrims safe from harm. Is that not so?"

"Exactly," he said and smiled at her. "I guess it's my destiny."

"You come from a noble family and have taken up a noble cause. It only makes sense to me," she said.

"What is your destiny, then?" he asked.

"As a female I'm limited. It's either marriage or the nunnery. Either way is a sacrifice."

"How so?"

She smiled. "Of course I'm sure you've never thought about it because you don't have to, being a male. But for me and my sister … I don't know if it's the misfortune of being educated and intelligent and, therefore, wanting more out of life than squalling babies or gardening in a convent."

"You don't want children?" Baldwin asked, shocked. He'd never thought that a woman might not want children. After all, everyone wanted children, didn't they? He was trying to think of a good answer. "You could have a governess take them when they cried."

She laughed and nodded. "I could if I married for wealth and position. Yes indeed. But what if I loved someone, let's say, oh I don't know, whom I met in Jerusalem. And he was gentle, kind and poor? I would end up with crying babies and maybe go mad."

"Somehow I don't see that happening–I mean the mad part."

"In our world, men make babies for women to raise," Ana continued.

"Of course! That's the way it works. It can't work any other way," Baldwin was trying to be quiet so as to not wake any nearby sleeping pilgrims but the conversation was irritating him.

"Then I have one word for you," she said.

He raised his eyebrows. "Which is?"

"Celibacy."

Baldwin pressed his lips together.

"From the 11th century the Catholic Church has ordained only celibate unmarried men and are *still* giving services in Latin. And ..."

Baldwin knew he should listen and not get into an argument with her, even though he wanted to. She was pretty, smart and probably way too feisty for him. Suddenly, in the back of his memory came a brief thought of Anastasia and her marriage to the cruel czar. What was her fate? Baldwin returned his attention to Ava.

"It was Pope Urban the Second," she continued, "the one who initiated the crusade that liberated the Holy City from the Muslims, who had priest's wives sold into slavery and then their children were abandoned. All in the name of purity and celibacy."

"But you're Catholic, are you not? You're going to the very city that Pope Urban said would save our souls. Do you not believe your own faith?"

"I do not question the greatness of Jesus, the two Mary's or John the Baptist. I do question the interpretation of holiness. What makes a person good?"

"I think," Baldwin said, but his next words were drowned out as the ship suddenly dipped and a gigantic, salty wave crashed over them. They both slipped on the deck but came up laughing.

"Refreshing!" Ava shouted as the other passengers struggled to stand in the wind.

The ship dipped again and the helmsman yelled, "Strike the sail!"

Baldwin took Ava's arm and they slipped and slid over the deck. She got in line behind the passengers who were hurriedly climbing down the ladder. Bernard was helping each one.

Ava leaned close to Baldwin's ear. "See you at dawn for prayers."

"God help us survive the night!" Rupert shouted just as Bhaiya came skidding down the deck and hit the cabin door with a thump. Rajeev opened the door and motioned Baldwin and Bhaiya to hurry in. He winked at Ava as he closed the door after his two traveling companions. As the ship rolled and crashed crazily on the water, Baldwin sat on his bunk with his back against the wall and asked the now wide-awake Rajeev about women.

"What is the role of women in the world?"

Rajeev raised his eyebrows. "Been having a conversation with Ava, I see. You, no doubt, stated the obvious, child bearing and serving men."

"I didn't put it that way but close. I think she didn't like my opinion."

Rajeev looked thoughtful. "You could tell her how we treat women in India. That might make her like you more."

Baldwin shrugged. "Not sure I …" Rajeev put up his hand to stop him.

"Don't deceive yourself. She's attractive and young. *You're* attractive and young. You could develop a close relationship, friends, lovers, who knows? She could be Parvati, you could be her Shiva."

"Cryptic as always," Baldwin smiled. "What does that mean?"

"In India we have a Hindu deity known as Ardhanarishvara."

"Oh, no. I can't even say that. She's Catholic anyway. Do you think she wants to hear about a Hindu deity?"

"Do you?"

"Yes, of course. I like your stories."

Rajeev nodded. "So will she. Ava is not a common woman. We have spoken together many times about India. She is very interested and said she would like to visit there someday. She will be impressed with you if you tell her about," he held his hand to his ear, "now listen, *Ard ha narish vara.*"

"Ard ha narish vara," Baldwin repeated to his life-long tutor. "Tell me, please sir, what I should know to impress her, just in case I want to." Baldwin grinned. "How will this deity be of interest to her?"

"It's a long story but worth knowing. It will be of interest because Ardhanarishvara is half male, half female."

Baldwin rolled his eyes and smirked, "You jest!"

"Both male and female energies are represented—the unity of opposites. I might add that we all have both opposite energies to some degree. When you accept who you really are and accept others for who they are—part of totality and not separate from you, then you understand the totality that lies beyond duality."

"Erm." Baldwin stared at his teacher. "Not exactly sure how that explains something that Ava will like. Not sure what duality means. It's obvious it's a male dominated world. She's a female who needs to be protected. I'm a knight who can do that. I don't understand what you mean when you *imply* that *I* have some female qualities. What is she going to think when I *imply* that *she* has male attributes?"

"She is very knowledgeable. I think she will understand balance. In her world where most women are not as well educated she has been accused of being masculine, or having masculine qualities. It is not something a refined, intelligent young woman wants to hear. I was going to tell her more about Indian culture but I think she would like to know that you are well educated, too, about other cultures and other ways of thinking."

"What? That isn't obvious?" Baldwin joked. "I do come from a noble family after all."

"That doesn't necessarily mean you have a brain. Many sons of great families are ne'er-do-wells. As the youngest son you won't inherit and you may have wasted your youth on games and frivolity."

"With you as our tutor? Frivolous? Not likely."

Baldwin put his chin on his raised knees and stared at the sleeping Bhaiya sprawled out on the floor. "You know what you are, don't you boy? A male dog. Leader of the pack. If you had one, that is. And I know who I am. A human male. I carry a sword. I defend the poor and downtrodden. I fight for justice and righteousness. I'm all male!" With that statement he turned with his face against the wall and tried to shut out the roaring wind and the rolling ship.

Rajeev smiled and curled into his corner thinking ... and you have an interest in nature, you can sew, make peace between your brothers, heal the sick and love your mother above all others. Balanced. Suddenly the ship tipped dangerously to one side. Bhaiya and Rajeev slid right into Baldwin's bed. Baldwin sat up and as the boat tipped again Rajeev scrambled up beside him and Bhaiya jumped up and lay across both their laps. The unnerved men held on to the panicky dog as the ship rolled.

"I wonder what's happening below," Baldwin said loudly. Even though they were sitting right next to each other, the wind made it hard to have a normal conversation.

"I'm sure Bernard is leading them in prayer," Rajeev shouted. "Everyone always prays to God when they're in trouble."

"I'm going to thank the Almighty One when he answers our prayers and stops rocking this ship!" Baldwin shouted back.

"It will be good to give thanks when the sun rises. Probably a good idea to give thanks everyday," Rajeev said. "But for now try and put your mind elsewhere." With that, Rajeev closed his eyes.

Baldwin did the same. His mind filled with images: Ava, Anastasia, Mary Magdalene and the demon were saying something to him–all of them at once. After awhile the exhausted men fell asleep sitting up with their backs against the wall and a wet, smelly dog on their laps. The storm abated around midnight.

Just before dawn Bhaiya was in a frenzy. He scrambling off the bed and repeatedly jumped up the cabin door. Rajeev woke with a crick in his neck. He yawned and rolled his head from side to side. Slowly he got off the bed, stepped to the door and opened it. Bhaiya rushed out barking crazily.

"Wha'?" Baldwin asked sleepily. His back hurt, his head ached and his shoulders were sore. He rolled his shoulders and rubbed his eyes. Rajeev turned toward him laughing.

"Come look or you won't believe me."

Baldwin yawned, stretched and stumbled sleepily to the door and looked out.

"Oh my God," he said suddenly wide-awake. He looked at Rajeev. "Ugh, the smell."

His head throbbed. Hundreds of fish and other sea creatures were wildly flapping on the deck. An unusually massive dolphin-like monster fish was lying on the prow. Bhaiya was running everywhere trying to catch a flailing fish. He'd corner one and it would furiously flop away. Laughing deck hands were picking up nets trying to catch the fish as they skidded around the deck. The tired, pale passengers slowly climbed up to see what the commotion was about.

"Fresh fish!" Rupert said excitedly.

Baldwin and Rajeev looked at each other.

"Obviously," Baldwin said.

"Englishmen are a strange lot," Rajeev said. "Rupert is a chef."

"No," Baldwin said. "He's English, therefore he can't cook. We Frenchmen know this for certain."

Rajeev smiled as a fish flopped up to his knees. He reached out trying to catch it. Everyone tried to catch one. Then the passengers started laughing and the fatigue and fright of the night were forgotten as everyone chased the fish.

"What is this?" Frau Berkowitz shouted holding up something small and squishy-looking with flailing tentacles.

"Calamari!" Rupert shouted as he rounded up more of the tiny squid.

"A French dish I believe," Rajeev said with a sideways grin at Baldwin.

"Get as many as you can Frau Berkowitz," Rupert said, "and I will make you a delicious feast."

Both Frau and Herr Berkowitz got busy catching the squishy squid and putting them in a burlap sack one of the sailors handed them.

"How's he going to cook them?" Baldwin asked Rajeev, but his friend just shrugged and tried to control the slippery fish he'd caught. The next moment the fish flipped out of his hands and over the rail into the sea. Their attention was drawn to the sailors at the prow trying to catch what looked like a small whale.

"It's worth a fortune!" Captain Marco exclaimed. "The sea's gift to us!"

Baldwin and Rajeev took a closer look at the strange creature. It was oddly shaped and had a very long thin tusk protruding out of the middle of its forehead. The sailors were shouting and Baldwin heard the words "sea unicorn."

"It's too big for the ship!" Captain Marco shouted! "Get the tusk and get it back into the sea!"

One of the sailors slashed at the point where the tusk protruded out of the creature's forehead and pulled it out. Then the crew pushed and pulled and finally got the bleeding creature overboard.

"What is it?" Baldwin asked the captain. The captain had the five-foot ivory tusk and was smiling broadly.

"It's a miracle this creature is in the Mediterranean as it lives in colder waters up north. Sometimes it happens though. Perhaps it was captured and got away or was caught in ice somewhere." He held up the tusk. "This could buy me a fleet of ships as it's worth much more than its weight in gold."

"Why is it so valuable?" Baldwin asked.

"Because," the captain replied, "this is what is sold as unicorn horn. Unicorn horn is said to heal many ailments."

"But it isn't a unicorn horn," Fergus protested. "The unicorn looks like a horse and is well-respected in Scotland for its power, purity and innocence."

"Power, purity and innocence," Bernard, overhearing them, restated. "Jesus and his blessed mother."

"The unicorn represents Christ?" Fergus asked in astonishment.

"But it's a myth," Héloïse stated. Bernard raised his eyebrows.

"The unicorn is a myth, not Christ," Héloïse smiled. She almost rolled her eyes but thought better of it. "Persians, as I recall from my studies, believed in a winged creature with a horn sticking out of its forehead."

"Wings?" Bernard said. "How wonderful."

"We've revered unicorns for centuries," Fergus said. "It's never been conquered."

"It couldn't be because it has never been seen!" Héloïse said.

"Never been seen but this fish-creature's horn is sold as unicorn horn and if people think it heals them then so be it," Captain Marco said. He pointed the horn like a jousting lance and strolled back to his cabin.

"Beware what you buy," Herr Berkowitz said shaking his head. "But the creature is part of Jewish folklore. I believe we call it a *re'em* and is mentioned in the Torah. But then the translations are not always accurate. That may have been an ox because it is big. Who knows?"

"There is a large animal with a horn on its nose that lives in Africa," Rajeev said. "I have not seen it nor know its name. Some of them are white. But I don't believe they look like a horse."

"One idea," Ava said," is that the playful unicorn missed Noah's ark and therefore perished in the flood."

"It missed the boat?" Baldwin said from across the deck. Ava smiled at him. Seeing them Héloïse did role her eyes.

With most of the fish either in the nets or back in the sea, Bernard raised his hands and cried to the morning sky, "Thank you Lord for saving our ship, our souls and serving up this feast of fish!"

Exhausted and smelling of fish, the travelers turned their faces to the rising sun and listened as Bernard said an exuberant morning prayer.

"Now," Rupert said when Bernard's prayer was over, "I will get a few supplies from below and if the fine sailors will start a small fire over here," he pointed to the enclosed area of clay earth and compacted wet sand where they normally cooked, "I will make you a breakfast fit for kings."

The sailors shouted their approval at this.

"I will get the dried pasta," Alfonso said as he followed Rupert. "We can steam it and put the fish over it."

Ava and Héloïse joined Baldwin and Rajeev.

"It was quite a storm," Ava said. "Elena Maria has not come up yet. She was very sick."

"We should probably get her up into the fresh air," Baldwin said. Ava looked at him curiously. "My mother ministered to the sick when needed," Baldwin said. I learned from her. The woman should come up."

"Yes, of course," Ava said. "I will convince her husband to bring her up."

Rajeev and the other passengers made a makeshift bed for Elena Maria to rest upon. Ava and Senior Ortega helped her up from below and walked her over to the pallet. She was deathly pale and could hardly walk. She lay down and closed her eyes. A tear ran down her cheek from the effort.

Baldwin knelt down and took her hand. He thought her skin looked grayish.

"Try to breathe deeply," he told her. Elena Maria managed a faint smile.

"It stinks," she whispered.

For a moment Baldwin didn't know what she meant, then realized that the entire ship reeked of fish. He probably smelled awful. Just then someone put his hand on his shoulder and a shot of energy went through him. He looked up to find Bernard standing over them.

"May I?" Bernard asked and bent down. Baldwin stood up to let the monk kneel next to Elena Maria. He noticed that his piercing headache had disappeared with the monk's touch. Bernard put his right hand on Elena Maria's forehead and raised his left arm to the sky as if pulling some power down to him. As Elena Maria trustingly looked into Bernard's gentle eyes the monk whispered, "Trust in the healing powers of Our Lord Jesus Christ and know that you are held in his arms and healed."

Elena Maria sighed. Bernard kept his arm up. Baldwin couldn't detect anything happening but Rajeev had his full attention on the kneeling Bernard.

"Faith alone will heal you," Bernard whispered. Elena Maria signed again and closed her eyes. Rodrigo Ortega gasped.

"Oh blessed Virgin, no!" he cried.

Bernard turned to him. "Shhh, she is only sleeping. See how softly she breathes?"

Rodrigo fell to his knees. Bernard knelt next to him. Then everyone, including most of the sailors who could, and the captain, kneeled and bowed their heads.

"Let us offer our strength and our silence to this beautiful woman Elena Maria who has faith in the Lord our Father and trust in the Divine forgiveness and healing of the Virgin Mary."

He fell into silence, as did everyone on board. The sea settled, the seagulls sat staring from the mast and the wind gently pushed the ship forward. After a few minutes Baldwin looked around and saw some of the men wiping tears from their tanned and craggy faces. He noticed Ava had her face in her hands. The silence was ... profound.

When Bernard looked up Rajeev stepped forward and started chanting. It was beautiful. Baldwin reached up to touch the cross his mother had given him. Tears streamed down as everyone watched the tableau of Bernard, Rodrigo and Elena Maria and listened to the soft, soothing sounds coming from Rajeev.

Bhaiya walked over, sat and stared at the sleeping woman. Baldwin caught his breath as Elena Maria opened her brown eyes and smiled. A soft pink flooded back into her face. She gently pushed herself into a sitting position. Rodrigo covered her face with kisses. Bernard quietly walked to the railing and stared out to the sparkling blue sea.

"Are those squid ready yet?" Captain Marco shouted. But he smiled as he said it. "We have only a day and a night until we reach Acre and my men are hungry!"

"Acre, our final port of call," Rajeev said.

Grabbing wooden bowls they headed over to where Rupert and Alfonso were dishing out the tiny squid over large amounts of pasta. Rajeev and Baldwin looked at each other as they took a bite. By now they were quite use to the unappetizing food on board. As they began to chew the tiny, slightly rubbery creatures their eyes sparked with joy. Delicious was not the word. Sublime was the word.

They overhead Rupert say, "it's a simple dish really. I bought some spices along the way. You must clean them of course, the squid I mean, and then as you can see I've added oil to this large pan and some garlic–you really can't have calamari without garlic–salt, pepper, some spicy red flakes. You can fry it of course, and at home I would have added lemon and parsley, but on a ship that may rock at any time, best to have a pan I can control."

The sailors were hanging on his every word.

"Three cheers for our English cook!" one of the sailors shouted. They all seemed to understand what he said for the next minute they were hip-hip-hooraying Rupert and toasting him with mead.

"It's excellent Rupert," Ana said. "If I didn't know better I'd think you were French."

"High praise indeed," Baldwin said raising his drinking cup.

"All right, all right," Captain Marco said when everyone was finished. "Line up men."

As the pilgrims watched, the sailors all came to attention in front of their captain.

"Tomorrow morning," Captain Marco said addressing the pilgrims, "we arrive at the port of Acre and you will leave us. Lead by Baldwin, who will protect you from bandits and pickpockets," he nodded at the young knight who nodded back, "you will take the much-traveled road up to Jerusalem. I say up because the Holy City is almost three thousand feet above sea level. With any luck you will be at the Gate of David on the western edge of Jerusalem by evening and gaze upon the center of the world where Jesus lived and died."

"Oh, just imagine," Frau Berkowitz said, her eyes tearing as her husband took her hand.

"As captain of this ship I am in charge of giving you instructions on how to act when you get there. Naturally, you will not show any bad behavior to the citizens of Jerusalem. As we have all gotten to know each other over these five weeks I know that there is not one person among you who would do so. As pilgrims you will show Christian respect to all you meet. You will not enter any Muslim mosque nor graveyard, nor carry off pieces of wall or other artifact from any site holy or otherwise."

He looked around then continued. "There is a small admission fee at the Gate of David. From there you will travel to the Hospital of Saint John, if need be, run by the Hospitallers. They have accommodations or you can travel further and find lodgings elsewhere. From there you can go your separate ways. Come, let us say farewell."

With that he lined up with the many men who made their journey a safe and successful one. With Bernard leading the way the pilgrims walked down the line, the men shaking hands or patting backs and the women curtseying. Bhaiya got the most pats he'd ever had. In the many weeks they had been together the passengers had gotten to know each other, the dog and most of the sailors well. It was both a joyful and sad moment.

As the sun blazed overhead, Bernard as usual intoned, "Let us pray." All bowed their heads. "Heavenly Father, we thank these skillful and brave men for our safe journey. Please look down lovingly upon your glad and weary travelers and open the gates to Jerusalem to us so that we can offer our souls to you as true penance for our sins. Let us regret without ceasing the faults of the past and firmly resolve to never again commit that which is so deplorable. No matter what sins we have committed, please forgive us. Let the tears of those repenting be like nectar to the angels in your sight. So be it."

Not one of the pilgrims could sleep that night and most stayed on deck, talking and looking at the stars. They were almost there. The holy of holies. Jerusalem!

CHAPTER TEN

THE FINAL ASCENT

1120 A.D.
On the Road to Jerusalem

"Let's leave as soon as they put down the gangplank and get a good start to this day," Baldwin said while standing on the deck in the cool, predawn mist.

"Not saying anything to our friends?" Rajeev questioned.

"They'll catch up to us but I want to get out ahead and see if I can spot any areas where bandits might surprise us."

"Thinking like a warrior. Good," Rajeev said. "Perhaps we can find some horses."

In the early morning quiet they packed their few possessions, then ate pieces of dark bread and fragrant cheese. At first Baldwin was going to wear his chainmail but decided against it, as it added weight didn't appeal to him at the moment. Although there may be thieves and bandits, he was fully capable of protecting himself at close quarters with his sword. He'd wear his chainmail after he was made a soldier of Christ, he decided.

Captain Marco was on deck. "I thought you two might go out as early as possible."

"We're going to look at horses," Baldwin said.

"Of course. What's a knight without a horse?" the captain said humorously. "Don't buy the first one you see. There are many who will try and trick you. More reputable horse traders are further down the road. They like to negotiate. Or you might try a camel."

"The spitting beast? My father told us about camels but we didn't believe him."

"You'll hear them complaining loudly even before you see them. Shaggy, smelly but excellent at crossing deserts," the captain said and smiled. "I advise you first to go down to the beach where many of the pilgrims are and bathe. You smell worse than my men."

Captain Marco bent down and spoke to Bhaiya. "Having a dog on board was a first for me. You are a real sea dog and can travel with me at any time." Bhaiya wagged his tail and allowed the captain to stroke his muzzle.

The captain stood. "The same for you my friends," he said and patted each man on the shoulder in farewell.

"Good luck selling the unicorn horn," Rajeev said smiling. "I hope it brings you good fortune."

Captain Marco grinned. The other sailors saluted as the trio silently passed them by.

"There are no doubt some things to help us smell better in the marketplace," Rajeev said as they walked down the gangplank followed by Bhaiya. As usual they found it difficult to walk on dry land. It took them some time to get their land legs back and to absorb their new, noisy surroundings. The smell was a combination of salty sea air, exotic spices and heady perfumes.

The colorful marketplace was busier than any other of the ports on their journey. Not only were there travel-weary people of multiple races, but also knights, their horses and attendants. Baldwin identified knights from all across Europe by the symbols they used on their cloaks. A feeling of expectation and excitement permeated the air.

"You'd better put your DesMarets coat-of-arms on so the other knights will know you," Rajeev said as he pulled out the tunic with the Baldwin designed symbol on it. He helped put it over Baldwin's shirt.

"Good thing I didn't put on the chainmail. The heat itself feels heavy. I'm saving the battle gear for ah, well, battle."

"Yes, your simple clothing will do, as long as you carry your sword. I'll hold your tunic and weapon and you can just go in the sea with your trousers," Rajeev said. "But first I want to see if there is attar of rose in this marketplace. That should help keep you smelling human instead of like a dead fish."

"I should have brought dried flowers from our garden at home," Baldwin said. "Do you think you'll likely find them here? Roses, I mean?"

Rajeev shrugged. "Perhaps some Persians are here with their goods. Rose water and rose leaf are popular in India but I doubt if many of my countrymen are here. The journey is a long one but people have been coming and going for centuries. Many peoples besides mine–Egyptians, Romans, Syrians–all like to be scented. Others, not so much. We'll see."

They walked through the marketplace admiring the many brightly colored goods people were selling. "Ah!" Rajeev suddenly said, "I think I see something I can use."

He stopped at a stand with baskets piled with mysterious herbs and vibrant spices of red, orange and yellow. He negotiated with a small, turbaned man who enthusiastically showed him many exotic ointments, powders and fragrances until they settled on a price for attar of rose and rose water, which Rajeev was delighted to find.

"My mother would love this place," Baldwin said wistfully. "My father, too. They adored their gardens and would love seeing all these herbs and plants used for cooking and healing."

"Perhaps this is where your father first discovered he had a love of herbs and their uses," Rajeev said.

"Probably," Baldwin said, then stood still for a moment listening. "Do you hear that awful noise?"

Rajeev smiled. "Camels."

The trio of tall knight, short tutor and scruffy dog headed in the direction of the bellowing beasts. On the sandy road between the bazaar and the beach beyond they spotted a line of light brown camels, grey donkeys and various horse breeds.

"I thought *we* smelled bad," Rajeev joked waving his hand in front of his nose. Black flies buzzed around the beasts. Baldwin reached out to pet the camel's nose but the animal shook his shaggy head and backed away. Baldwin looked at Rajeev and rolled his eyes.

"Perhaps father was in jest when he said he rode one of these things. I don't see how it's possible." Bhaiya stared at the beasts while tilting his head from side-to-side.

"I think the horses are a better idea," Rajeev said as they strolled past braying donkeys.

The horses were worn-out looking and thinner than any horse Baldwin had seen. "They certainly aren't battle horses," he commented.

"None of them look if they could walk very far," a female voice said from behind them. The two turned to see Ava, Héloïse and Bernard standing there.

Baldwin and Rajeev smiled in greeting.

"Where are the others?" Rajeev asked.

Bernard answered, "The Berkowitz' and Elena Maria and Rodrigo are still on the ship. I think neither lady is feeling well. Rupert and Alfonso are still at the street shops. I'm not sure where Fergus is."

"Captain Marco said you were off early to look for horses," Ava said. "We're going to the seashore for a bit of a wash." She smiled at Baldwin. "I can't believe we're heading toward water when we've been on it for weeks."

"We can get one of these, ah not so fine beasts, when we get back from a romp in the sea," Baldwin said, then blushed. "I mean we'll feel refreshed at least." Ava smiled.

"I smell smoke," Héloïse said sniffing the air.

"Cooking fires, I believe," Rajeev said. "The beach is not far away and I understand from talking with the sailors that knights and tired pilgrims may be camping there."

"You know everything," Baldwin said quietly to Rajeev as they all started toward the shoreline while the two women talked to each other. Bernard walked quietly behind, his small cross in hand.

"People talk to me," Rajeev said and grinned. "It's a gift. Now go be the gentleman I taught you to be and escort the women. As you can see, Bhaiya is already in the lead."

Bhaiya was ahead walking between the two ladies and being patted from both sides for his escort duties.

"But I smell like fish," Baldwin protested.

"As do they," Rajeev said, "therefore, they won't mind."

Baldwin caught up to the women and Bhaiya ran over to Bernard's side where he was also greeted with a pat on the nose. Bhaiya sniffed the staff Bernard was using for walking but found it uninteresting. Smiling, Rajeev followed while trying to take in everything he saw.

"When we get to Jerusalem, what do you want to see first?" Baldwin asked the women.

"The Church of the Holy Sepulchre," both said in unison.

"It's where Jesus was crucified, buried and resurrected," Héloïse said.

"I want to go there and then rest in a hostel if we can find one," Ava said. "Oh, look at all the people on the seashore!"

They saw hundreds of people of all descriptions at the shore. Some were eating over cooking fires and others were jumping around in the sea. Knights were either sitting at long tables eating and drinking or standing in groups talking about their various campaigns. Children were running through the crowd selling trinkets.

"I think we ladies will try and find an indoor bathhouse," Héloïse said. "And you Bernard? Are you going to let the waves wash over you?"

"Bathhouse for me, also," he answered.

"I'm going in," Baldwin said flatly. "God knows I don't want to smell like fish when I enter into His presence."

Bernard nodded, crossed himself and brushed dirt off his white robe.

As they hurried through the throng, Bernard stopped to talk with some black-robed monks. Héloïse and Ava continued until they found a large boulder to sit on at the edge of the shoreline. They stripped off their shoes and stockings, then raced into the water and ran back, not wanting to get too wet or jump into the waves. Laughing, they splashed each other, picked up shells but didn't venture further out.

As suggested by Rajeev, Baldwin stripped down to his trousers and boldly walked into the water. Bhaiya stared at him as if he were crazy and laid down in the wet sand just out of reach of the incoming tide.

"Come on Bhaiya!" Baldwin coaxed. "You smell the worst."

Bhaiya didn't budge. Baldwin jumped into the waves, stripped off his breeches and threw them to Rajeev. The Indian wasn't close enough to catch them and had to charge down the shoreline to pick them out of the water. He laughed as he held Baldwin's clothes and let the water splash up to his knees. The waves were modest and Baldwin dog-paddled around, dipping down to wet his hair trying to get some of the odor off. The water was not cold but was refreshing. As he jumped around he saw Ava staring at his shirtless body. He thought about jumping higher so she could have a complete picture. Rajeev was grinning at him.

Baldwin called, "Are you coming in?"

"You have to come out first," Rajeev yelled. "I think Bhaiya here needs a dip."

"He didn't much like it when we threw him into the water at Venice," Baldwin reminded him.

Rajeev just shook his head. "If we don't get him in our noses will regret it."

"What about the baths at the hostels?"

Rajeev shook his head. "As friendly as he is, I still don't think they will allow him in."

Suddenly feeling bold, Baldwin walked out of the water, picked up his dog and carried the wildly struggling beast into the ocean. He glanced sideways to see if Ava was looking. Both she and Héloïse were laughing. Bhaiya jumped out of Baldwin's arms and immediately swam for the shore. Rajeev ran several steps away as the dog started shaking the water off his matted coat. Everyone was laughing.

"Come on out!" Rajeev called. "The mademoiselles can stare or not. All the children playing in the ocean are naked. You are just a much bigger child."

"Very funny," Baldwin said as he once again marched out of the water and grabbed his trousers from his friend. He then realized he couldn't easily get them back on while sinking into the wet sand. He used Rajeev's shoulder for balance and awkwardly got back into his clothes.

The hot sun was already drying him and his still stinking dog as the trio walked to where the two women were brushing sand off their feet.

"I don't think we can put our stockings back on," Ava was saying to her sister, "just our shoes."

She looked up and saw Baldwin. "I think we need to go back to the ship and find out how Elena Maria and Frau Berkowitz are doing."

Baldwin was disappointed that she hadn't commented on his ocean antics. Just then they heard Bernard hailing them.

He greeted them with, "My fellow monks have suggested that I help persuade the horse seller to give us a decent price. They have given me some suggestions on how to negotiate."

"If I may," Rajeev said to Baldwin, "I will escort the mademoiselles back to the ship while you and the kind abbot find horses. Perhaps we will find our fellow shipmates in the bazaar. We can then all journey together to the Holy Land with your protection."

With that as their plan, Rajeev, Ava and Héloïse took a shortcut along the seashore back to the ship while Baldwin, Bernard and Bhaiya went horse shopping. After an hour they were all back at the Starburst to find Elena Maria almost too weak to walk. She was sitting on a large coil of hemp rope with her husband standing beside her. Bernard rushed over, took her hand and spoke softly to her. She smiled and nodded. After a moment she put her arms up and both men helped her stand.

"I must get to Jerusalem," she said. "Nothing will stop me."

Baldwin stepped forward. "You can ride the horse," he said. "He's a sturdy beast." He looked over at Frau Berkowitz who was quietly talking to her husband. "Frau Berkowitz will sit behind you on the horse." With her ample padding Baldwin knew that at least Elena Maria would feel comfortable with Frau Berkowitz behind her.

"Oh, ya," Frau Berkowitz said looking over at her husband who nodded.

As they departed, Rajeev once again waved to the few sailors who had remained on board while everyone else had gone ashore. He paused a moment at the end of the gangplank where stood a sad looking, mottled brown horse. Fergus was holding its reins.

"One of those humped-backed beasts may have been a better choice," Fergus said in his deep Scottish brogue. "I dunna think this poor animal has much in 'em." He waved flies off the beast's flank.

Rajeev stared at the poor dusty looking brute as Baldwin came up behind him. "I now know what the word 'downtrodden' means," Rajeev said. "Doesn't compare to a sturdy Ardennes, does it?"

Baldwin shrugged. "I'd say father wouldn't approve but then he rode a camel. You should have heard Bernard assure the seller that this rather dubious looking creature wasn't worth its weight in gold, as the horse trader swore. As a matter of fact, when Bernard got through with the man I think he was going to pay us to take the horse away. Bernard was very, very persuasive," Baldwin said.

"Bernard is impressive," Héloïse said overhearing them. "He'll have a lot of authority one day, I'm sure."

"I'm not sure we got a bargain on this beast though," Rajeev said. "If he lasts the journey we'll be lucky."

"He'll do," Baldwin said. "You should have seen what else was for sale. This old fellow was the best of a sorry lot."

They watched as Bernard and Rodrigo Ortega helped Elena Maria walk slowly down the gangplank. Her husband lifted her onto the horse and with some shoving Frau Berkowitz managed to get behind her. Baldwin took the rope reins and with everyone walking in single file made it safely through the crowded, odorous marketplace and onto the much-traveled uphill road to Jerusalem.

Out on the open road the group gathered closer together. It was hot, the desert air dry, and the land barren-looking to the travelers. Señor Ortega walked on the left of the plodding horse and Herr Berkowitz on the right. The others were reluctant to walk behind the animal so gathered around Baldwin for the journey.

Two hours later they stopped to give the horse a rest and let the riding ladies stretch their legs. Not use to riding, their bottoms were sore and their legs stiff. The rest of the pilgrims had tired feet, aching bodies and itching bites from annoying bugs.

Knowing they had hours to go Bernard suddenly said, "We're on the rode to Jerusalem! We make but little sacrifice compared to our Lord Jesus."

As smiles broke out, Ava pointed to a cloud of dust coming down the rode toward them. Suddenly, Baldwin dropped the horse's reins and drew out his sword. Rajeev drew his knife and Señor Ortega told the travelers to get behind him and held his cane ready. Bernard had his small cross in hand and started saying a prayer under his breath. Fergus pulled out an impressive-looking dagger with a bronze blade and a carved wooden handle. Bhaiya growled. Rupert and Alfonso unsurprisingly had knives, too, which they had recently purchased at the marketplace. Herr Berkowitz and his wife both had small knives concealed in their clothing. Ava and Héloïse, too, had taken Captain Marco's warning of dangers on the last leg to the holy city and had small, sharp knives. They both picked up substantial stones, just in case. Only Elena Maria remained unarmed.

Yelling and shouting unintelligible words, six men on horses rushed straight out of the dust.

"Arab bandits!" Rajeev shouted.

Baldwin realized he had almost no chance of fighting them off as he was standing on low ground but he raised his sword and shouted, "We are poor pilgrims and have nothing you need!"

One of the men said something to the others, they laughed and looked over at the women. Bhaiya suddenly started barking furiously, but much to everyone's surprise, wagged his tail and shot off between the horses then came rushing back chased by another dog. They both ran crazily around the shocked pilgrims and the much-amused bandits. Everyone watched as Bhaiya started digging a hole right in the middle of the road. He looked back at the other dog, then started digging again. Baldwin thought his dog must have gone mad in the sun.

At the sound of someone's voice, the bandits all turned then started animatedly talking at once. A turbaned man with a trimmed beard and flashing black eyes rode between them, raised his hand for silence and stopped his magnificent black stallion in front of Baldwin. He dismounted. The man looked over at the dogs.

"I believe your dog remembers my Didi and is trying to impress her," he said in perfect French. His smiled dazzled.

Baldwin's jaw dropped in astonishment. It was the man who escaped from the pirates with his dog and stole the lifeboat from the Starburst.

"How did you live?" Baldwin blurted out.

The man's smile widened. "I knew I would survive when Allah sent me you with this." He drew back his riding cloak and held out Baldwin's dagger, hilt first. The bandits started murmuring to each other again. "How could I not survive with such help?"

Baldwin lowered his sword, then reached out and took the knife he had dropped so long ago to help a desperate stranger in a rowboat trying to escape pirates.

"I have a very long name but most know me as al-Hakim. This is my dog Didi. I believe we are now all friends."

"I am Baldwin DesMarets, on my way to join a group calling themselves The Knights of Christ."

"Ah yes," al-Hakim said. "They are only a few in number, less than a dozen, yet they are already known as fierce protectors of travelers. These bandits who have come upon you once traveled in much larger groups. I am glad I will not have to save any more like you. I would get a bad reputation."

He laughed then turned and said something to the bandits. After he finished talking, two of them dismounted and waited patiently holding their horse's reins.

"These are not my men but marauders on the road who prey on pilgrims such as yourselves. However, they know me and now that I have presented you with a knife and explained that you are my brother for helping me, they will see your group safely to Jerusalem. There are many more along the way who do not wish you well but, seeing these rascals, they will not bother you."

Baldwin sheathed his sword. "How did you know we were French? You speak it almost like a native."

Al-Hakim smiled. "I am a well-educated man who happens to have some excellent teachers. It was not hard to determine that you are French. You have a sword, which means you are a nobleman turned knight. Almost all of the knights here are French. The King of Jerusalem ... French."

Rajeev stepped next to Baldwin and bowed to al-Hakim. "Young Baldwin was named in honor of Baldwin of Boulogne, First King of Jerusalem," he said. "I am Rajeev. Thank you for your protection." He bowed again with his hands together. "I must ask, how is it that you travel with a dog named Didi?" They all looked around as Bhaiya was still dancing around Didi, barking, backing off and turning circles as she sat and watched him. "Didi is a word from my culture as is the name Bhaiya."

"Your dog's name is Bhaiya?" Al-Hakim asked. "It is interesting that they have names from the same culture. You are Indian, yes?"

Rajeev nodded.

"I am much interested in your country and speak a very small amount of Hindi. Didi means sister. It fits her. Although she thinks she owns me."

Rajeev was about to speak when they heard coughing. It was Elena Maria looking very pale. Rodrigo was fanning her with his hat.

"We must start again," Baldwin said. "This horse may not be a thing of beauty but Señora Ortega cannot walk well. She is very weak."

Al-Hakim looked at the horse. "That is definitely a beast of burden."

By this time the others had collected around Baldwin, curious as what this stranger was saying.

"Please sir," Señor Ortega said, "we need to get there soon. My wife needs help."

Al-Hakim motioned one of the two Arabs who had dismounted and said something rapidly to him. The man grimaced and sounded like he was protesting but shrugged and nodded.

"This man has volunteered his faster horse. This other man will lead them ahead of us. I suggest you ride with your wife," al-Hakim said to Rodrigo. "Do not worry. The man will not dare do you any harm while you are under my protection. He will take you to David's Gate for entry into Jerusalem. At the gate they will direct you to the place overseen by monks who heal the many weary, worn out and ill travelers."

After profuse thanks, the Spaniards got on the stallion and Rodrigo put his arms around his wife. The bandit mounted his horse, turned and led the way up the hill. The other bandit shifted his feet and waited for al-Hakim to give him directions. Once again al-Hakim spoke rapidly to him. The man turned, mounted behind another bandit and all but two of the bandits rode off in a dusty cloud.

"I have instructed these two to stay with you while the others go to set up tents just off the road. There is a small oasis known to them where they will get you water. You should shelter there when the sun is highest or your companions may tire from the heat. When it is cooler you can start again and reach Jerusalem by evening."

Bernard stepped up. "That is very generous of you," he said. "You are of what faith?"

"Ismaili Muslim," al-Hakim answered. "We have great respect for different cultures." He looked toward Ava, Frau Berkowitz and Héloïse and treated them to his dazzling smile. All three women looked mesmerized.

Ava cleared her throat. "If those were not your men are you traveling by yourself? Are you perhaps a spice trader or …" her voice trailed off.

Al-Hakim grinned. "I am a man of many talents. Would you ladies like to ride my horse while I walk with my friends?"

"I would!" Frau Berkowitz said immediately.

Ava and Héloïse looked at each other. "I think I will walk with Bernard," Héloïse said.

"I'd like to ride, yes," Ava said.

"Your poor beast can plod behind," al-Hakim said.

Rajeev noticed al-Hakim had not answered Ava's question and had changed the subject.

"Help us up then, won't you?" Ava asked al-Hakim.

Baldwin just stood and stared at her. Al-Hakim easily helped both women on his steed, then took the reins to lead them. The others all started walking beside him and asked many questions. Bernard was fascinated that Muslims were worshiping in Jerusalem. Al-Hakim related to them the history of the city since the crusaders conquered it.

To Baldwin he said, "I understand that your group of knights have been granted housing at the al-Aqsa mosque, which the crusaders renamed the Temple of Solomon. It's part of the royal palace, which is thought to be built over the temple. I have heard that the new knights, now called the Knights Templar by the local population, are very strict with their religious initiates and that they have to scrub the floors of the mosque. This amuses me greatly."

"It seems you know a lot about them," Baldwin said.

"I make it my business to know," al-Hakim said. "They are defenders of their faith and I of mine." He looked intently at Baldwin. "Are you prepared to scrub floors?"

"If that is what is required to serve God, then yes."

Bernard added, "To be humble in the eyes of God and to serve Him well, is the highest cause our young nobleman here can have."

"My knight–brother," Al-Hakim said, smiled, nodded and went on answering questions from each of the others. Fergus wanted to know about weapons and al-Hakim showed him the knife he carried with a curved blade. Rupert asked about food. The Berkowitz' were interested in his knowledge about trade from different countries. The last leg to Jerusalem was made more interesting by al-Hakim's presence.

"I am interested in one day visiting India," al-Hakim eventually said to Rajeev. People, especially Jewish traders, have traveled from here to there for centuries. At one time it was called the spice road. For some reason Jews and Indians get along while we Muslims and Christians are always fighting among ourselves or each other. Why is that?" He looked at Bernard.

"Is that so?" Bernard asked. "I will have to give your observations some thought."

"Perhaps they relate on a spiritual level and are not trying to convert each other by killing," Héloïse said. "They manage to believe what they believe and let others believe what they believe."

Al-Hakim smiled. "Intelligence and beauty. A most admirable combination."

Héloïse smiled.

"We are all more similar than we are different," Rajeev put in. "I would be honored to discuss more about my country with you, al-Hakim."

Al-Hakim nodded. "I would be pleased to continue our discussion."

From her vantage point on the horse Ava interrupted, "I can see tents in the distance. We are almost there!"

At this the small group hurried their steps and were soon at the two tents—one for the women and another for the men. Al-Hakim helped the women dismount his horse and spoke to the Arab men. One brought water to his horse while others held back the tent flaps and showed the weary travelers their temporary lodgings. Fruit, water and lightweight robes were inside each tent.

"Baldwin," al-Hakim said, "you are my friend and brother. We will meet again. Rajeev you are now my friend, also."

He turned to the women who had just emerged from their tent exclaiming how wonderful it was. "Unfortunately, I have urgent business in the Holy City that cannot wait. But I do not regret the distraction."

He smiled at the three woman and all three curtsied. Baldwin rolled his eyes but grinned at al-Hakim's magnetism.

"These tents will protect you from the broiling sun. Rest for several hours before you start your journey again. Jerusalem can be overwhelming the first time you see it and you should be refreshed."

With that he mounted his horse, put his hands together and bowed to Rajeev. He said something the Indian seemed to understand. Then he turned his horse and galloped up the road.

"He is such a learned man," Rajeev stated just as Didi ran after her master and Bhaiya ran after Didi.

"Bhaiya no!" Baldwin shouted. The dogs disappeared.

"Don't worry. I believe he's in good hands," Rajeev said.

"But he's never run off like that before," Baldwin protested. "I mean, he charged off the ship but this is different."

"True love makes fools of us all," Rajeev said and smiled. "Come let us take our new brother's advice. I'm tired and in need of refreshing and refreshment."

Several hours later they started out on the last leg of their long journey, using the horse Bernard had bargained for as a packhorse for water and food. Three bandits were in front and the others followed. Along the way there was a landowner who'd blocked off the road and was charging a toll. When he saw the Arab bandits he bowed low and waved the pilgrims on.

In spite of the heat, dust, sore feet and sunburned faces, emotions ran high as the pilgrims finally arrived to stand in line at David's Gate. Hundreds of other pilgrims lined up behind them. Ava and Héloïse held hands, while the Berkowitz' quietly wondered how Elena Maria and Rodrigo were faring. Excitement shone in the men's eyes. Baldwin said a silent prayer of thanks.

With Rajeev translating, the small group thanked the bandits who then touched their fingers to their foreheads in salute and disappeared back down the road.

Each pilgrim was lost in thought until Bernard said, "Finally! We've arrived in heaven!"

With great anticipation they stood in the long line of pilgrims waiting to get into the gate to the holy city of Jerusalem.

CHAPTER ELEVEN

DARK KNIGHT OF THE SOUL

1120 A.D.
Jerusalem

"You'll have to walk your horse through the bazaar," the exasperated sounding man said at David's Gate. He was wearing a beige robe that matched the color of the desert road they'd just left.

Baldwin laughed as he patted the horse on its drooping head. "I don't think this old fellow will make it that far." He turned to the others. "Take your belongings off this beast and we'll let him go. He's not worth selling."

"Perhaps someone will steal him," Fergus put in. "They'd be helping us out if they did. Let's give him to that boy over there."

Once the horse was unloaded, Fergus took the animal's reins and said to a young boy in tattered clothes selling dubious looking sweets. "Blessings to you."

He handed the surprised boy the reins and walked off leaving the child staring after him. Quickly recovering, the boy disappeared into the crowd with the horse in tow.

"Well done!" Rupert exclaimed from his place in line.

"Anyone in your group sick or in need of help?" the gate attendant asked in a bored monotone. The travelers looked around at Frau Berkowitz but she shook her head. "Everyone in our group is fine," Baldwin stated in a firm tone.

"There are guides to the holy sites, hostels and lodgings. Pay your entry fee over there. Welcome to Jerusalem," the gatekeeper said in the same tone and waved them through.

Once inside the holy city their senses were assaulted: the colorful clothing, the fragrant spices, the people maneuvering around each other and the sheer excitement of walking in the footsteps of Jesus. It was a gigantic bazaar made up of all the different peoples of the world. Baldwin grinned at Rajeev whose eyes were tearing from the joy of it. The tired pilgrims were suddenly energized. They gazed around walking from stall to stall, admiring beautiful silks and cotton clothing; brass pots of various shapes and sizes; colorful fruits and vegetables; fish, meats, sweets and more herbs and spices then at any of the ports they'd been to. Holy water was for sale and crosses to wear as jewelry, for decoration or simply as a memento from Jerusalem. Baldwin was amazed at the sheer variety of goods. When he saw the crosses— gold or silver, jewel-encrusted or plain—he put his hand up and felt his mother's precious cross through the fabric of his tunic. Nearby, Rajeev was looking at black pepper and salt when a man enticed him to inspect a selection of precious gemstones. The Indian was impressed with the quality but not the price.

It was extraordinarily noisy. People were haggling in different languages. Baldwin was surprised to see Muslims selling their wares alongside merchants made up of races he'd never seen before. Two young boys were beckoning them over to a stall that advertised tours to the Holy sites. Their sign was written in multiple languages. Baldwin felt he didn't need a guide; they'd planned where they wanted to go for months and knew the layout of the city.

After a short search the Berkowitz' spotted their Jewish relatives and enthusiastically rushed off. Frau Berkowitz waved back at her fellow travelers and shouted, "Make sure you come see us!"

As the other pilgrims walked toward the sites that interested them or stopped at the many stalls along the way, Baldwin, Rajeev,

Bernard, Ava and Héloïse walked toward the Church of the Holy Sepulchre.

"I must see this holiest of places before I go to the Temple Mount," Baldwin said excitedly.

"Yes," Bernard said reverently, "where Jesus was crucified, buried and resurrected."

"We know," Héloïse said with a hint of sarcasm in her voice.

Baldwin wondered how those two were getting along. They were both so knowledgeable and opinionated.

"I hope Abelard will come here some day," Héloïse was saying.

Baldwin leaned over to Rajeev and whispered, "Who's Abelard?"

Rajeev whispered back, "The man who is her tutor, like I'm yours. Only …" his eyes twinkled, "I believe the relationship is much, much closer and she mentions him to make Bernard jealous."

Baldwin frowned. "He's an abbot. He's not supposed to get jealous."

"He's a man first an abbot second," Rajeev said. "She's made quite an impression on him and he her. But Abelard got there first."

Baldwin raised his eyebrows. "Oh."

He looked at Ava who was walking ahead of them. "He's also Ava's tutor then?"

"She doesn't mention him. She may …" he was interrupted as something big, furry and chestnut colored jumped up and almost knocked him over.

"Bhaiya!" Baldwin exclaimed as Rajeev recovered his balance. The dog turned and danced around both of them and then shot off into the crowd.

Shaking his head Rajeev said, "You go ahead. I'll find him and come find you."

"You'll have to wait for our young knight outside the Temple of Solomon," Bernard explained. "Dogs won't be allowed. I'll be there to see my uncle."

Rajeev smiled. "No matter, I'll be well occupied with the sites of this great city." Turning to Baldwin he said, "I'll find Bhaiya and wait for you to emerge a holy knight." Before Baldwin could say anything, Rajeev pressed his hands together, bowed and hurried away.

Perplexed, Baldwin watched his friend disappear into the crowd. He thought for certain that he and Rajeev would enter the repurposed mosque together, but it seemed that Bernard would have that position. As they threaded their way through the crowd they passed a building where weary-looking pilgrims stood in a line.

"What is this place?" Baldwin asked a stooped man at the back of the queue.

"Inside are people who care and heal us," the old man said. "They are called Hospitalliars."

"Oh, I want to see inside there," Ava said stepping forward.

"There's a woman's hospice just over there," the man said pointing, "if you need to rest. It's a sad day here as the much loved monk who ran the order has died. His name was Gerard and he was the Grand Master of the Hospitalliars."

"I am indeed sad to hear that," Bernard said. "I shall go inside and see if I can be of some assistance."

"We'll come with you," Héloïse said while Ava nodded. Bernard strode to the front of the line as the two women followed. He turned to the people waiting and raised the small cross that he always carried in his hand. "We have come to assist in this holy work."

A bald man with a long beard stepped out of the building and nodded to Bernard. "I am Raymond du Puy and am much grateful for your assistance during this mournful transition for our Order of St. John of Jerusalem." He turned and the three followed him in.

Baldwin stood alone in the street. No one was with him, not even his dog. At first he thought he'd go to the Church of the Holy Sepulchre but then decided he couldn't wait to present himself to the French knights who had formed the Poor Knights of Christ and the Temple of Solomon. Or what the locals called the Knights

Templar. He asked the old man at the end of the line directions to the Mount Temple. The man pointed and Baldwin turned away from the headquarters of the Hospitalliers and walked toward his future.

The lively sounds of a busy Jerusalem were distant as Baldwin retired early. Tomorrow would be a life-changing day, a day he'd long looked forward to, a day when he would give himself over completely to God.

That afternoon when he'd entered the wing of the royal palace on the Temple Mount given over to the Knights Templar he immediately saw a brown robed monk with shorn hair on his knees scrubbing the floor. His thoughts flashed back to what al-Hakim had said about Christians cleaning the floors of the Muslim mosque. He bit his lower lip and shook his head. He tried not to smile, but failed. The monk looked up, put his finger to his lips to indicate he was in silence and winked. It was Baldwin's friend Thierry. He looked completely different without his knight's chainmail and sword and with his cropped hair and simple brown robe. Thierry pointed toward a door and watched as Baldwin went in.

Eight men were seated around a large wooden table staring at a small box that sat in the middle. All stood as the young man entered. Most were dressed in brown robes or simple tunics and breeches. He recognized several from the Champagne region just south of his village.

"Sirs," Baldwin said, "I am Baldwin DesMarets of France here to dedicate myself to your noble cause."

"*Bonjour*," said a tall, brown-haired man with a short beard and long mustache. "We've heard of your coming and of course know of your family's good reputation. I am Hugues de Payens. I'm humbled to be the Grand Master of our order who wish only to serve God and protect the pilgrims who come to see this holy place. There is much devastation and slaughter of travelers between here and Jaffa. We few have found through fierce dedication, purity of heart and a humble soul that we are capable of defending these worthy travelers. But with the help of you and other noble knights we can cover a larger area and defend all of Christianity. Are you willing to renounce the world and dedicate your life to our religious community?"

Baldwin was momentarily captivated by Hugues' intense blue eyes and direct speech. Reluctantly he looked at the floor and nodded, hoping he seemed humble instead of proud of himself for being there. After he looked up as each man announced his name and welcomed Baldwin: Godfrey de Saint-Omer, Payen de Montdidier, Archambaud de St. Amand and Geoffrey Bison.

A man who looked as swarthy as Captain Marco spoke next. "We two," he said indicting the modest monk standing next to him, "simply go by Gondemar and Rossal."

Baldwin noted Gondemar had the same strong Portuguese accent as the captain. Rossal nodded but said nothing. Clearly these two were more monk than knight. Last to introduce himself was André de Montbard.

"Ah, I traveled with your uncle Bernard," Baldwin said.

"That is great news! Where is he? We have so many things to discuss with him."

"He stopped to talk with the new Grand Master of the Hospitalliers. He was offering his advice. I assume he'll be here soon," Baldwin replied.

The men looked pleased.

"We are indeed eager to speak with him." Hugues held out his hand. "Your sword Baldwin. After you have endured our initiation ...," he looked around at the men. "I do not use that word endure lightly." The monk/knights nodded. None smiled. "I do not use the word *endure* lightly Baldwin as the initiation is meant to test your merit before God. If you pass then your sword will be returned. You will have a choice of horse and, if needed, a squire. These will not be your property but your tools in the service of our Lord Jesus and his mother the Divine Virgin Mary. Anything you possess may be taken away at any time if needed by someone else in the order. As for money, you will have only what a poor monk needs and nothing more." Hugues de Payens glared intensely at Baldwin, "Do you understand?"

"With all my heart," Baldwin replied quietly and handed over his sword.

Hugues de Payens admired it. "This ruby makes it very distinctive."

"A present from my parents," Baldwin said while looking at it.

"All those attachments will soon be gone." Hugues motioned for a monk standing on the outskirts of the room to come forward.

"Come, let me have Hogarth show you to your room. Your initiation will be in the morning after breakfast."

As he tried to sleep thoughts filled his mind. Where were Bhaiya and Rajeev? What would be his assignment? Would he be scrubbing floors like he saw the new initiates do? Or polish swords or perhaps minister to the sick and needy? After tossing and turning he remembered the breathing technique Rajeev had taught him. He filled his lungs with air. He coughed. The room was small and windowless, the air stagnant. He tried again. Breathe in through the nose and out through the mouth. Again and again. Soon he fell asleep.

The dream started. "No!" he wanted to shout but was frozen in the darkness of the dream. He was in the strange country with the peculiarly dressed people where his beloved Anastasia lived. He was guarding her as she slowly walked along a snow-covered path. She stopped and put her hand on her back and moaned. Her belly was swollen with child. She was so beautiful, like the Madonna must have looked when she was carrying the Christ child. Anastasia's baby would not be born in a humble place but in an elaborate bed with the finest linens and women to attend her.

Baldwin turned in his sleep. Once again he was guarding the Czar's bedchamber. He could hear the women with Anastasia urging her to push. Then he heard the baby cry. He smiled and tears brightened his eyes. The physician rushed out the door to summon the Czar who came majestically striding in followed by several men wearing sumptuous silk pants and tunics lined with furs and decorated with glittering jewels.

After a moment the Czar shouted, "What is this? A girl? How dare you!"

The women ran from the room. He heard Anastasia cry out then the Czar stomped out followed by his men. Baldwin swallowed, turned and walked into the room. He caught his breath. Sun was streaming through the window casting a golden light on Anastasia and the child she was holding in her arms. Her tears were lit by the sun as they ran down her cheeks. Baldwin could see a rainbow in every drop.

He walked to the side of the bed. "Did he hurt you?" he asked quietly.

She looked down on her sleeping child and a tear dropped on the child's forehead. Baldwin had never seen anything so stirring. It touched his soul.

"Or the baby?"

Anastasia shook her head. "I thought he was going to slap me," she said. "With the rings it hurts, but he just pinched my arm hard and left."

"You mean he's hit you before? Why didn't I know about it?" Baldwin asked in a low voice that barely contained his anger.

"I would stay in or cover myself with veils. Or sometimes you were away."

Baldwin drew out the words, "More ... than ... once?" Then clamped his teeth. Anastasia could see he was trying not to rage against her husband, the Czar.

"What do you think?" she asked softly looking at her child. "Is she beautiful?"

"Second only to her mother."

"You'll look out for her if something should happen to me?" Anastasia pleaded, suddenly sounding anxious.

"What? No. Anastasia nothing will happen to you I swear on my life."

Anastasia smiled. "She is little Anastasia, named after me. Little Resurrection. Promise me you'll be her knight."

Baldwin got down on one knee and took his beloved's hand.

"I will be as devoted to her as I am to you," he said and kissed her palm.

Anastasia touched his cheek and they stared into each other's eyes. Baldwin was about to speak when a woman came through the door carrying a small gown obviously meant for the baby. The knight rose and walked past the woman to once again guard the door.

The night sounds of Jerusalem continued in the distance as in his small, dark room Baldwin shook his head, moaned and woke. His thoughts were disturbed. Why was he dreaming about a woman he'd never met? He'd never been to a country called Rus. This was the first time he'd ever traveled outside of France. Who was she to him? Was she part of another life like Rajeev had talked about? What karma did he have with her? Why did he keep dreaming about her? Most of all … what had happened to her so long ago?

It was still dark when Hogarth woke Baldwin and in a whisper told him what would happen next: matins, a light breakfast in silence and then to see Hugues de Payens for his initiation. Excitement overtook Baldwin and the dream forgotten for the moment. He was about to become a Soldier of Christ! Yet, something from the dream still lingered, something dark and dreadful. Not the demon, something else. He shook it off. He had bad dreams all his life. But also good ones of Mary the Mother of Jesus and Mary Magdalene. Odd. *Almost* all his dreams were about women. He smiled. Well, he was a man after all, a knight, and a protector of the righteous devoted to God.

Baldwin dressed quickly and followed Hogarth to the chapel

for matins. About twenty men were present. He was pleased to see Bernard of Clairvaux in the front of the chapel. The abbot spoke briefly in the same uplifting tone that he'd used on their sea voyage. At the end of the chanting Hogarth motioned for Baldwin to follow him.

They silently ate bread, cheese and a light soup at a long table occupied by men who were paired with each other. Hogarth and Baldwin shared the bowl of soup, which Baldwin thought an odd meal for daybreak. He tried to share equally with Hogarth. This was part of his training as a humble monk he realized, but it was difficult not to just pick up the bowl and pour it down his hungry throat. It seemed like barely a moment when Bernard himself walked up to Baldwin and indicated he should follow him. Hogarth patted Baldwin on the arm in what was meant to be reassuring but didn't quell Baldwin's suddenly jumpy stomach.

Silently, they walked through a door of white muslin curtains. On the other side most of the men Baldwin had met the day before stood in a semi circle. Several of them were dressed in their chainmail and had swords by their sides. The others were dressed in their brown monk clothes. Candles were burning in the still dark morning and what looked like an alter was in the middle of the room. The small box that Baldwin had seen the day before was placed upon it along with a silver goblet.

Hugues de Payens spoke. "As a Knight of Christ and a humble servant of God you will no longer own any personal possessions. Your fine clothes will be given to the poor and you shall wear the robe of a peasant. Your sword will now be in the safe keeping of the knights of Christ. You shall wear no jewelry of any kind nor keep anything from your family. They no longer exist. Only God exists and we his holy servants."

Baldwin flushed and bowed his head.

"Strip yourself and stand naked before God."

Baldwin looked up. All the knights were looking directly at him. He started to slowly take off his shirt then, resolved to do this, quickly stripped off his clothes.

"Your cross," Hugues de Payens said.

Baldwin inhaled. He reached up and fingered his cross just as his mother used to do before she gave it to him. He pulled it off and clutched it, letting the cross cut into his hand making it bleed. A knight stepped forward and Baldwin handed him the cross, smeared with blood.

All looked at the Grand Master as he asked, "Poor Fellow Soldiers of Christ and of the Temple of Solomon, what do we believe in?"

"Poverty, chastity and obedience," the men intoned loudly. Their voices were magnified in the room.

Baldwin stood still as de Payens walked forward holding a goblet.

"We the Poor Fellow Soldiers of Christ and the Temple of Solomon purify your body and soul."

He poured the goblet of water over Baldwin's head. It cascaded off his nude body onto the floor. "Baldwin DesMarets," de Payens solemnly intoned, "by taking this oath you will give allegiance to the Poor Fellow Soldiers of Christ and no other. If you so agree then say, 'I swear.'"

Baldwin cleared his throat. "I swear."

"Do you swear to love the God above and his son Jesus the Christ and no other?"

"I swear."

"Do you swear an oath of poverty and to claim no ownership of any kind and to give all that you now posses to the Poor Fellow Soldiers of Christ?"

"I swear."

"Do you swear a vow of chastity and to have no impure thoughts of any kind of man, woman or beast."

Baldwin licked his lips. Armpit sweat trickled down his sides. "I swear."

"Do you swear to be devoted to discipline, chastity and prayer?"

"I swear."

As if he just thought of it, Barnard stepped forward and asked, "Do you vow poverty, chastity, obedience and *piety*?"

"I so vow," Baldwin answered quietly.

Barnard nodded to Hughes.

"Do you swear to honor and protect your fellow knights?" Hughes asked.

"I swear," Baldwin answered, his voice now harsh with emotion.

"Kneel," Hughes commanded.

Baldwin knelt with both knees on the stone floor and bowed his head. Someone came up behind him and started cutting his hair until his long locks lay beside him. He felt soft wisps of hair stick to his neck, back and arms.

Then Hugues de Payens stepped forward and once again poured a goblet of water over Baldwin's head while saying, "Your life before this now meant nothing. From this blessed moment you will forever be righteous and pure in the eyes of God."

Baldwin kept his head bowed.

"Now go with Hogarth in silence. He will instruct you how to serve our Lord with your poverty and humility."

Baldwin moved one leg behind him to try and graciously stand. He felt his shorn hair under his toes. He rose unsteadily as Hogarth walked toward a lower staircase. Baldwin followed. As he walked toward the staircase he heard the sound of someone sweeping. Then he felt remnants of his hair sticking to his back, arms and under his toes. It itched but he did not scratch it nor brush it away.

As he followed Hogarth Baldwin knew he was about to be given a task, such as scrubbing the floors, to show his humbleness to God and obedience to the Knights Templar. The air was hot and his skin started to dry. As they descended the stone steps the atmosphere became slightly cooler as they kept walking. It was a steep descent and Baldwin felt slightly unsteady on his bare feet. He put his hand out on the gray stones to steady himself and felt their coolness. His stomach rumbled and he wondered when he would eat again and when he would be given the peasant clothes he would now wear. His mouth was dry and he licked his lips hoping to still find a drop of water lingering there. Then he smelled a familiar odor—hay and horses.

At the bottom of the stairs was a long corridor with lit torches, two on each wall. The end of the corridor opened to reveal an underground stable with at least 20 horses tided to long rails, ten on each side. The horses were standing in straw, which smelled strongly of excrement. The only light came from the torches on the corridor they had just come down and from torches that he could see on the walls of another corridor beyond the stalls.

Hogarth turned and faced him. "You are to muck out the stalls until the Master assigns you another duty. You will sleep down here. In the morning you will find your peasant clothes at the foot of the stairs. At the top of the stairs and to the right you will go to our place of worship. Your day starts before sunrise at four with Matins. Today's breakfast was a feast. From now on, after we honor our Holy Mother you and I will share a bowl of bread soaked in goat's milk. We will always share a bowl as a sign of our poverty. You will return here and care for the horses until the third hour when you will return upstairs for prayer. You will maintain this routine in silence and humility until told otherwise."

Hogarth looked around the stable. "I believe you will find everything the horses need within this room."

With that he turned and briskly walked away leaving Baldwin damp and slightly bewildered. *What about my needs? Of course, I only need God*, he remembered.

It was only slightly cooler in the subterranean cavern. Baldwin wondered how long it was and guessed he would have plenty of time to go exploring. In the meantime, he would feed and water the horses, which were loosely tethered to a rope that was strung between wooden pillars. They were standing and shitting on straw. Realizing he had a full bladder, Baldwin did the same.

As Baldwin walked down the line patting noses he whispered, "I will call you all Bucephalus," then clamped his hand over his mouth. *Silence in the name of God*, he thought. *Naked in the name* of God, too, as rough straw stuck to his bare feet and clung to his legs. Feeling foolish he stood on one foot and scratched his ankle, then tried unsuccessfully to brush some of the sticking straw off. Black flies bit him.

Sighing, he located the grain and water and the buckets for each. Looking around he spotted what looked like a well in the distance. The entrance to this underground grotto must be beyond it, he thought. Thinking the word *grotto* reminded him of his trip to the Mary Magdalene shrine. This place was far different than that. Here was just an underground cavern, obviously manmade. He put his hand up to finger his mother's beloved cross, but of course it was gone. Everything and everyone was gone. No friendly pilgrims whom he had gotten to know and love. No Rajeev or Bhaiya. They had run away. Now he was in the hands of God alone and HE asked for total sacrifice and offered nothing but silence in return.

Baldwin sighed again as the fatigue of his long travels, excitement of finally reaching his destination and the heart-wrenching ceremony, all set in. He leaned against the stone wall. After a moment he turned and jammed his face into a corner. He raised his arms as high as he could over his head and pressed his palms into the stone feeling the stretch all along his exhausted body. Silently he stood there, his eyes closed, feeling the stone on his naked skin and sweat roll down his back. He could feel where bits of his shorn hair stuck to his neck and straw to his ankles. Both itched but he mentally refused to brush anything away. He imagined that soon his body would be covered with insect bites that he could either scratch until they bled or try to ignore the pain they inflicted.

Slowly he opened his eyes and wedged his face even harder into the corner until the gray stones blurred. He licked one to see if it tasted like salt. It tasted of nothing. He was now nothing. Behind him he heard the horses shaking flies away from their heads, snorting and pawing. They seemed far away. He inhaled deeply letting the stable odor of dung and hay wash over him. It was a smell so familiar. He remembered when he and his brothers protested when their father made them muck out the horse's stalls on their estate. He'd give anything to be back in France again. Back home. No, he was God's now, body and soul. He pressed his cut hand over his heart where the crucifix had hung, leaving a small spot of blood. Slowly he slid down the wall until he collapsed his head against his knees.

"Mother," he whispered.

He sobbed.

CHAPTER TWELVE
SECRET ASSIGNMENT

12ᵗʰ Century
Jerusalem

Baldwin didn't know what woke him—his aching shoulders, itching bug bites, strange sounds or his terrible thirst. Somehow, he'd fallen asleep while curled into a tight ball. Slowly he straightened and brushed matted straw from his face. He rubbed crust out of his eyes and examined the cut in his hand. It had stopped bleeding.

He heard the horses, mice and rats rustling in the stale smelling straw, but there was something else. He was sure it must be the dead of night yet something seemed brighter. Using the wall for a brace, he stood and surveyed the room. The two torches at the foot of the stairs had been recently lit. Then he noticed in the semi-shadow that there was a bundle of something on the bottom step.

The horse next to him snorted and pawed the straw. Baldwin patted its nose then relieved himself. Brushing his sweaty, bug-bitten skin as best he could, he walked awkwardly toward the steps, flexing his legs and shoulders as he moved. "Bless you Hogarth," he whispered in a rough voice before remembering he was in silence.

On the stair was a wooden bowl of water with something small beside it wrapped in a rough cloth. A folded light brown robe with a rope belt, hose, undergarments made out of a scratchy material and serviceable shoes were on the next step down. Baldwin picked up the bowl and sipped the water. He wanted to down the entire contents but knew it was also for bathing. He unwrapped the scratchy cloth and found a small, olive green cube inside. He sniffed it but it had no fragrance. Then he remembered that most of the knights were French and this was French soap made of olive oil, sea salt and ash. At home his father had experimented with adding fragrance but had so far been unsuccessful. Sighing at the thought of home, Baldwin carefully used the small amount of water, soap and cloth to scrub his body and shorn head before he dressed.

Yawning, he silently walked down the row of horses patting each one on the nose. Then he got busy fetching the buckets of water and oats. Although it was barely perceptible, he heard someone coming down the steps and turned. Hogarth nodded and beckoned Baldwin to follow.

A stiff-legged Baldwin climbed slowly after his fellow monk until they reached the chapel, which was glowing inside with candles. Bernard of Clairvaux stood in front of the chapel reciting the ritual prayer. Baldwin listened silently as the monks chanted. It was beautiful and soothing to his bruised soul. Next he followed Hogarth to the long table for their simple breakfast of goat's milk but instead found a thick soup made with vegetables and some kind of grain, which the two of them shared. Although he was famished, Baldwin was careful to share the unusual breakfast soup equally with Hogarth. They also shared equally thick slices of bread and cheese and some watered down wine. Baldwin wondered why the extra food but couldn't ask.

When they finished, Hogarth put his spoon down, looked at Baldwin and whispered, "Grand Master wants to see you in his room."

Baldwin nodded and raised his eyebrows. He didn't know where the Grand Master's room was. Hogarth immediately understood and indicated, "Follow me."

Hogarth walked down a short hallway, knocked and the door was open by Hugues de Payens. When Baldwin entered he also saw Bernard. Hogarth bowed but did not enter. Instead he closed the door leaving the three men staring at each other.

The men smiled at Baldwin.

"We were just discussing the future of our Poor Knights of Solomon's Temple," Hugues said. "We have many plans and after learning more about you from brother Bernard we feel that we can take you into our confidence."

Confused by what was being said Baldwin merely nodded. His arm was itching but he stood quietly, trying not to scratch.

"Oh you may speak," de Payens said pleasantly. "Silence during meals but now we want your opinions on many things. Please sit."

They sat around a small table in the middle of the room. It was almost as sparsely furnished as the room Baldwin had slept in on his first night. But it was larger and had a few pieces of intricately carved wooden furniture–it had once been a temple after all. Several candles burned along with some incense that smelled to Baldwin like frankincense. He noticed that the small box that he had seen during his initiation was laid upon a silk scarf, which was resting on top of a chest of drawers.

Bernard spoke up, "After spending some time with the new Master of the Hospitalliars I have some ideas for a type of uniform that will unite our men. Many of the orders favor black but I think white tunics, of course, which my order favors. It represents the purity of our cause. What do you think Baldwin?"

Baldwin cleared his throat. "Ah," he said hoarsely. "White definitely and perhaps a red cross representing ..."

"Jesus and his holy blood," Bernard jumped in enthusiastically. "Yes, yes. Something functional the men will wear at all times to remind themselves and everyone else of our holy mission to fight for God and righteousness."

Hugues interrupted, "A sand color might be more practical Bernard. I've been here awhile and we do need tunics to cover the chainmail to keep the hot desert sun off. But white is not easy to keep pristine. It might be considered prideful."

"White is so pure and stands out," Bernard countered. "For now Baldwin you will wear a light brown robe and a white tunic over your chainmail if necessary."

Hugues shrugged and continued, "Before you came in we were discussing the guidelines for our order. Abbott Bernard will develop them further and when we expand beyond just the few knights already here …"

"With success in our missions to help the weak and defend the pilgrims, then I will present our guidelines to the pope," Bernard said promptly. "My fellow Christians will be passionate about these holy defenders of truth and righteousness and many more will join us. I've made a list of bishops and abbots who have influence with Rome and will, with our clear mindedness and devotion to the rules, agree with our cause."

He stood for a moment and paced behind his chair while rapidly ticking off names as if he was giving a sermon that had to include the twelve disciples and all their friends.

"Matthew, bishop of Albano, is a good friend. Renaud, archbishop of Reims. The various bishops of France, of course, Count Theobold of Nevers, and …"

"However," Hugues interrupted before Bernard could name everyone he knew, "we have something very important that we feel you are especially qualified to do."

"A special and holy mission," Bernard said sitting down again. His eyes blazed with zeal. "Two, actually. One is that you will help us entice knights to come to Jerusalem. You will recruit when traveling along the ancient trade routes. Although you could travel by sea, we want you to go by land to show yourself and meet the people who could join our cause. Not only knights but the support staff that is needed: squires, cooks, washer women, and so on."

Baldwin sat stunned. This was completely unexpected.

"First I'll give you some background on why we've felt compelled by God to form an elite force of warriors and what we want to accomplish," Hugues said leaning in. "It starts with Rome." Just as Bernard had done a moment before, he stood and paced while gathering his thoughts. "You see, Baldwin, we don't agree that the Catholic Church should be headquartered in Rome. It was after all the Romans who put our Lord Jesus on the cross. It makes more sense to us to have church authority in France."

Baldwin sat quietly and stared back and forth at the two men. Mutely he nodded not really understanding where he fit in.

Bernard continued to explain in a conspiratorial tone, "We'll be working toward that move and will use noble young knights such as yourself as examples of the purity of France. After all Jesus' devoted follower Mary Magdalene and Lazarus, the first bishop of Marseille, and Maximin, the first bishop of Aix-en-Provence, were sent by God's holy winds to France. That is merely one change we are working to accomplish as you start on your holy recruiting assignment."

"I have been in Jerusalem long enough to know that there are many things we don't know about Jesus and his healing powers," Hugues continued.

"I, for one," Bernard said, "think that he was trying to teach others his wisdom. He was saying that humankind is capable of greater blessings than the church allows. I think God, and therefore Jesus, was more human than the church gives him credit for."

Baldwin swallowed. He wasn't sure where this was going but he knew these were perhaps the two most pious men from France and he was blessed that they were talking to him.

"Of course," Hugues continued thoughtfully, "he was certainly a great healer. The Hospitalliars are good examples of helping the needy and healing the sick. Although, maybe not in so spectacular a way as our Lord."

"As you know," Bernard continued, "I stopped by the Hospitalliars and spoke with their new Master. I think some of their rules and wisdom, along with Saint Augustine's rules, we can adopt. But we are mostly inspired by the rules of Saint Benedict. Hugues and I are currently creating the specific behavior of the

Templar Order along with designing a new uniform to wear that distinguishes the Knights Templar from other knights."

Hugues de Payens leaned forward. "It's unfortunate but after the crusade many knights turned to robbery and debauchery. We are going to change that."

"That's why we have a special assignment for you," Bernard said. "You are uniquely qualified for this great task. The second part of this holy mission is that not only do we want you to go out and recruit for our order," he glanced over at Hugues, "we also want you to travel where Jesus traveled as a young man. The fact that he traveled is one of those secrets that everyone knows. There are many ancient families here who can tell you stories of Jesus as a youth. Not much is mentioned in the bible. But surely he made himself known along the way to India."

"India?" Baldwin questioned his voice rising.

"Yes, with Rajeev as your guide you will be able to travel along the ancient trader's road and find stories about Jesus. I'm sure there are many miracles performed by him. Those stories have been passed down for generations by the families he helped. We want you to write them down and draw pictures when you can."

From below the table Bernard brought up the bundle of possessions that Baldwin had to relinquish when he entered the temple. He took out the pictures that Baldwin had drawn while he was on the ship and showed them to Hugues.

"Remarkable," de Payens said. "This couple is so life-like. A wonderful skill."

Baldwin suddenly felt cold. These two men were commenting on his private pictures, a personal record of his adventures and memories. They were being careless with them. He watched as they looked at the drawing feather from Reginald, the precious parchment, and his personally ground charcoal. He swallowed hard.

Hugues continued, "There must be artifacts, too, that have been taken from this holy city. We want to collect those to keep them safe."

Hugues stood, picked up the small box from the dresser and put it in the middle of the table. "This," he said reverently, "is a splinter from the cross on which Our Blessed Lord Jesus was crucified. We will take it to battle as a symbol of our holiness–to protect us and give us strength."

Inside the box was a two-inch piece of dark, brown wood. Baldwin stared at the two men and the precious splinter. He put his hand over his heart where his cross had hung. The Templars had his cross now but did they know it was brought back from this holy city by his father over twenty years ago? He guessed not.

"You'll have one of the best horses, your own sword to carry and this," Bernard said.

As if by thinking of it Baldwin had made it appear, Bernard held out Baldwin's precious cross and dangled it in front of him. Baldwin was confused. Was this a test to see that his possessions were still precious to him? That he had not taken his oath of poverty seriously?

"You may speak," Grand Master de Payens said.

"I came here to be a knight to defend the pilgrims and serve God," Baldwin protested.

"This is an assignment by your Grand Master," Bernard said peevishly. "Being a Poor Knight doing battle for Christ means not only obeying God but following orders from Grand Master de Payens. Nothing is dearer to Jesus Christ than obedience."

Baldwin bowed his head. "Of course," he whispered. "I will follow your orders to the best of my abilities."

"You will go with me tomorrow to see the sights of Jerusalem," Bernard said. "Brothers can only go out in twos and only by permission."

"You have my permission," Hugues de Payens said and smiled. "It will be good for you to see the holy sites to inspire you on your journey."

That night Baldwin tossed on his hard bed. He still thought what Clairvaux and de Payens said was really a test. He could journey away from Jerusalem to protect the pilgrims, but to India? He thought of the knight's red cross and had visions of it being like a target on his chest that the unholy pagans could aim at. He thought of his lifelong training as a knight—he often beat his brothers in a sword fight, was an excellent horseman, and was skilled at archery. He thought of his brothers—where were they now? What were his parents doing in their home in France? Would they be disappointed that he was not to go into battle? He was trained to be a knight like his father! That's what he should be doing.

Baldwin tossed some more, his thoughts tumbling together. He'd been through so much already in his young life. On his way to Mary's grotto he had thwarted bandits and saved his mother from a terrible fall. He'd survived storms at sea, bloodthirsty pirates and horribly bad water and food. He had everything taken away from him, including his dog and his dignity. And maybe worst of all, he'd seen a demon and he knew it was coming after him. All through the night his thoughts raced and by the early morning he was blurry-eyed and exhausted as he silently walked to the chapel.

After the usual silent breakfast Baldwin met with Bernard who handed him a white tunic with a small red cross stitched over one shoulder.

"I want to try this out on the citizens of Jerusalem," Bernard said. "To see what effect it has on them. You will accompany me into the holy city as my guard to see the relics and holy sites. Here is your sword. And your cross."

Baldwin swallowed as he clutched the cross, willing the tears to stay out of his eyes. Willing that he looked indifferent to receiving it back. Then he looked at the hilt of his sword. The red ruby his mother had so thoughtfully chosen for him had been removed.

Bernard noticed Baldwin staring at the sword. "You have taken an oath of poverty. We utterly forbid any brother to have jewels or any ornamentation on his sword, saddle, bridle or harness. Of course I have made a small exception by giving you back your cross. However, I feel since it represents Christ and not vanity you may wear it as a sign of your deep faith."

Baldwin nodded, squared his shoulders and decided to speak formally to Bernard. "Thank you Reverend Father." He thought for a moment. "Should I put on my chainmail?"

"Not this time," Bernard answered sounding pleased. "We're being pilgrims but also introducing you as a holy knight. You should look like a knight and a monk at the same time. You will wear your sword belted around your robes. But I had one of the monks make you this simple cloak with the red cross on the shoulder," he said while fastening the flowing cloak at Baldwin's neck. "However, I may change the design so the red cross is over your heart. As we go out to see the holy sites you will not speak. The pilgrims and true believers will see you as strong and humble. A true servant of God!"

Baldwin fastened the precious cross around his neck and tucked it under his monk's robe. He belted on his sword and straightened the cloak so the red cross would lie over his right shoulder. Bernard slapped him on the back and nodded his approval. Silently they left the Temple of Solomon and walked into the noisy, ancient city.

Because Baldwin was in a hurry to get to the temple when he first entered Jerusalem, he'd glanced at the shops and people but hadn't really taken them all in. Now while silently walking beside Bernard he couldn't help but notice the variety of people, clothing and dialects. All shades of brown-skin peoples, from pilgrims who had traveled great distances in the sun to Arabic nomads of the desert. Christians, Jews, Samaritans, Muslims and many peoples Baldwin did not recognize were all gathered together to see the sites.

Women in gauzy veils covering their mouths; undernourished, dirty beggars; fat and thin merchants; knights, servants, holy men and monks wearing the color of their orders; excited children and crowds of pilgrims were all swarming through the sacred city. Baldwin looked at his sunburned skin. He wondered how soon his head would become sunburned, too, now that his hair was cut short. His white cloak was hoodless. While people stared at them, Bernard guided the way, pleased that people were noticing the noble, young monk/knight.

The entire town seemed to be one big bizarre divided into categories: bolts of cloth, shoes, shiny accessories that could be woven into designs; weapons of every variety; tents, rugs and carpets; religious artifacts (Baldwin thought they were of dubious origin): herbs, oils and spices; fired clay drinking and cooking vessels from plain to elaborate; delicate jewelry of ancient and modern designs and delicious-smelling, colorful food that made Baldwin's mouth water and his stomach growl. These were just a few of the various wares that Baldwin could see.

But it was the knowledge of walking where Jesus walked to his crucifixion that thrilled Baldwin's heart. Some pilgrims were walking barefoot and weeping at each step. Others were clutching prayer beads or crosses and shaking with excitement or ecstasy. Some looked lost and were asking directions or trying to stay in groups with their guides. So many people were praying at different sites that it was hard to get through. But Bernard with his sweeping gestures and enigmatic smile got the crowds to let them pass by. While they were about to enter the church of the Holy Sepulcher where Jesus was crucified and buried they heard a familiar voice call, "Bernard!"

They both turned to see Héloïse walking behind them.

"Oh!" she exclaimed when she realized that the man standing beside the abbot was Baldwin. "Baldwin you look so …"

Bernard put up his hand. "This is a new recruit for the Poor Knights of The Temple Of Solomon. He is in silence contemplating his sins."

Baldwin kept his eyes cast downward wondering what she had been about to say about his appearance.

Héloïse looked directly at Bernard. "He who is without sin cast the first stone," she said haughtily. "He's too young to have too many sins. The Baldwin I know has always had good intentions and that's what counts."

"That kind of thinking will surely lead to an afterlife in hell," Bernard said shaking a finger at her.

Here we go, Baldwin thought. *The two of them debating the meaning of Scripture.*

As several pilgrims *shushed* them Héloïse changed the subject. "I really wanted to ask Baldwin more about seeing Mary Magdalene's grotto. Now I won't have a chance, but seeing the Chapel of St. Helena will be fascinating. She looked over at Baldwin. "He's not going to be in silence forever, is he Bernard?"

Baldwin wished the two of them would stop talking about him as if he couldn't hear them. He wished she'd go away. Then he wondered where Ava was, then wished he hadn't thought of her. Thinking about women was a fault. He really was contemplating his sins, he thought.

As they entered the chapel dedicated to Emperor Constantine's mother Helena, they bowed their heads and said their silent prayers. It was a powerful feeling and Baldwin silently rededicated his heart and soul to God. As they exited the chapel Héloïse turned left while Bernard and Baldwin turned right. She didn't say goodbye or give them a backward glance. Bernard frowned and Baldwin wondered if the abbot had feelings for the intelligent and beautiful Héloïse. *He who is without sin …* Baldwin shook the thought from his head.

The newly initiated Templar was glad that he was allowed to actually see the holy city. Many people had noticed him and Bernard had chosen to explain that he was a holy knight, a Knights Templar, here to protect the pilgrims. Most nodded or said that they knew of this Order and were glad of it.

When they returned to their headquarters, Baldwin was exhausted but dutifully went to the chapel to pray. Later that evening after supper Bernard gave Baldwin his traveling instructions.

"You will travel as a monk but when you enter taverns, hostels or villages you will wear your white cape and speak of the glories of joining The Order Of The Poor Knights Of The Temple Of Solomon. I had thought to send Hogarth with you but he is needed here. However, with Rajeev by your side I know you will do well."

Baldwin looked at him curiously. "How am I to find Rajeev?" he asked quietly.

"I have been to the Hospitalliars and he has been helping them. I have told him of your holy mission and, as the good converted Christian that he is, he has agreed to accompany you. You will leave now, go to the Hospitalliars and find him."

Baldwin so much wanted to ask about Bhaiya but knew this might be seen as attachment so remained quiet.

"Keep a record of evidence of Jesus walking the path to India. I know of one family who tells stories that their ancestors knew that Jesus accompanied his uncle, a merchant I believe. Upon their return, Jesus healed the sick."

Bernard opened the outside door, handed Baldwin a bundle that included his chainmail, wished him good luck and shut the door. Just like that Baldwin was walking the narrow street toward the Hospitalliars hoping to find Rajeev.

As he entered the main thoroughfare two familiar-looking dogs shot by him closely followed by his Indian friend.

"Ah, there you are," Rajeev said catching his breath while staring at Baldwin's cropped head.

Baldwin unconsciously brushed his hand over his skull. He grinned and shrugged.

"The saintly Bernard has told me, or rather ordered me, to accompany you to my homeland."

"Yes," Baldwin said.

"A very important mission."

"Yes."

"A gentleman with two horses is waiting for us outside the gate. Follow me."

Waiting for them outside the gate were two dogs and one al-Hakim.

"It seems as if our dogs have fallen in love," the Muslim grinned. "I cannot separate them so I will have to go with you."

"But we are going to India," Baldwin said, "over land."

"You will thank me then," al-Hakim said. He held up a skein. "I brought water."

Later, the three companions said their prayers each in his own way and made their beds under a starry sky. The air was clear, crisp and cold. All three stared at the stars and crescent moon.

"How many stars do you think there are?" Baldwin asked.

"More than my brain can fathom," al-Hakim said. "As we stare at them do they stare back?"

Rajeev grinned. "We don't know much about stars or planets do we? But if we are here perhaps others are there."

"Others?" Baldwin asked. "You mean people or creatures or angels? Maybe angels are looking at us?"

"And laughing because we are so small," al-Hakim said, yawned, rolled onto his side and fell asleep.

"I wish it was daylight all the time," Baldwin said. "There are too many creatures hiding in the dark."

"The dark is as important as light," Rajeev said. "One can't see the light without the dark. We can only see the stars because of the dark. No need to fear the dark."

"When Hugues de Payens told me about my travels he said that my lodgings should not be without light at night."

"Because?" Rajeev asked curiously.

"Enemies of purity and righteousness live in the shadows. God forbids us to be wicked. We must be careful of shadowy enemies," Baldwin intoned.

"Interesting thought," Rajeev said. "Good thing there are plenty of stars then. Shadows can only be cast by the sun anyway." He yawned and closed his eyes.

"Forgive me, I am talking too much. I must try to be more

silent as instructed," Baldwin said dutifully. He quietly watched a star shoot across the sky, relaxed and fell asleep.

In his dream he woke in a cold room in a distance land in another time. He saw something draped over his chair. Picking it up he realized it was a child's traveling cloak. Little Anastasia's. How and why was it …? Dread filled him.

He dressed quickly, grabbed the cloak and ran out. He knew where *she* was. Where she had been going for weeks. Up on the highest tooth-shaped parapet, staring out through one of the crenels. He had always watched but usually she said nothing. Except the last time she was there she'd turned to him and said, "Little Anastasia smiles when she sees you. You know she can walk now and eat solid food."

Of course he knew. He'd watched the child take her first steps; watched her cry when her teeth grew; watched her run to him instead of the Czar, who never looked her way. It was so odd that Anastasia would mention it. Her behavior had been dreamy lately and distant. When he guarded their bedchamber he'd heard the Czar brutally take her again and again. He'd seen the man's anger when she hadn't conceived after a year. Everyone had seen that his mistress was with child. He often rode with his mistress on hunts leaving Anastasia behind to stare at them from high atop the castle. Clutching the child's cloak Baldwin ran. At the top of the steep steps he saw her standing at the far end, staring.

"Milady!" he shouted and kept running. She turned. "Why have you given me this?" He called as he neared her.

"She needs someone to love her as no one ever loved me, because I didn't do my duty and give the Czar a son. Duty above love, how can that be?" Anastasia sorrowfully asked turning toward her journey's end.

She lifted her beautiful, azure silk dress, stepped up on the crenel and jumped into the cloudless blue sky.

Baldwin sat up screaming, "No, no, no! *I* loved you! Anastasia! Anastasia! *I loved you!*"

He felt a strong hand grip his shoulder and looked up into

al-Hakim's eyes. "Courage," al-Hakim said. Rajeev crouched down beside him with a concerned look.

"What is it my friend?" al-Hakim asked. "Who is this Anastasia who haunts your dreams?"

Baldwin shook his head and did not answer.

CHAPTER THIRTEEN

NEW TRUTHS

12th Century
Trader's Road

Rajeev and al-Hakim quietly packed their things, called for the dogs and left Baldwin to his own thoughts. But they didn't get on their horses. They waited. Finally he turned to them.

"I have a story to tell you. It's about a woman."

They nodded, sat cross-legged and motioned for the dogs to sit. Baldwin paced, then told the story of Anastasia, his deep love for her and how he never told her.

When he was finished Rajeev said, "You are remembering another life. One you had long ago."

"Is that possible?" Baldwin asked.

"Yes," al-Hakim answered. "The experience you had then was so strong that you brought it with you into this life."

"Assuredly," Rajeev said. "You have some karma with this woman."

"Ah, yes, karma," Baldwin said. "I'm beginning to understand that."

"Can you remember what happened without dreaming it?" al-Hakim asked.

"No, I don't think so," Baldwin answered sadly.

"Maybe you can," Rajeev said, "with a little help. We will ask you questions and you will answer them without thinking."

Al-Hakim nodded. "Speak what comes to mind."

Baldwin shrugged and kept pacing.

"Did she know you loved her?" al-Hakim questioned.

"No. I think she thought I was just doing my duty as her guard. I never touched her. Although I wish I'd killed the czar."

"Oh no!" Rajeev said loudly. "That would be very bad karma. No, no. Tell us what happened with the little girl. Why were you holding the cloak?"

Baldwin gave him a puzzled look then looked off into the distance.

"Yes," he said quietly, "I do remember holding the cloak. It was green, like the forest." He paused in thought. "And running. I remember running. Not just me but everyone. Only … they were running toward the courtyard and I was running toward the nursery where the child was. When she saw me she reached up and I wrapped the cloak around her."

He stood still, gazing into the distance.

"Where did you take her?" Rajeev asked.

Baldwin shook his head. "No thoughts."

"Look around you," al-Hakim said.

A perplexed look crossed Baldwin's face.

"You were standing in the room holding the child. What did the room look like?"

Baldwin paced. "Ah! There was a large tapestry on the wall. It was tan and green and had strange animals on it. Winged creatures. Lions and horses with wings. I pulled it aside and went through the door hidden behind it."

He paused. "I ran to the stables and mounted a horse that was already saddled." He shook his head. "We galloped away. I don't think anyone followed us."

He put his hand on his forehead. "Ooohhh, my head hurts." He took a few steps awhile, bent over and retched.

"How long has this woman come into his dreams?" al-Hakim asked Rajeev quietly.

"He's had vivid dreams since he was a child. Some good, some that frightened him."

"So," al-Hakim said, "the long ago knight took the child into the forest of a far away place. I wonder if he stayed with her or gave her to some forest people?"

"Do you think that's important?" Rajeev asked quizzically.

"If the dream is real–meaning it actually happened in his past–then her descendents ..."

"If she had descendents," Rajeev noted.

"Yes, if she had descendents then it may give him some peace to find them."

"Perhaps," Rajeev said. "But I think he needs to find himself first before he can delve into his past. Or meet up with his past."

"Find himself?" al-Hakim asked. "What does that mean? He's a Frenchman, knight, noble and a seeker of truth. He's not lost so how can he find himself?"

Rajeev grinned. "I think you know what I mean, al-Hakim. Who is he when you take away all of those identities? Who are you, really?"

Al-Hakim laughed, "I am many things. Perhaps everything. Perhaps nothing."

Baldwin returned wiping his mouth on his sleeve. "I throw up and you two are discussing ...?"

"The deeper meaning of life, I think," al-Hakim said.

Rajeev carefully looked at Baldwin. "Feeling better after your terrible dream?"

Baldwin rolled his shoulders to ease the tension. "This was just about a woman and a baby. I've had much worse dreams than that."

"Which were?" al-Hakim asked.

"Which are none of your concern," Baldwin said. He sat down and stared at his two friends. He wasn't about to discuss the demon.

"Ah well," al-Hakim stretched, scratched and yawned. Didi and Bhaiya stood, stretched, scratched and yawned also. "Let's journey on and see what the day brings."

After prayers they mounted their horses and journeyed on until they reached a caravan of tradesmen with many camels, a few horses, donkeys and goats. A rough looking man rode out to meet them. After a brief talk he determined that they were not bandits but simply wished to follow the procession for added protection. He let them ride behind at a distance.

It was a wise choice for the trio to follow along as merchants and nomads had traveled the trail for thousands of years. It was hard-packed, but rutted, fairly wide and free of brush. The leaders of the caravan knew where water was hidden, how to preserve it for the long trip and how to protect themselves from marauders.

After awhile al-Hakim said, "If I hadn't studied about it I'd believe this earth is flat."

"How do you know it isn't?" Rajeev asked with a twinkle in his eye.

"Observation," al-Hakim said. "One can learn a great deal by simply looking. Many if not most people don't see when they look. They assume what they've been taught is true and never think much. If all would look how nature thrives they would have happier lives, I think."

"To live more naturally, is good," Rajeev said. Suddenly the dogs stopped to look at something on the ground. Al-Hakim dismounted and began picking up off the sand what looked like rocks.

"What are you doing?" Baldwin asked curiously.

"We are in the fortunate position to be behind this caravan where the animals are dropping their dung," al-Hakim said.

"The stench is not what I'd call pleasing," Baldwin said crinkling up his nose.

"It's not this wet dung that is interesting but the dried dung that has been baking in the sun for awhile."

"Don't tell me you make incense out of it," Baldwin said. "Rajeev has told me this about cow's dung."

Al-Hakim smiled. "You may notice that there are not a lot of trees in the desert. Trees are precious. We do not make campfires out of them. We use dried dung, brush and twigs. Sometimes add a drop or two of fragrant oil."

He put some dried dung in a sack then bent down and wiped his hands in the sand.

"Dung is useful everywhere," Rajeev said. "I can smell the incense wafting this way from the caravan. Frankincense and myrrh that they've previously brought from my country to use along the way."

Baldwin looked at the two dogs walking along steadily with their tongues handing out. "Listen you two. Rajeev and al-Hakim are going to collect your excrement, sell it and make their fortunes. I, a poor knight, will benefit from their kind donations."

Both dogs stared at him and seemed to shake their heads. Rajeev and al-Hakim laughed.

"Who are the traders? What do they bring and what do they take back?" Baldwin asked curiously as he brought out his parchment to make notes and draw.

Al-Hakim grinned. "Arab traders and Jews have been plying their wares since long before the time of King Solomon. As you have just come from the temple that Solomon built you probably know he needed cedar and cypress trees for his many building projects. As I said, you don't want to cut down trees when you live in the desert no matter how grand the temple."

Baldwin thought back to the temple and realized that he'd seen cedar-lined walls and intricate carvings. The box containing the precious sliver from Christ's cross could be from Solomon's time, he realized.

Al-Hakim continued, "Perfumes, beautiful cloth, eating and drinking vessels were all traded along with slaves, furs, exotic musk and spices. Whatever was considered precious. Incense, of course. They traded both by sea and along the route we're traveling."

"India is an ancient land," Rajeev said, "with many beautiful items to trade."

"Ah," al-Hakim said staring in the distance, "the caravan is stopping at an oasis at the edge of those foothills. "I will take our animals for a drink and come back here. I think it's best to keep our distance."

He dropped his sack of dung. "Here knight, let's see how you do making a small fire." He handed over a small box of flint and steel to start the fire.

Baldwin made a face but set to work and soon had an adequate fire going. Al-Hakim returned with the horses and several skeins of water. As the sun set, al-Hakim unfolded his prayer rug and bowed toward Mecca, Rajeev and Baldwin sat cross-legged and said the Lord's Prayer. Then Rajeev chanted. They felt settled and peaceful.

Suddenly, one of the dogs growled. In one motion al-Hakim drew his scimitar and in a quick move cut at something on the ground. Reaching out he pulled a two-foot headless snake up for everyone to see. "We feast!"

As the two dogs dived for the snake's head, al-Hakim brought it's slightly bloody body over to the low burning fire, put it on a flat rock and cut it into two-inch pieces.

"You did that so quickly," Baldwin said with a look of admiration.

"It's easier to manage when you cut the head off a thing."

Rajeev gave him an interested look, then reached into his pouch and brought out spices while al-Hakim brought out a small vial of oil. As Baldwin watched in fascination, the Muslim shook a few drops of oil on each piece, and then Rajeev added the spices. The dogs, having finished with the head now gathered around pushing toward the carcass with their noses. Al-Hakim threw a chunk of snake and the dogs chased after it.

"Make yourself useful," al-Hakim said to Baldwin and find us some stout sticks."

In a moment, Baldwin brought back three sturdy foot-long sticks he'd scavenged from the ground. Al-Hakim skewered pieces of snake on each stick and threw two more pieces to the dogs. The he showed Baldwin how to roast the snake.

Rajeev and al-Hakim watched as Baldwin took his first ever bite of roasted snake. He shook his head. "It tastes like chicken."

The two men nodded while carefully pulling off the pieces of snake with their teeth.

"Ideally I would add some vegetables, maybe some mint," al-Hakim said. "But for our feast tonight I will add these."

He reached in his tunic and pulled out a small bag of dates. He gave three to each of his companions. The dogs eagerly walked over but al-Hakim shook his head. Instead of dates he threw his roasting stick and the dogs chased after it.

While the wind blew gently and small animals called to each other, they finished their meal of snake and dates and threw the remaining sticks to the dogs, who licked them thoroughly and then played chase with them.

Rajeev asked quietly, "When you cut the head off, were you also referring to an army perhaps? Eliminating the leader and then the body of the army would be easier to manage?"

Al-Hakim grinned. "Insightful aren't you?"

Baldwin looked from one to the other, not understanding what they were talking about.

"The problem with that," Rajeev continued, "is that another head will take its place and the troops will follow him. You cannot control another you can only control yourself."

"Lead by example is what you're saying," al-Hakim stated. "Maybe yes, maybe no." He shrugged. "But eliminating the leader rather than attacking the legions that follow him makes more sense to me." He wiped his hands in the sand.

"It never works in the long run," Rajeev said.

"Ah well, none-the-less, duty calls."

Rajeev shook his head. "Duty to what?"

Al-Hakim shrugged. "More like to whom. I'm leaving tonight while it's cool."

"Leaving?" Baldwin asked, perplexed by the entire conversation.

Al-Hakim stood, brushed himself off, untied his horse from a bush and mounted. The other horses snorted and swished their tails.

"I have something important to do. Keep traveling and I will meet up with you in a few days if not sooner."

"But …" Baldwin stammered as al-Hakim turned his horse and rode into the night. Didi followed. Bhaiya followed Didi.

"Bhaiya!" Baldwin shouted. Bhaiya turned, wagged his tail and then trotted off after Didi.

"He'll be fine," Rajeev said.

"Who? Bhaiya or al-Hakim?" Baldwin shook his head. "Both troublemakers."

Rajeev laughed as he stood and cleared his throat. "I should be back before they catch up with you."

"What?" Baldwin stared at Rajeev, not believing what he was hearing.

"I have some cousins I must see. They live not too far. I will take al-Hakim's advice and start out tonight before the day gets too hot."

"How can you see where you're going?" Baldwin asked.

"The moon and stars will guide me," Rajeev answered. "Besides, earlier I asked one of those caravan travelers for directions." He looked up. "I can follow the stars." He grinned. "My cousins only speak Hindi and I know you'll appreciate a bit of quiet along your journey. I will only spend a few days and then catch up with you. You can stay close to those who are going your same way. No harm will befall you."

"I'm not worried about that," Baldwin said as he watched Rajeev mount his horse. "I'll probably make great time without you two," he added stubbornly.

Rajeev smiled, waved and disappeared into the night.

Baldwin sat in the dark desert silence, which was neither completely silent nor completely dark. He could hear the distant murmuring and singing of the people who were by the oasis, the grunting of their camels and the scuttling of small animals. His horse pawed the ground, swished his tail and snorted. "We've been abandoned Bucephalus," Baldwin said. He poked the fire, rolled up in his thin blanket and fell asleep.

The moon had been full, he was sure of it. But now everything was pitch black with a cold heaviness that permeated the air. Baldwin shivered. Something was blotting out the light … something blacker than darkness. I'm dreaming, he thought. Is my mind playing a trick on me or is it just a trick of the light?

But he wasn't dreaming. As he deliberately opened his eyes wider and stared out into the dark, a pair of fiery red orbs stared back. They slowly moved out of the blackness toward him. A sliver of ice crawled from the base of Baldwin's spine into his head. His insides felt cold, empty and soulless. He heard words in his mind. *Come. Come.* He knew rather than saw that a bony finger was beckoning him. He could hear the swish of a garment sweeping the ground as the dark demon turned away.

The moon and stars reappeared as the blackness retreated up the steep incline of the foothill, easily climbing over sand and stone. Baldwin rose, unsheathed his sword and followed, slipping and sliding on the steep terrain.

He climbed until he found himself on a narrow ledge. He noticed caves that couldn't be seen from below were set back into the cliffs. The demon was waiting for him by a cave entrance. With a laugh the demon disappeared into one. Baldwin scrambled to the entry, scattering small stones as he went.

He turned on the narrow ledge and saw the caravan with its sleeping occupants far below. Their campfire burned low. He thought of calling out to let them know he was above them and walking into sure danger. Then he thought they might think he was a thief leading a group of bandits and they would be terrified. No he wouldn't bother them. He would walk into hell alone. He was sure it was hell, where else would a demon go?

Holding his sword high, he courageously, or foolishly, walked into the dark, cold cave. *Odd.* The cave was familiar. Then he remembered the dream he had when he fell asleep in Mary Magdalene's grotto. He'd dreamed he was in a massive cavern with high rock walls dotted with cave-like openings and no ceiling that he could see. Baldwin remembered he'd seen something that looked like a flying lizard that breathed fire. As he carefully walked down a sloping path his senses were on alert for any movement, smell or sound. If there was fire, then here was the path to hell.

Mary Magdalene had said something to him in her grotto. What was it? The words came back; *There is more to life than most people know and more creatures above and below us than you can imagine.* Yes and what else had she said? Something about illusion.

Blackness jumped in front of him. Baldwin shouted and thrust his sword forward. A low laughing sound met his ears as the demon jumped up on the cave wall, his claws cutting deep into the gray earth and sandstone.

"What do you want?" Baldwin shouted.

The demon made a mewing sound and spoke in a high-pitched voice.

"You," it mewed.

"Why?" Baldwin asked while carefully watching the demon. The creature was slowly inching its way higher. Baldwin stepped away trying to get the advantage but knowing the demon could jump on him any moment.

"What am I to you?" Baldwin asked trying to distract the thing enough so he could get near with his sword.

The demon grinned. "Isn't it obvious? I'm your worse nightmare. Your tarnished soul. Your *e v i l* self. I'm everything you don't want to be and yet you are."

Baldwin put his free hand over his cross.

"Ah," the demon said, "you look for Jesus? He left his mark here, you know. Just follow me and I will tell you all about the *real* Jesus. Poor man. Poor, poor man. His hands looked dreadful."

"He was crucified," Baldwin recited angrily, "dead and buried. He descended into hell to save our souls. Is that where we're going? Hell?"

"If you'd like," said the demon and jumped. Baldwin was ready for him.

"On the third day he rose again and ascended into heaven," Baldwin screamed while jabbing his sword directly into the demon's chest.

Laughing, the demon jumped away. No wound appeared. Baldwin brought his sword up but stopped as a loud roar boomed above them. A lance came down out of the shadow, caught the demon and threw him toward the trail leading downward.

"Get away," a voice hissed. Baldwin started after the demon but two lances crossed in front of him blocking his way. Who or *what* was holding them he couldn't tell as they were standing in shadow. Only their gloved hands were visible. Baldwin tried prying one hand away but its grip was too tight. He noticed the glove was made out of a scaly, snakeskin material. He peered into the shadow as the hissing voice spoke.

"You are too young and naive to know the purpose of your demon," the voice hissed.

"*My* demon? Not *my* demon," Baldwin said as he tried to look past the lances to see where the demon had gone.

"Oh yes, your personal demon accidently brought back by your father when he returned from the Christian crusade. This demon you've had for a long time, yesssss?"

Baldwin looked into the shadow and nodded. "It's haunted my dreams since childhood. How did you know?" he asked and rushed at the crossed lances. They held and he backed away.

"We know it's not your time to kill your demon," the voice said. "Not your time to enter into hell."

"This path does lead to hell then?"

"So you are taught to believe. It's called hell to keep such noble young humans like you away. It's called *home* to us." A soft glow outlined the shape of the speaker.

"Humans?" Baldwin repeated hesitantly. Even though the cave was warm, he shivered. "What do you mean? Aren't you ...?"

A heart-stopping roar bounced off the cavern walls overhead.

"Ah. Our dragon is getting curious about you. Watch out, here he comes."

An enormous, lizard-like monster with shiny, multicolored scales and talons bigger than Baldwin flew straight at him.

"No Deleto! He's not fire-proof!"

The dragon dropped down until his monstrous face was only a yard from Baldwin's. He paused, sniffed, reared back and sneezed. In a cloud of smoke Baldwin was blown out of the cave and slid on his back all the way down the mountain.

───────◆◆◆───────

Two days later Baldwin woke under a palm tree with a throat-clenching thirst, scrapes, bruises and cuts all down his back and arms. Everything ached. After a moment he felt something damp and soothing on his forehead and looked up into Ava's gentle eyes. She was sitting beside him, patting his forehead with a moist, rose-scented cloth. Baldwin groaned.

"He's returned," a familiar voice said in slightly accented French.

In a moment al-Hakim bent over him and put a water skein to his lips. Baldwin opened his mouth and let the water dribble down his throat. Ava smiled as she carefully pressed the damp cloth over his eyes. He inhaled, coughed and tried sitting up.

Ava gently pushed him back. "You have a lump the size of a chicken egg on the back of your head and thorns sticking out from all over your body."

Baldwin frowned, confused.

"You slid all the way down the mountain on your back," Ava explained. "Your sword was gripped tightly in your hand."

"Fortunate," al-Hakim added. "A true knight."

Ava continued, "Many rocks slid with you. The leaders of the caravan heard the noise, investigated, saw you were breathing and moved you under this tree. They thought you wouldn't last long. I've been traveling with the group and saw it was you, even though your hair is ah, well, missing."

Baldwin ran his hand over his head. "Cooler."

Rajeev grinned. "At least he's making jokes."

Ava smiled and continued. "I realized that Rajeev must be somewhere nearby and said I would stay with you while the caravan traveled on. Fortunately, I have good survival instincts." She shook her head. "It didn't bother Abraham Ben Yiju, the caravan leader, one instant to leave us out in this desert. He did leave me your horse, my camel, water from the oasis and food."

"I showed up the next morning," Rajeev said. "Your clothes are not as torn as one would think from such a slide. But still in need of repair."

"We came in the afternoon," al-Hakim said just as Didi and Bhaiya bounded forward. They both sniffed and sneezed repeatedly.

"Of course," Baldwin whispered through his cracked lips. "It sneezed. The force pushed me out over the cliff and then down the mountain."

Rajeev and Ava stared at each other as al-Hakim gave Baldwin another sip of water.

"No need to talk now, my friend," al-Hakim said. "No doubt you'll be stiff and sore. We'll camp here awhile longer."

As the two dogs lay down next to him Baldwin nodded and closed his eyes. He could feel Ava still gently wiping his forehead. She mustn't do that, he thought. He'd just taken a vow to stay away from women ... stay the hell away from women. But she hadn't been beckoning him to hell. His confused mind drifted. There was something important he needed to remember. His companions watched as Baldwin's breathing became deep and rhythmical.

"What do you think happened?" Rajeev asked. "Why was he on the mountain in the middle of the night? Why does he smell of smoke?"

"Looking for something? Following something or someone?" Ava asked quietly. "He was away from the caravan, up on those cliffs, but it was a full moon so the camp guards saw the rock slide with him in it. He was passed out when they got to him."

"He had his sword gripped so tightly in his hand," al-Hakim noted, "that he must have been confronting something. An animal of some sort. He's lucky he didn't cut himself with it."

Although seemingly sound asleep Baldwin could vaguely hear a word or two of his companion's conversation. *Animal*, he thought. But whom had he been talking to in the darkness of the cave? Why did whatever or whomever it was know about him? Maybe it was an angel. But *no*. It looked like … No it couldn't be. A memory of Goswin's scaly pet lizard flashed into his mind.

When the guard had warned of the dragon's approach he had momentarily moved into the light. He was as tall as Baldwin with strange iridescent skin. Scaly skin. Almost the same as the dragon's. When he or *it* had stepped forward to distract the dragon away from Baldwin it had said, "They escape sometimes. About every thousand years." Did he mean the dragon or the demon? Or both?

But, of course, dragons were a myth. No such thing. He'd imagined it. But then there was the story of Saint Martha taming a dragon with holy water in Tarascon, France. A dragon in France. Baldwin's mind raced. What was said about Jesus? Baldwin was trying to remember something else. Ah, yes the guard wasn't speaking French yet Baldwin understood what he said. A strange language with an odd lisp or hiss. Yet *I understood it* Baldwin mumbled.

Rajeev looked at Ava who was still stroking Baldwin's head. "What did he say?"

"I understood it," Ava said. The three exchanged puzzled looks.

Baldwin remembered what else Mary Magdalene had said in her grotto. *Know this, there is an interconnectedness of all life and the separation between our inner and outer worlds is but an illusion.*

He groaned. The three companions and two dogs watched him for a few more minutes and then started on a small meal.

"Why were you with the caravan?" al-Hakim asked Ava.

"For the adventure, I guess. Héloïse has gone back to France on the same ship as Bernard. They are probably arguing religious points every minute of the way. I wanted to go on and see more of the world. Your part of the world actually Rajeev."

"I'm pleased," Rajeev said. "It will be a pleasure to have you travel with us."

"No," Baldwin whispered.

Al-Hakim looked over at him. "Did he say, 'No'?"

"I took an oath," Baldwin rasped out. "Can't be around women."

Ava's mouth dropped open. Rajeev shook his head and al-Hakim walked over to where Baldwin lay and felt his head. "You must be delirious."

Rajeev spoke. "Unfortunately, he did take an oath. He can't even speak to his own mother nor write her letters. Although these new poor Knights Templar revere Mother Mary they see women as temptations."

Ava shook her head. "Try living without us, you rude …"

Al-Hakim interrupted, "No wonder they already have a reputation of being fierce when it comes to defending the pilgrims," he scoffed. "I'd be crazy if I had to stay away from women. I'd definitely want to kill someone."

"From what I understand," Ava said sarcastically, "it was our dear Abbott Bernard who came up with most of the rules. It doesn't make sense to me."

"Did Jesus have something against women?" al-Hakim asked. "Muhammad had many wives. All educated and intelligent. He had many children."

"Aren't you glad you're a Muslim then?" Ava quipped. "What do you think Rajeev?"

"Women are Goddesses in my country. We have temples of worship. There were many great women in the bible so I'm not sure why the Knights Templar have that rule unless it's a matter of focus."

"Focus on killing in the name of God," Ava said. "The world is crazy."

"Oh I think he's just supposed to kill us pagans," al-Hakim joked.

"I don't think I'll be comfortable traveling with a Baldwin who doesn't speak to me," Ava said. "The two of you and the dogs can take care of him," she said angrily.

"I'll be more than happy to escort you back to the caravan," al-Hakim said. "I'd be delighted with your company. I believe we can catch up to them in a day or so."

Ava smiled at him. "You don't think I'll corrupt you along the way do you?"

Al-Hakim laughed, "I hope so!"

Rajeev just shook his head. "Perhaps I should do the escorting."

"No!" Ava and al-Hakim said in unison.

"We'll leave as soon as it gets cooler," al-Hakim said. "Don't worry Rajeev, I don't have to take an oath to behave myself."

At sunset after saying their prayers–al-Hakim on his rug facing Mecca and Ava bowed over her folded hands–they mounted their animals. As Ava's camel lurched up from the ground Didi and Bhaiya stood.

Al-Hakim looked at Didi and made a stay motion with his hand. Both dogs sat.

"Two moons at the most," he said to Didi, who put her head down.

"Even animals obey you," Ava said as they rode side-by-side. "You are a man of many accomplishments."

"I was raised on a mountain with many playful animals. They understand much more than most people give them credit for," al-Hakim said. "They can be taught."

Ava considered this a moment then changed the subject to

something that was bothering her. "Bernard and his gratuitous rules that Baldwin now so mindlessly follows. He and my sister Héloïse don't see eye-to-eye on women's roles in the world."

"Baldwin has limited his world to what he has been taught to think instead of paying attention to his own feelings," al-Hakim said.

"From what Rajeev has told me, Baldwin was taught since very young to be a knight and knights are brave and strong. Now he has found a group of men who combine that with what they think Allah, or God, wants. Humility and bravery. I like the bravery part but humility not so much," al-Hakim beamed his bright smile.

"I admire knights," Ava said. "But ... I want respect and courtesy along with their noble deeds. I may be part of the fairer sex but I'm certainly not the weaker."

"No indeed," al-Hakim said. "In Arab historic literature a Fáris, which translates as a Knight, is an excellent horseman skilled in weapons. He also had many virtues: dignity, eloquence, kindness ..." al-Hakim sat straighter in his saddle. "I do look dignified and eloquent on my horse don't you think?" He flashed his radiant smile.

"Oh yes and you are kindness personified," Ava smiled back.

They chatted amicably under the stars as they guided their horses along the much-traveled, rutted road until they reached the caravan at sunrise. Al-Hakim immediately noticed that the caravan was not moving and the guards had their attention on a group of hooded men who were riding swiftly towards them from the surrounding hills. Al-Hakim drew his scimitar and galloped toward them, intercepting them at the bottom of the hill. He waved and shouted. After a few minutes of shouting at each other, the men turned and disappeared back over the mountain.

Al-Hakim rode up to Ava as she rejoined the caravan. "You keep doing that," she said. "You chased off the bandits when I was on my way to Jerusalem and now I assume they were also bandits that you have chased away."

Al-Hakim bowed. "Do I qualify as a gentle knight, milady?" he joked. "Saving you, the weaker sex, from a terrible, terrible fate?"

She shook her head but smiled at him. "What did you say to make them turn around?"

"Simple. This is a caravan of my many wives and they shall not be touched unless they want the wrath of Allah to rain down on them."

Upon hearing al-Hakim's words the guards scoffed.

Ava continued. "You are an educated rogue who has my thanks and gratitude for safeguarding me. One day I hope to repay your kindness. I also wish that one day I find out why marauding bandits obey you. They knew you."

"I am a rogue as you say."

He turned to the guards and quietly asked them a question. One nodded, turned and pulled something that looked like cloth out of a pack from behind his camel. Al-Hakim traded some coins for it. A man in a long-striped robe stepped up, hailed al-Hakim and motioned him to get down off his horse.

"Please, I am Abraham Ben Yiju the leader of this fine caravan. I thank you for returning this beautiful lady to us. We would be honored to have you join us."

Al-Hakim thanked him for his hospitality but stayed on his horse. "I have to attend to our traveling companion until he can ride again. Perhaps we will catch up to you later," he said and touched his hand to his head and then his heart. "A good journey to you all. May Allah protect you."

Swinging his magnificent stallion around, he rode back in two days to his two friends, two dogs and two problems—a bruised and bettered Baldwin and an expecting Didi.

Back at their small camp, such as it was, the ever-resourceful Rajeev was trying to get Baldwin to move his limbs. He was rolling him from side to side when al-Hakim trotted up, tied his stallion to a bush and dropped a bundle next to the Indian. Rajeev unfolded it to find a long, loose-fitting robe with full sleeves.

"This will be much more impressive than his torn clothes," al-Hakim said. "Lucky he wasn't wearing his white cloak. Has he told you what he was doing on the mountain?"

Rajeev shook his head. "We discussed his mission and the new rules he insists he has to live by but he goes mute when it comes to what he did or saw."

Rajeev smiled. "The Templars think that the young Jesus came this way as a boy with his uncle to trade goods. When he came back as an adult he performed miracles. They think stories of these miracles were passed down from generation to generation. Baldwin is supposed to keep a record of any words about this. They think Jesus made it to India."

"I heard Tibet," al-Hakim said sitting next to Rajeev and looking at Baldwin.

Baldwin put his arms in the air trying to flex them.

"I'm unhappy with you," al-Hakim said to Baldwin.

"In addition to being blown off a mountain and slowing down our journey?" Baldwin asked through parched lips.

Al-Hakim nodded. Baldwin and Rajeev stared, waiting for him to continue.

"Good thing Ava is a strong woman and was able to tolerate your insult," al-Hakim admonished him.

"Oh no, not you, too. Rajeev has been chastising me for days. But I have taken an oath."

Rajeev turned to al-Hakim. "His oath is very strict, no talking to women for they are corrupters. No talking much in general."

"I do not think Allah has created us in His image to be boring," al-Hakim said.

"To be holy and obey," Baldwin said defending himself.

"I will make you some holy water then," al-Hakim said, "to help keep your soul clean."

Baldwin looked at him curiously. "How do you make holy water?"

Al-Hakim looked him straight in the eyes. "You boil the hell out of it."

Baldwin burst out laughing, as did Rajeev and al-Hakim.

"Baldwin gasped. "Please don't make me laugh again it hurts all over."

"We will wait until you heal. You're young. It shouldn't take long to start your journey again," al-Hakim said. He touched his forehead and then his heart. "May peace be with you."

Rajeev smiled. "We've come but a short way and yet the adventure has already had some lessons. We are just beginning to learn about life, my friends."

"Yes, I know," Baldwin said while slowly stretching his arms and legs. "Words don't teach, only experience."

His companions nodded.

Baldwin carefully looked at the two smiling men sitting across from him. One, his long-time tutor, the other his new friend. Both raised so differently from him and yet kindred spirits. They laughed together, discussed life together, traveled together in peaceful coexistence and protected each other as comrades in these terrible times. Would they be there for him when he faced the demon again as he knew he must?

In his innocence Baldwin did not know who his friends *really* were or what they were capable of. As his life's journey continued, time would tell.

EPILOGUE

Al-Hakim was a tall, wiry boy surviving as best an orphan could when the old man of the mountain found him, brought him into the compound and trained him to be a warrior along with other young boys the old man had collected.

His education was extensive. The compound consisted of a massive library filled with ancient writings inscribed on various scrolls. Timeworn rocks with strange pictures and signs had been discovered and added to the library for the boy's education. Languages, science, biology and astrology were taught along with a belief in reincarnation. His mentor, the "old man" would not allow his "warriors" to wear armor due to an astrological belief that there is a certain time for every death and one can neither postpone it or rush it. Therefore, no armor was worn.

This suited al-Hakim's unencumbered style perfectly. His only weapon was his scimitar, which he used extremely well. The only thing al-Hakim really disagreed with about the beliefs that were drilled into him, was martyrdom. He liked himself and his world and didn't want to leave it too soon. But, a belief of the religious-political group was sacrifice and he knew his whole life had been dedicated to being a glorious assassin.

When al-Hakim joined Baldwin and Rajeev, his plan was to disappear so he wouldn't have to explain why he wasn't dead. He'd done what he was asked just didn't stay to be cut down by the guards of a certain leader he had assassinated. Throwing himself on someone else's sword wasn't his style. After all, why die with so much knowledge in one's head? He thought himself too smart for such a waste.

As for Rajeev, he hadn't been exactly truthful when he'd told Armand and Baldwin the story of his upbringing. A Christian couple hadn't saved him, although he did study with them. He *had* worked for the incense maker but only to learn how the peasants lived and at an older age then he had described to Armand and Baldwin.

He did not know if he was an orphan or had been given to monks for instruction. His first memories were of living in a temple and being trained by his guru in the philosophy of "everyone being right." It was still something he was trying to understand.

An intelligent and insightful boy he learned easily yet always wanted to learn from experience. His studies were diverse: music, literature, languages, astrology, astronomy and medicine among them. But he was fascinated with how the temple was constructed and after much persuasion the monks has also let him learn stone masonry. Rajeev put much of that hands-on knowledge into making stone inscriptions.

Now this Indian master of many things had become Baldwin's tutor, friend and soon his spiritual guru. It was, he knew, his *dharma* or duty to teach the young man and his unlikely friend al-Hakim about a way of living that most people did not understand.

<hr />

Going to India are they, the demon thought. Wonderful! The place is full of Rakshasas. Divine devils, like me. Shapeshifters, like me. Warriors like my devoted Baldwin. Not that I need any help keeping the knight's mind on fiendish things—sacrificing his true nature to a hopeless cause. I don't like it though that a Christian, Muslim and Hindu are traveling together and getting along. That can't last. I will infect his mind and turn his heart. His friend's, too. All it takes is belief in my illusion. Manipulating reality is so much fun!

Printed in the United States
by Baker & Taylor Publisher Services